*living
on
impulse*

# LIVING ON IM

DUTTON BOOKS

*cara haycak*

# PULSE

DUTTON BOOKS | *A member of Penguin Group (USA) Inc.*

PUBLISHED BY THE PENGUIN GROUP
Penguin Group (USA) Inc., 375 Hudson Street, New York, New York 10014, U.S.A. |
Penguin Group (Canada), 90 Eglinton Avenue East, Suite 700, Toronto, Ontario M4P
2Y3, Canada (a division of Pearson Penguin Canada Inc.) | Penguin Books Ltd, 80
Strand, London WC2R 0RL, England | Penguin Ireland, 25 St Stephen's Green, Dublin
2, Ireland (a division of Penguin Books Ltd) | Penguin Group (Australia), 250 Camber-
well Road, Camberwell, Victoria 3124, Australia (a division of Pearson Australia Group
Pty Ltd) | Penguin Books India Pvt Ltd, 11 Community Centre, Panchsheel Park, New
Delhi - 110 017, India | Penguin Group (NZ), 67 Apollo Drive, Rosedale, North Shore
0632, New Zealand (a division of Pearson New Zealand Ltd.) | Penguin Books (South
Africa) (Pty) Ltd, 24 Sturdee Avenue, Rosebank, Johannesburg 2196, South Africa |
Penguin Books Ltd, Registered Offices: 80 Strand, London WC2R 0RL, England

CIP Data is available.

Published in the United States by Dutton Books,
a member of Penguin Group (USA) Inc.
345 Hudson Street, New York, New York 10014
www.penguin.com/youngreaders

DESIGNED BY HEATHER WOOD

Printed in USA | First Edition
ISBN 978-0-525-42137-5
1 3 5 7 9 10 8 6 4 2

*To my beautiful family . . .*
*you make happiness real*

—C.H.

*living
on
impulse*

I have a mad impulse
to smash something . . .
to commit outrages.

—HERMANN HESSE

*In early April,* Mia hits the department store downtown on the Commons. It's a school day. Lunch hour. Going round the revolving door she gets that feeling—an energy passes through her, like an electrical charge. She likes it. She wants to close her eyes, just spin and go dizzy inside the carousel of glass. Her choices spinning round her.

To steal or not to steal. Let the door decide. If she lands inside she'll take what she came for. If she's left on the pavement she'll call it all off. Today she only goes around once, because as soon as she sees the marble floor and cool glass counters, it's as if the polished shine of the place beckons her in.

She never goes straight to the target. Control is key. Taking her usual route, Mia dabbles in cosmetics and buys a peach-colored lip gloss with cash. She ponders a display of gold and silver earrings, lifts a pair of hoops to her ears, vetoes them with a glance and moves on. She's careful not to rush. Rushed is nervous. Deeper in, she faces a sea of denim. Racks of stonewashed, diesel-grungy, incredibly expensive, and daringly low-waisted jeans tempt her. She has a dozen pairs at home. She casually fits herself into a cropped jacket, reads the price tag as if she wants it, then shrugs it off her shoulders like a skin she no longer needs, places it back on the hanger. She's a shopper with some time, just looking. It's all fine.

The shoes wait on the second floor. She steps onto the

escalator. There's that charge again, like a buzzing *zap*. The heat is all in her face. She checks herself in the wall of mirrors as she rides up, relieved it doesn't show.

From the landing, she can see what she came for. Now she must count her steps to slow down. One Mississippi and two . . . She counts the people in the shoe department . . . three working the floor and a fourth at the cash register. Five, six, seven women shopping. Getting closer, she sees one older lady who has several open boxes at her feet. She's holding a fluffy white dog that looks like it just came from the groomer.

Everyone shops at lunch. That's what makes it safer. That's why it's a green light. That's why she cut school to be here now, and why if she chooses quickly she'll be able to get back in time for her next class.

She hunts now, eyes eagle-sharp. There are sandals for a new pedicure, for impressing a first date on a hot night, for lounging by the hotel pool, for becoming someone she is not but could be—jeweled flip-flops and wedges and pointy slingbacks. But she's hoping for something extra special. Today she's looking for the wear-them-on-your-sixteenth-birthday pair. Shoes that say, "Watch out, world. Mia Morrow is here." She has no idea what that might look like.

And then from the corner of her eye she spots silver leather straps, spaghetti-thin, crisscrossing a bleached wooden platform.

*Go slow.*

So slowly now, she walks over and picks up the shoe, holds it in front of her face. There is a throbbing in her temple and a voice in her head that says, *Perfect for you.* Mia reads the price tag. Two hundred and twenty-five dollars. The voice says now, *Even if you can't afford them.* Mia shivers, knowing that the sandal is already hers; it had just been waiting there for her to arrive. She looks around for a salesperson, and seeing no one ready to help her, she slips the sandal inside her large handbag.

*Got it.*

She's done this before. Sometime soon, the floor manager will notice a shoe missing from the display racks and after pointlessly nagging his salespeople to find it, he'll accept the fact that it's gone and that he has to put out another. Why not the mate? Mia will just come in and pick up the other shoe from the very same shelf. Maybe even tomorrow.

No need to linger now. She has the perfect, perfect thing for the Mia she wants to be, a person who might have been lost to her but now was found. Her sixteenth birthday, which is less than three months away, is going to be the best ever.


Mia made it all the way back through the spinning doors. As soon as she stepped outside, a man appeared from nowhere and took hold of her arm. "Excuse me, young lady." He was football-player big and wearing an earpiece connected to a wire that disappeared beneath the collar of his ugly blue jacket. "I'll need to inspect your bag before you go."

Her heart was hammering. "Who are you?"

"I'm a security agent for the store, miss. Now here's my advice to you. If you cooperate, this will go much better.

Make a fuss and you'll be sorry. Okay? Now step back inside with me."

He escorted her to the same counter where she'd purchased her lip gloss and gestured that she should put her bag on top of the glass display case. A thought flashed through her mind that she should have worn gloves to do this. That way her fingerprints wouldn't be on the merchandise.

The agent said, "Please unzip your bag."

Mia felt that electrical charge again, but this time it jangled her, left her gasping for breath. She watched, paralyzed, as he pulled her things out—the new tube of lip gloss, a fashion magazine with the headline TIME TO SPRING FORWARD, her address book, a pack of tissues, a small bag of makeup that the man unzipped and ran his fingers through before placing aside, a comb and hairbrush, and her gold key ring with the Irish friendship symbol that her best friend, Gael, had given her last Christmas.

Then he removed the silver sandal.

The agent turned it over, saw the fat price tag. She silently cursed herself for not scratching that off already. "This doesn't belong to you, does it?"

"Of course it does! How else would it get in my bag?"

"What are you doing with one shoe?"

The words came out of her, a cloth that wove itself. She hoped there were no holes—that while she talked it all made sense. "I bought it last week, then I wasn't sure I bought the right size, so I came back to try it on in the next size up. I brought this one back so I could compare. But I couldn't get a salesperson to help me. They were too busy." *Whew. Done. That should work.*

"That's your story?" The agent carefully put Mia's belongings back in her purse, everything but the silver sandal. "You're going to have to come with me."

"What for?" Mia shrieked. "That's my sandal, you asshole!"

He didn't answer her. The agent slung her purse over his shoulder like a carcass he'd bagged and led her away by the elbow. In the makeup mirrors she passed, she saw how her black hair hung down limply in her face as he jostled her along. She did not look good like this.

"Where are we going?" she asked, suddenly nervous.

"Roger Brady. Head of security. He loves a good story. You two should hit it off."

They got on an elevator and rode in silence to the top floor. It opened on a long, empty hallway. There weren't any windows, only closed doors. The walls were scuffed and dirty-looking. Mia's mind raced double time. She'd have to stick to the lie. Bought it last week . . . this is outrageous . . . I'll never shop here again. . . .

She was led to a tiny room where a bald-headed man sat behind a desk. "Thank you, James. Please wait outside. This won't take long." Behind his desk was a bank of video monitors. Ten of them broadcasted images of different areas of the store in black and white. The control panel looked as if you could land the space shuttle with it. She looked back at the bald guy.

He smiled and gestured to the monitors. "Like it? It's our new security system. State of the art. Shall I show you how it works?"

"No."

"Oh, I think you'll be interested to see a particular video

we captured today. Take a look." He swiveled around in his chair. "See this screen?" He pointed to a monitor on the bottom row. With a flip of a switch, it lit up with a picture of the shoe department. The date and time scrolled across the bottom of the frame. "There you are, upper left-hand corner." Sure enough, Mia was right in the frame. "I'm going to fast-forward to the good part." He turned the knob so that Mia's journey through the shoe department happened in triple time. On-screen, she didn't move with the kind of stealth she imagined. More like a hungry bug searching haphazardly for a meal, zigzagging in and out of the aisles. The tape slowed down to normal speed. "Here's what I want to show you," he said.

On-screen, the sandal in question went into Mia's bag. He pushed another button and the camera captured her departure, following her as if by magic all the way down the escalator, into the cosmetics department and out through the spinning doors.

"We have cameras throughout the store," he explained. "This is all admissible evidence in court. You will be convicted of shoplifting." He opened a desk drawer and pulled out a pile of blank forms.

Mia watched herself on the monitor as she followed Big James back inside, watched him go through her stuff. She heard herself say, "That's my sandal, you asshole!"

The bald guy scowled at her now. "Nice language. Let's see some ID," he said.

There had to be a way out of this. But Mia couldn't think of what it might be. She took out her wallet and handed over her student ID. He looked at it and wrote on the form.

"Mia Morrow. I used to know a Constance Morrow." Now he looked at her again. "You're not her daughter by any chance, are you?"

She was. "No. Not that it's any of your business."

"Address, 69 West Adams Street. Apartment 2. Is this current?"

It was. "I live on Gregson Way now. Number 249."

They finished filling out the form with as many lies as Mia could manufacture, and when they were done he told her she'd have to wait until the police could pick her up.

"I can't believe you want to send me to jail for stealing a sandal," she said bitterly.

He shook his head. "You remind me of your mother."

"I don't look anything like my mother."

"I'm not talking about your looks."

Mia decided to keep quiet before she gave him any more vital information.

"She still working up at the university?"

"How would I know?"

The bald guy then spoke into an intercom on his desk. "James, you can take her now."

Mia was led across the hall and into another room. "This could take a while," James told her. "Better get comfortable," he said, indicating a metal chair. It was the only thing in there.

And then she was alone.


Mia couldn't think of any way out of the trouble she was in. Michele and Gael, her closest friends in the tenth grade, wouldn't have the kind of money she'd need for bail. Unless they asked their parents, which they were unlikely to do, because they wouldn't want their parents to know their friend was going to jail. Grandpa Andy would rescue her if he could, but he was too frail to get down to the police station on his own, and she *really* didn't want him to know what she'd done. Too bad the small allowance he gave her wouldn't be enough to cover bail. It wasn't even enough for a pair of sandals.

Mia had no father to turn to for help. He was long gone. So her mother was her only way out of jail. Mia was sure of that. It was the worst part of all of this. She knew exactly what her mother would say about the situation she was in. "Don't you ever think?" She'd never hear the end of it.

Mia wished she'd never seen the silver sandals. Never wanted them. Never ever had the thought they'd make her happy or feel anything at all.

She checked her watch. She'd been waiting nearly an hour. You'd think cops would come right away, shoplifting being a crime and all. She wondered if the hallway was still as empty as before. Maybe then she could throw her jacket over her head to fool the cameras and then . . . Mia devised a getaway in her head. But when she walked to the door, opened it and looked out, she found James there.

"Can I help you?" he said coldly.

*Drat.* "Um . . . Is there a bathroom I can use?"

James led her down the hall to a ladies' room with two stalls. "You got five minutes," he said, and turned to walk back down the hall. She went in.

It was grungy in there, with dingy black-and-white tiles on the floor and a couple of sinks stained with age. The metal stall doors were covered with graffiti. She read what was scratched there.

*This place sucks*

*J.V.* ♥ *L.D.*

*If u cn rd ths thn u r . . .* and next to that the person had drawn a picture of a spiral. Mia figured it was supposed to look like a screw. Whoever drew it wasn't much of an artist. But then again, she couldn't draw, either.

Mia took out a quarter and tried to scratch at the stall. It was shiny and new, but it wasn't sharp enough to make a clean mark. And so she started to flip it instead. "Heads I get off, tails I go to jail." The coin glistened as it spun on the tiled floor, then stopped. It was tails. She threw it again. "Heads I'm out, tails I'm stuck for good." It twirled in the air then fell on its face. Another flippin' tail. "Hah! Okay, one more time. Heads I win the lottery, tails . . . tails what? . . . Okay, tails Grandpa Andy gets better." She tossed the coin high this time. It landed on Grandpa Andy. Mia raised her arms and cheered silently.

She should have been home soon to make his dinner. He was probably sitting all alone and wondering what was keeping her. Ugh! What if she never got to make him dinner again? How was she going to get out of this mess? *Could* she? Mia exited the bathroom, her worries now spinning around her again.

James watched her walk back down the hall, but instead of sending her back to the empty room, he directed her to the bald guy's office. "They're waiting for you."

Mia turned the doorknob, ready to face her fate, then froze.

Bald-headed Brady had indeed figured things out. Her

mother was there now, still in her work uniform, a pink short-sleeved dress stained with something that looked like blood but was probably tomato sauce. This was bad. She'd obviously raced over from the university's cafeteria in a panic. Mia wished her mother had at least changed before she came down here. She looked awful. Hairnet and all. How could she stand to let anyone see her like that?

Her mother apparently wasn't happy to see her, either. Constance sat there looking like some kind of beast had entered the room. "If I thought she had any remorse for her actions," the bald guy said, "I might act differently."

"I'm sure she does," her mother responded. "How could she not?"

"Right. She's sorry she's caught, not sorry for stealing. And she lied to me for a half hour while we filled out those forms. She won't even admit what she did. Which is very typical criminal behavior, by the way." He gave her mother a meaningful look.

Her mother rolled her eyes at him. "How many people do you know who are sorry at the time they do something wrong? That always comes later."

"The point is, if she isn't made to pay for her actions, she'll never learn that they're wrong. Think about that, Constance," the bald guy said sadly. And at that moment Mia realized that these two actually knew each other. "Do you want her to keep on stealing for the next few years," he continued, "until she's caught by someone else, and possibly for a much worse crime?"

Her mother didn't speak for a minute, then said, "It's her first time, Roger. Come on."

Constance? Roger? So they were on a first-name basis. The bald guy looked ten years older, but she realized that was only because he had no hair.

"Yeah, Roger," Mia said. "Come on."

Her mother gave her a warning look, and Mia was silenced.

"If you think she hasn't stolen before," Roger said, "then she's conning you, too. I won't just let her go. She shouldn't be let off without paying some kind of price."

"You're right. She should pay. How much were the shoes she stole? Two and a quarter you said, right?"

Roger was nodding in a resigned way. Mia could sense her mother cooking up a plan. And then she got even more nervous than she already was.

"Here's what I propose." Constance looked sternly at Mia. "She should pay the store back for the shoes she tried to steal. You'll keep the shoes, and you'll keep the cops out of it. Unless of course, she defaults on the debt. If she can't or won't pay, then you can press charges. How's that?"

"I'm going to be charged for something I don't get to keep!" Mia yelped. "That's not fair!"

Roger and her mother looked at her like she was a crazy person. Then they laughed. They both laughed!

"Wonder how I guessed she was your daughter?" he said to Constance. "Must be some fun around your house."

*If you only knew,* Mia thought.

Then Constance said, "For that impulsive comment, I think she should pay even more. So let's call it three hundred even, shall we?"

Mia glared at her mother. Constance was into her business

for the ninety-millionth time, and Mia didn't like it. This was *Mia's* life. *Her* choices. Wasn't it? She almost wanted to go to jail just to prove that it was.

If only she could fly away. Get real tiny and buzz right through Roger's open window. Then all of a sudden it hit her . . . that's how she'd save herself . . . get tiny. She'd do what her mother wanted. Besides, what was three hundred dollars? She'd find a way to get it. She'd be fine.

"Okay," she addressed her mother. "I'll do it."

Her mother's face relaxed. Roger was nodding. "I hope this teaches you a lesson, young lady," he said.

"Thanks, Rog. I owe you one," her mother said.

"What are friends for, I guess."

She patted his shoulder. "You are so nice," she said.

He shrugged, like it wasn't the kind of compliment he wanted to hear. There was some history between them for sure. Enough to agree to the whole crazy debt thing. He showed them out of the office.

Big James followed Mia and her mother through the store and outside, too. He watched them walk down the sidewalk. "Be good," he called out to Mia.

"Oh, she will!" her mother answered for her.

And out on the street, Mia felt her mood lifting, because it suddenly occurred to her that she could hold a yard sale of all the goods she'd ever stolen, and in that way she'd be able to raise the kind of money she now owed the department store, thanks to her mother.

*The stony silence* that fell between them as they walked home felt as harsh to Mia as what she'd just lived through at the store.

Soon they were away from the Commons, the old main street that had been closed to traffic a few years back and was now a boutiquey shopping district of five blocks anchored by the department store. They passed the old Methodist church, then crossed the bridge over the gorge that separated their more run-down neighborhood from the rest of things. Mia felt like she knew every ugly crack in the sidewalk of this small college town in upstate New York.

Mia tried to break the tension between them. "So who was that Roger guy?"

Her mother glared at her. "The guy who just saved your butt, that's who."

"No, I meant how come you know him?"

"We went to high school together."

"Oh." Mia took a breath. "Did you go out with him?"

"Yeah. Once. Or twice. I think."

"You don't remember?"

"Well, it was a long time ago."

"Huh." Mia couldn't picture it, though for a split second she tried. For purely personal reasons. Constance was still a teenager when she had Mia. What if she was dating Roger Brady when she'd gotten pregnant? Could he be the guy who got her pregnant?

Nah. The bald-headed head of security wasn't the bad-boy type, the kind her mother said she used to "waste her time on." The kind of guy Constance said Mia's father was. Mia had no idea who her father was. Whenever she'd asked her mother about him, all Constance would talk about were ugly things. Sometimes Mia thought she'd go crazy wondering. But she'd stopped asking Constance about him because she hated hearing that the guy was a loser.

It didn't matter that she didn't know him. He was still her father. So it was better not to think about it. Mia pushed the thought of Roger and her mother out of her head.

They stopped for groceries at the little market close to their house. Constance had settled back into silence. All of a sudden, the thought of having to spend the entire evening with her angry mother seemed more punishment than Mia could stand.

"Are you going back to work tonight?" she asked. "Your shift doesn't end till nine tonight, right?" Constance had a permanent job working the food line at Butler, the main dining hall at the university up on the hill. The university was the reason most people lived in town. Either you were a student or professor, or you worked some service job up there, like her mother. Mia's grandfather had been a professor of biochemisty, though he retired due to his illness.

"They had to call someone to fill in for me since I didn't know how long it would take to . . . you know . . . help you. Bet they'll dock my pay." Her mother worked every weeknight: from lunch shift at one through dinner until nine at night. She never took a day off, and now she sounded pretty pissed about missing this one.

Once she'd paid at the checkout and had placed her change safely back in her wallet, Constance asked Mia, "So, what are you going to do for money now that you have a debt to pay?"

Mia sighed as they got back onto the street. She didn't want to let her mother in on her plans just yet. "I'll think of something."

"Like what? That's what I'm asking you to contemplate right now."

"I'll sell off a bunch of my stuff. Like at a yard sale," Mia told her. "I should be able to raise what I need that way."

"What stuff?"

"Clothes I don't wear anymore. And some of my CDs." Mia started talking fast because her mother was giving her that look, her face a frowning mask. "I'll do it on a Saturday, so there'll be plenty of people around. I can put up flyers at school and on the Commons."

Constance shook her head.

Mia stopped walking. "Why not? What's wrong with that?"

Constance stopped, too. "It's too easy. You'll sit out with all your stuff on the street for a day, and then it'll be over. This is a punishment, Mia. Do you understand what I'm saying to you? You're a shoplifter, and you almost went to jail today. I'm not going to let you off that easy. You're going to have to get a job."

Mia groaned. She should have known. Constance had been after her to get a job for a year now. Mia hated the idea. Why do some dumb job that didn't pay anything? And Grandpa Andy was against it, too. He didn't want his granddaughter doing menial labor. He said it wouldn't prepare her for anything worthwhile in life. Constance tried arguing that there was nothing wrong with honest work. That way Mia could earn money for all the silly things she wanted. Besides, Mia was her daughter, so she should be the one to decide what was best for her. This was only last month, and it had gotten really ugly. "The girl has a brain. Unlike you. So forget it!" he'd yelled. Then there was her mother's stunned face when he announced he'd up Mia's allowance, sending a clear message that the whole idea need not be discussed further.

Mia could see their house now.

She decided to ignore her mother's request until she could speak to her grandfather about it. He was sure to be against it, as he had been in the past. She unlocked the door and went upstairs without waiting to see if her mother was coming after her.

They lived in a three-story Victorian, an old firetrap divided into three apartments, one on each floor. It was owned by Grandpa Andy, who lived on the ground level. Mia and her mother had the second story, and they rented out the third to a guy named George LeRoy. He was divorced and a garage mechanic, and he had a huge crush on Constance. As soon as he heard the front door open, he appeared at the top of the stairs and came clomping down. Even her mother's ugly uniform didn't seem to dampen his enthusiasm. "Let me get those bags for you ladies."

"Hey, George," Constance said. "I don't want to trouble you."

"No, no. It's no problem. No problem at all." He took the bags out of their hands.

Mia unlocked their apartment and George went down

the long hall to the kitchen, which was in the back. Up front was a small parlor with a water-damaged ceiling, dingy stained-glass panels in the front windows, and a door to a terrace with some plants that looked as if they were done with living. Down the hall were two bedrooms for Mia and her mother, at the back was a kitchen/dining room where they spent most of their time, and out back was a porch stacked high with garbage bags and all the recycling. The whole place was more than a little run-down, with crooked windowsills and uneven floorboards. They couldn't afford to fix it up. The best they could do was pick out some fun colors to paint the walls—toffee for the kitchen, pretty apricot in the hall, and cornflower blue for the parlor—but Mia still thought the place looked kind of sad.

George made some small talk, how's work, that kind of thing, then Constance said, "Well, it's time for me to get food on the table."

After they heard the upstairs door shut, Mia said, "He just wants to ask you out. How long are you going to watch him try to work up the nerve?"

"The last thing I need is a boyfriend living over my head."

"It's just dinner."

Constance shrugged and fixed herself a drink. Part of her evening ritual, though usually it took place a few hours later. Mia knew it well. Three fingers of gin, a splash of tonic, and a slice of lime squeezed hard over the clear liquid before stirring it with her finger. Just one. Constance said it took the edge off.

"Or you could go for drinks," Mia tried.

But Constance wasn't having it. "Put the groceries away and I'll make dinner."

"Shouldn't I check on Grandpa Andy?"

"I'll take care of him when we're done."

"Oh, okay." This wasn't what she wanted, but Mia did as she was told, emptying the grocery bags. Her mother was going to talk to Grandpa Andy before Mia got the chance. "I could go down to him after we eat," Mia said.

"Don't you have homework?"

"I don't know. I mean, yes, but I don't know what it is."

"Right. Because you missed school due to almost getting arrested." Constance tossed a frozen lasagna in the microwave. "Set the table now."

Mia took two knives and forks from the drawer and set their places with paper napkins that Constance kept in a holder on the table they'd bought from a furniture outlet. It wobbled a little when you cut your meat, but they ignored it. They ate dinner this way, like two characters in an old-time novel, sitting up straight at the unsteady table. To Mia it was pointless to act as if they were a proper family, eating a proper meal together. They were a mother and daughter who could barely stand each other most of the time. Why pretend to be something else?

"We haven't finished talking about what you're going to do for work." Constance finished her drink and chopped up salad fixings. "I might be able to get you a place on the food line," she said. "Starting pay is six and a half an hour."

*Shite!* Mia thought. This was her evil plan all along! Butler Hall was a dreary place that hadn't changed since it was built more than a hundred years ago. Lots of dark wood everywhere, on the walls, the tables, the chairs. A real dungeon. And her mother could easily keep an eye on her the whole time, too. There was no way.

"I don't know what else you can do," Constance contin- ued. "As Grandpa Andy says, working at Baskin-Robbins isn't life-enhancing enough. And if you don't pay the de- partment store back . . ." The bell on the microwave rang. ". . . I don't know what's going to happen to you. Grab two plates, will you? " Mia did as she was told, but she could feel her anger rising.

Constance pulled the steaming lasagna out of the plastic wrapper, divided it in half, and heaped it onto their plates. Mia watched her as she worked in their tiny kitchen, ma- neuvering the spatula with about as much care as she did on the food line. Constance didn't spill a drop, but she didn't treat it like food, either. Or treat Mia like her daugh- ter. Mia took the plate her mother shoved at her as if she were just another student, got some salad for herself, and sat at the table.

Her mother did the same, then launched in once more. "So . . . should I ask the boss if we can make a place for you? It's a good job, Mia."

Mia really didn't want to talk anymore. *Really didn't.* She looked up from her plate. "You're kidding, right? What's so great about serving bratty college kids that nuclear waste?"

Her mother ignored the comment. "Did I tell you I'm about to get promoted? They're opening up a new position, as a management trainee. I'll learn to negotiate contracts with vendors, and keep the books, and all kinds of other things. I'll get a twenty-five percent pay raise. I've worked hard, and it's finally going to pay off."

Constance seemed genuinely excited, but Mia didn't care at that moment. "So now you'll order the slop instead of shoveling it out," she shouted. "Who cares? You work in a stupid cafeteria. Grandpa Andy thinks you could do a lot better. And so do I."

Constance pounded the table with her fist. "I'm in the food services industry!" she shouted back. Then she immediately stopped herself. She took a deep breath. "Someday, Mia, you're going to learn you can't just act without thinking." Constance stood and tossed what was left of her lasagna in the trash. "I've had it with your behavior. You're grounded. No going out for a week. No phone, no TV. Get it? And if you don't pay back that debt, you'll go to jail. Now go to your room and think about that."

Mia was glad it was finally over. She walked down the narrow hall and slammed her bedroom door real hard. But it didn't make her feel better. Not one bit.

She heard Constance walk out of the apartment. Heard her go down the stairs, heard her go into Grandpa Andy's apartment.


Mia was surrounded by the deep purple walls of her bedroom. Dark as a womb, the color always made her feel safe and quiet and back in touch with her own heartbeat. She felt the tension draining from her, and she breathed in the quiet. Silvery curtains shimmered at the windows, wafting in the warm evening breeze, a present from her mother a few birthdays ago. But she didn't want to think about the good things her mother had done for her. It only made her feel bad again.

Why did it always have to be war? Sometimes Mia thought if it were just her and Grandpa Andy living together, things would be fine. If he weren't so old. And sick. But after a fight like this, she wished her mother would go away—just vanish like a puff of smoke. No more Constance. Because then life would be so easy, so much better.

Mia sighed. That wasn't going to happen.

And that wasn't really what she wanted. She didn't want her mother to go away. She was already missing a father, and that stunk. What she wanted was for Constance to get a life so she wasn't so focused on what Mia was doing. So it wasn't so completely depressing to live with her.

Her mother never ever went out. She had some work friends but no one she'd hang out with afterward. And she never went on dates, though she had plenty of offers. Mia was sure it had to do with her missing father, who sounded like he was a total mess. "He was always getting high. Or drunk. Chasing girls. I'm glad I never married him. And you should be glad, too."

But Mia wasn't glad. Her friends' fathers might be weirdos or get angry at stupid things, but they could also fix bike tires and cheer at soccer games, and best of all, they made her friends' mothers happy. Instead, Mia had to live with a mom who was uptight all the time. She couldn't help thinking that maybe if she had a dad, a good one, she'd have someone to talk to about that.

Another sigh. That wasn't going to happen, either.

Mia heard voices coming from the downstairs apartment. Her mother saying something about "learn to handle" and "time to grow up." Her grandfather's gruff voice answering with "develop her mind" and "meant for better things."

Mia thought about calling her friends. Just talking to

them would make her feel normal again, but she would have to explain why she didn't come back to school that afternoon. Gael would be worried about her near miss with the law, and their other friend Michele would deliver the usual pep talk about how she had to pull herself together. Mia didn't think she could handle either reaction at that moment, so she'd have to save the confession for tomorrow.

Mia flopped down on her bed and emptied out her black bag, reaching for that fashion magazine with the SPRING FORWARD headline. Beneath the typeface was a photo of three laughing girls walking toward the camera as if they didn't have a care in the world. It looked so fake. How could anyone be that happy?

Then the voices got louder. "SHE'S MY ONLY HOPE!" That was her grandfather, bellowing now. Mia could imagine his angry face, and her mother's full of hurt. Mia tried returning her attention to the magazine, but she couldn't concentrate. Flipping fast through the pages, Mia searched frantically for something beautiful to look at.

And then she found it. A layout about summer sandals. Glittery, embellished with beads, beautifully constructed in impossibly bright colors. She wanted every pair. There were no faces in the layout, only legs. And that gave Mia an idea.

She looked up at the wall behind her desk at a collage she'd been working on for weeks. It was a figure of a woman with eight pairs of arms wearing snakeskin, corduroy, tweed, linen. Eight pairs of hands wearing rings, bracelets, fake nails, gloves. She was a creature from out of this world, a goddess, and spinning in her orbit were shiny pressed-powder

compacts and silvery gadgets every girl couldn't live without . . . cell phones and digi players and handbags in every
color of the rainbow, all cut from magazines and glued to
the purple wall.

Mia went over to her small white desk and the white
shelves beside it that held all her various art supplies: glitter, glue, pens, pencils, and colored tissue paper. She took
her scissors from her desk and carefully cut out all the magazine legs with their shiny sandals, taking care to preserve
their exact shape. With a glue stick she began pasting the
pieces where she wanted them all around the body of the
goddess on the wall.

As she worked, the voices downstairs faded away, but all
of a sudden she was interrupted by a loud bang. Mia froze
and listened to the sound of her mother sprinting up the
stairs. She came through the front door and marched right
into Mia's room without knocking. Mia still held the glue
stick in her hand.

"What happened?" Mia asked her mother. "Is Grandpa
Andy all right?"

"No. He's not. He's the same as always. But that doesn't
matter anymore. I'm here to tell you not to expect an allowance from him anymore. You're going to have to earn your
own money from now on." Mia just stood there with her
mouth agape. There was nothing else she could do. Nothing to stop her hell-bent mother from messing with her life.

"What are you going to do about that?" Constance asked
triumphantly. She positively glowed. "Any thoughts?"

Mia knew her mother thought she'd won, that Mia would
have to work at Butler after all.

"Yeah. I'm going to look for a job that's worthy of my time."

The look on Constance's face turned sour. "Well, you're not going to get paid to paste pictures on the wall. Get to bed now." And with that she stomped out.

Mia ignored the command and stood back to admire her work. It might be true that no one would ever pay her to make a wall collage, but that didn't mean it wasn't important. Because it was beautiful and out of the ordinary and something her mother would never do.

*The next morning* Mia's snooze alarm didn't go off and so she had to walk double time if she wanted to catch the school bus. It picked up kids ten blocks away, in a nicer neighborhood, where her friends Michele and Gael lived.

A steamy breeze rippled the morning air, and beads of sweat ran down her back. She was trying hard to think of a way to tell her friends about the department store fiasco that wouldn't sound so bad. She could lie and say it was all a big mistake. Or not tell them at all and just say she went home sick. But they probably wouldn't believe her.

And the truth was going to cause trouble. She could feel it.

They'd all been friends since elementary school. Mia used to think the three of them were a good team. Michele was smart and practical. Gael had the warm heart. And Mia was the spirit of adventure, pushing them to try things and take risks. Pick up that worm. Ride bikes to the other end of town. Leave an anonymous love letter in your crush's locker.

But as they grew up, they didn't seem to mesh together in quite the same way. They were growing uneven, their differences coming into sharper focus. It wasn't just that Michele's and Gael's parents were professors and expected big things from them. Their parents actually liked them, and Mia thought having that kind of backup made everything much easier for them.

She was coming into their neighborhood now. Row houses were replaced by single-family homes, each with its own pretty little yard out front. It seemed to Mia that everything had room to grow bigger around here. The trees and the houses and maybe even the people inside.

As she expected, when she turned the last corner she spotted her friends waiting at the bus stop with the rest of the other kids. Gael peered down the street, looking for her, a worried frown creasing her brow. "Where have you been?" she shouted out when she saw Mia.

Michele only half-turned and squinted down the street at Mia, a far less enthusiastic welcome. "The prodigal student returns," Michele drawled as Mia reached the bus stop. "What did you do to deserve the afternoon off?"

Gael bumped her friend's shoulder. "Quit it. So what happened to you?" Mia looked into Gael's freckled face. Her bright red hair gleamed in the strong sunlight. "We didn't know if you were hurt or something equally awful, and we didn't know what to do. We were so worried about you. Weren't we, Michele?"

Michele shrugged. "I thought you cut, then I wasn't so sure."

Gael went on. "If we reported you missing and then you'd only left school . . . you'd get in trouble. But there's a whole lot worse things that could happen to you than detention."

Mia smiled and patted Gael's freckled hand. "Poor girl. I had no idea I worried you so."

Gael pulled her hand away. "I'm serious, Mia."

Mia was startled. "I'm sorry . . . I didn't realize that you'd get so upset. But I'm fine, so stop worrying, okay?"

Gael sighed deeply. "If you say so."

The school bus screeched to a halt, and the doors opened. The girls waited for the younger kids to board and then made their way down the aisle to the back. The three of them squeezed onto a single bench with Gael in the middle, and as the school bus bounced and rumbled along, Michele leaned over and said, "So, Mia . . . are you going to tell us where you went or not?"

For the first time since the beginning of her ordeal, Mia felt ashamed. She turned to look out the dirty window and tried to gather enough strength to confess the whole embarrassing mess.

"I kind of got arrested. Almost."

Michele's smug expression vanished in a flash and Gael went all wide-eyed. "You were sort of . . . in jail?" Gael stammered. "You . . . What happened?"

"Take it easy. It was no big deal."

"You were shoplifting," said Michele, recovering her matter-of-factness as if she'd known it all along.

Mia nodded.

"Where?" asked Gael.

"At the department store on the Commons."

"I told you that would happen someday," Michele commented dryly.

"I only had one shoe in my bag. They didn't press charges."

"Did you cry? Do you have a record? Is your mother mad?" Gael asked.

"No and no, and if by *mad* you mean insane, then yes, she is. I'm grounded for a week."

"What are we going to do with you?" Michele was shaking her head.

"Buy me some new shoes?" she answered flatly, annoyed by Michele's parental tone.

Gael playfully slapped her arm, a little too hard. "Mia! You're impossible."

"Any remorse?" Michele said, looking at Mia like a fussy old schoolmarm would. "Feel anything like that at all?"

"I definitely feel bad I got caught."

"Is that all?" Gael asked, sounding shocked.

"No. That's not all. I'm glad I'm going to school today instead of jail. Although the two may not be so different from each other. Mandatory attendance and all."

"Yeah, but you're about to be paroled from school very soon," Michele said. "So try not to blow it, stickyfingers." Michele wagged a finger at her. "Be smart."

Michele turned away then, and Mia secretly stuck her tongue out at her friend.

"Were you scared?" Gael asked.

"Yeah, actually, I didn't think they were going to let me go." Mia told them about her mother showing up to make a deal.

Michele said, "My parents would have had a heart attack."

"Mine would have cried for days," said Gael.

"That's because they care about you. All my mother cares about is making me do what she wants me to do."

Her friends were silent for a moment.

"Well, we care about you." Gael put her arm around Mia's shoulder, and Mia felt the beginning of tears sting her eyes.

"How are you going to get the money for the store?" Michele asked.

"I don't know," Mia told her. "But I'll figure something out."

From her friends' worried faces Mia realized they weren't so sure about that.

The school bus pulled into the circular drive in front of the school, and the doors flew open. As soon as Mia saw the brick prisonlike building, she was reminded of more pressing matters. "Hey, you guys . . . I need to copy someone's math homework."

Michele looked like it didn't matter to her whether Mia needed help, but Gael pulled her notebook out. Still, it was Michele's paper Mia would rather copy from. Michele had enough ambition for two people, studying all her waking hours with the endurance of a robot. Mia had no idea how she did it. And math was her best subject.

The girls sat together on a low wall as Mia neatly duplicated the proofs on Gael's paper, while other students mingled outside the school, waiting for the bell signaling first period to ring. "Is that one right?" Mia asked, pointing at one of Gael's answers. She had no idea if it was right or wrong. The only thing she was sure about was that Michele would know the correct answer.

Michele peered down at the page. "No. You need to multiply by $x$ over $y$. Not the other way around."

"Great," Gael said. "Now I'll get that one wrong."

"You want me to do your homework, too?" Michele said to her.

"Who wouldn't?" Gael shot back.

Mia finished up. And then, still in a pissy mood, the three of them went in through the school's front doors. In the reinforced glass there, Mia saw reflections of her fellow students, looking gloomy. All trapped for the day.

By the time they arrived at math class, most of the other students were already in their seats. The teacher arrived moments later. Mr. Sabatelli picked up a piece of chalk and wrote on the blackboard. *POP QUIZ.* There were groans throughout the room. "Take out your notebooks, everyone," Sabatelli instructed the class. "Write your name at the top of a blank page. No talking now."

For Mia it was as if all the air got sucked out of the room. The only thing she knew was that she wouldn't be able to answer most of the questions. She dropped her head onto the wooden desk. It smelled like pencil eraser and sweaty hands. In the darkness there, she reviewed the little she remembered of past math lessons. Parts of equations flashed before her eyes. They blurred and turned into a bunch of squiggles that didn't add up to anything.

There was only one thing to do. Mia opened her notebook and tore out a piece of paper. In large letters she wrote, *HELP ME,* then crumpled it up and threw it, aiming for Michele's desk. It missed, landing with barely a sound on the floor. Paper hitting linoleum equals near silence, thank God. Michele regarded it out of the corner of her eye and then ignored it. Just left it there! Even Gael looked surprised, but Sabatelli was getting close and she turned away, too. Mia let out a deep, dry cough, bent over, and scooped up the crumpled paper. She sat back up, feeling a rush of blood that made her light-headed.

And she found Sabatelli standing in front of her desk. "I'll take that, Miss Morrow," he said, pointing at the ball of paper she clutched in her lap. Mia put it into his hand.

"Interesting," he said, smoothing out the paper on Mia's desk. "Tell the class what's written there, Miss Morrow. Speak up so everyone can hear."

Mia shot a burning look at her teacher. In a low, barely audible voice, Mia said, "Help me." There were nasty snickers from several of her classmates. "Shut up," she said under her breath.

But Sabatelli heard her. He said, "That's enough, Mia. Want to tell me who this note was intended for?"

Michele began to tap her foot, fast, her leg jittering up and down. Sabatelli looked at Michele for the briefest of moments, but Michele kept her eyes glued to the blackboard. He turned back to Mia. Just then she understood that he had no intention of pulling Michele into this mess. She was his ace student. His favorite. She was safe. Life was so unfair.

"You're excused from this exam, Miss Morrow. And your grade will be zero."

Her blood boiled. "Drop dead," Mia said.

Sabatelli grabbed her by the upper arm and yanked her out of her seat. There were gasps throughout the classroom, while her two best friends looked on horrified as Sabatelli dragged her up the aisle. Mia's heart raced in her chest from fear and shock and knowing she'd made a big mistake, and she could only hope Sabatelli didn't feel her pulse racing where he held her arm, because she didn't want to give him the satisfaction of knowing just how scared she was. No one had ever laid hands on her like this before. She didn't dare look at him as he firmly and silently led her into the carpeted wing of administration. The next thing she knew, she was left standing in front of Principal Kent.

Principal Kent considered her for a moment. "This is the second time this month you've been brought here," he said quietly. "Why do you do the things you do, Mia?" Looking into Principal Kent's calm gaze, Mia felt all the dark energy inside her begin to let go, and she found herself actually wishing she had an answer to his question.

"Take a seat on the couch outside in the hall," he said.

And that is where she spent the rest of the morning, thinking about how everything was going wrong for her.

After school let out, Mia spotted Michele and Gael waiting for the bus that would take them all home. She decided to pretend as if the whole math thing wasn't a big deal. "Hi, guys," she said breezily as she approached. "Hope your day was better than mine."

Gael spun around. "That was really freaky today, Mia," she said. "Sabatelli looked mad enough to tear your arm off."

"And then he sat staring at me all through the exam," Michele told her. "Probably waiting to see if I'd cheat with someone else."

"I doubt that," Mia said bitterly.

She didn't want to talk about math class anymore. There was nothing good to say about it. The sun was high in the sky, and the warm air felt like a caress. "Listen, it's too nice out for homework at the library, don't you think? Why don't we go for a swim at the reservoir?"

"Are you kidding?" Michele said.

"It's only April. The water will be freezing," Gael said, giving Mia an odd look.

"And I've got tons of homework," Michele added as she continued reading some class printout.

"Okay, then. Why don't we go hang on the arts quad up at the college? We can study up there."

Michele snorted without looking up. "Oh, sure."

"We will work. I promise. What do you think, Gael?"

"I'm up for it. I'd rather be outside if I'm going to have to do lots of reading."

"And you?" Michele asked Mia. "What will you do while we work?"

Mia returned Michele's barbed look. "Well, Principal Kent made Sabatelli give me a take-home exam, to make up for the quiz."

"I'm not helping you with that, either," Michele shot back.

"Did I ask you? Clearly it would be pointless."

"What would you prefer, that I sat outside Kent's office with you all morning, instead of acing that quiz? I've been studying hard since the start of term. You almost got me in big trouble."

"You almost got yourself in big trouble. You're lousy at looking not guilty."

"Why should I learn to look like something I'm not?" Michele shouted. "I don't have to look not guilty because I didn't do anything wrong."

"Stop it, you guys," Gael interrupted. "I'm sick of fighting. I'll help Mia with math. Are you coming to the quad or not, Michele? We're not going to beg."

Michele looked at Gael. "Yeah. Yes. I want to. I just need to work, you know?"

"We know!" Gael and Mia said in unison.

Michele smiled at them. "I'm sorry. Am I turning into a drag? I am, right?"

"You're not that bad. Yet!" Gael said.

Michele relaxed. "I'm sorry I didn't help you, Mia. It's just—"

"Forget it," Mia said. "I just don't want to fight anymore, either. Not with you guys. I feel all the bad stuff that happened this week is making me act crazy. I'm sorry. But I don't want it to mess us up."

Gael shot a look at Michele that Mia read as telling her to act nicer. She could have kissed her for it. And for the first time that day, Michele regarded Mia with a look of deep sympathy. "We're trying to understand," Michele said.

"Enough about what happened," Gael said. "Let's just move on."

They ditched the school bus and started to walk up the long, steep hill to the university. They were sweaty by the time they reached the arts quad in the center of campus. The sun was still strong and cast sharp shadows through the tall old trees dotting the expansive lawn. All the students had switched into summer gear at this first sign of good weather, hanging around in shorts and sandals, with their fat backpacks resting on the grass beside them. Most had their faces tilted up to gather rays, though a few had their books open, pretending to study or trying their best.

Michele had insisted on a place in the shade so they could work. Sitting away from her a little, in a patch of warm sunlight, Gael and Mia worked through math problems together.

"Where did you leave off in the book?" Gael asked.

Mia opened her math textbook and flipped through the pages, trying to remember the last time she did homework. "Here it is. I have to do all these questions, figuring out the area of these different shapes. Real useful stuff."

"Okay. Let's see . . ." Gael scanned the page. "Here's a good one to start with. It's pretty easy." She put on a professorial voice. "What is the area of a right triangle when the base equals four and three-quarters and the height is eight?"

Mia looked into the distance, as if the answer were out there. On the other side of the path from where they sat, a few guys played Frisbee. They wore their shirts tucked neatly into their jeans like models in the J.Crew catalog, in a sort of preppy-sexy way.

"What formula do you need to figure this out?" Gael asked.

"I'm not sure."

"You'll need to memorize this. So write it down," Gael told her. "The area of a right triangle can be figured out by multiplying the base times the height times one half. Okay?"

The Frisbee game was heating up. Those preppy guys were jumping into the air now. Mia forced herself to return her attention to the problems she had to work through on the page. "Now convert the fractions to start. Four and three-quarters becomes . . ." Gael droned on.

"Uh . . . yeah, I remember now. Four times four is sixteen plus three . . ." Mia started to write out the equation, but the excited voices of the players distracted her again. She looked up. One boy had hair so blond it looked like summer wheat blowing in the wind. He was too far away for Mia to tell if he was really cute or just had nice hair, but he could run fast, accelerating to catch up to the disk flying ahead of him.

"Are you still trying to figure it out, Mia? Because I could swear you're more interested in that Frisbee game," Gael said.

Mia pulled her attention back. "Sorry. Got sidetracked."

"Am I wasting my time here?"

"No. But is it my fault they're so loud? And really attractive? Look at that blond guy. Total Adonis. No wonder I can't concentrate."

Gael laughed. "You are too much."

Michele shushed them. Gael rolled her eyes, then said, "Now you can start canceling out. Two goes into four . . ."

"I know. I know."

"So do it!"

Nearly an hour went by like this, and then the three of them seemed to lose some steam. Michele put her pencil down first, making it safe to talk. "I have to memorize dates from the Revolution through World War Two," she sighed.

"Yeah, it's a snore," said Gael. "But we've got to get good AP history grades if we want to get into our first-choice schools."

"Want to get together and do drills over the weekend?" Michele asked Gael.

"Sure. Saturday?"

Mia didn't want to stay out of the conversation, but she wasn't in their advanced history class. And she wasn't planning on college. Couldn't imagine there was one that would want her. Not one that Grandpa Andy would respect, and he was the one who was going to have to pay for it. Her mother had already told her that.

Mia forgot all that for the moment, because the Frisbee flew right to them and landed at their feet. As the blond guy swooped in to pick it up, he locked eyes with Mia—his were clear and light blue and seemed to twinkle at her. The other two girls fell silent. "Sorry!" he said, and she saw how bright and white his smile was. Then he was gone.

"Wow. He *is* cute," Gael whispered.

"Yeah, if you're into the type who knows he's good-looking," Michele said, as if she didn't care.

Gael laughed. "So how about you, Mia?" she asked. "Will you need more help with math homework this weekend?"

Mia silently stared off in the direction of the game.

"Are you listening? Have you heard anything we're talking about?" Michele said.

"Yeah, I am," Mia said. "It was blah blah blah grades and blah blah blah college. Right?"

"So what are your plans?" Gael said, sounding alarmed. "What are you going to do if you don't go to college?"

"Something else, I guess."

"Mia, you're not thinking straight," Michele said. "College is the next logical step. You have to finish high school, of course."

Mia felt her mood shifting. Here was another difference,

and it was a big one. It felt like this was the last moment in their lives before they became adults who had nothing in common. All because Gael and Michele were going to college and she wasn't. It wasn't just about her grades, because some community college might be a solution for her despite her grandfather's disappointment. But Mia didn't really want to go. She didn't believe college was the only thing you could do with your life.

"Why is every high school grad supposed to march down the path toward more years of school?" she asked them, wishing she could lose the anger in her voice. "Aren't there any other choices?"

"Like what?" Gael said, trying to sound encouraging.

"You can't choose to do nothing," Michele added.

"I know that."

"You have to go to college or you'll wind up like some kind of townie loser." Gael abruptly stopped speaking. Then added, "I mean, you have to think more realistically about this."

"When the right thing comes along, I'll know it," Mia said, as calmly as she could. "And I don't think it's going to be more studying and more school."

"If you say so," Michele said doubtfully.

Looking away now, Mia didn't notice the discontented look her two friends shared. The Frisbee game had ended, and the blond guy headed down the diagonal path that led toward the dorms.

When she turned back to her friends, they looked different to her. Less like friends. Mia stood up and stammered. "I . . . um . . . I should go."

"Right now?" Gael asked.

"Yeah," Mia said, her voice zombielike. She gave half a wave. "I'll see you later. Okay?"

Mia walked off, following that same diagonal path. She was out of earshot when Gael said, "She just left as if we meant nothing to her. Didn't even thank me for helping her."

Michele answered, "She's on another planet."

"And it's spinning out of control," Gael added in agreement.

# 4

*Mia followed the* blond Frisbee player down the slope toward the White Hall dorm. She definitely wanted him to notice her again, but that wasn't what made her walk after him and away from her friends.

Okay. So she didn't have a plan for her life. It was a problem and she knew it, but it didn't help to have them nag her about it.

Grandpa Andy always said she was meant for something special. She had to believe it. Had to. Why couldn't they? When the right thing came along, she would know it.

The blond guy entered the common area of the dorm, and she went in after him. Staking out a somewhat hidden spot near a vending machine, Mia watched as he emptied his mailbox and noted that it was on the far right, two up from the bottom. He sorted through his stuff as he left the room. She let him go but checked the name on his box. Peter York.

On her way out of White Hall, she glanced at a bulletin board jammed with paper notices. One of these stood out in large black letters.

### LOOKING FOR WORK?
### SEARCHING FOR A CAREER?
#### COME VISIT THE JOB BOARD
#### CAREER SERVICES CENTER/LEON HALL/2nd FLOOR

Mia let out a hoot. This is exactly what she meant by "the right thing would come along." She needed a job and now, because of her urge to follow gorgeous Peter York, she might find a really good one. Or at least something better than cafeteria slave.

The job board was in the main administration building. A few students were there looking for work, too. Mia quickly found out most of the jobs listed were work-study positions she couldn't apply for, since she wasn't a college student. After that there were jobs that you had to be a graduate student to get, with experience in the departments that were offering them. Next came administrative jobs, but she couldn't type sixty-five words per minute or create Excel spreadsheets.

She was about to give up when she got to the end of the hall and found a few jobs listed as "No Experience Necessary." There were only three index cards there. One was for a telemarketing job that you did from your home, but it only paid a commission if you made a sale. Another was with an advertising company looking for someone to put flyers up all around town, but they needed someone with a driver's license and a car.

The last card was for a lab assistant in the university's entomology department. It had a contact name and phone number and listed the salary as "To Be Determined." She wasn't sure what to make of that. Why wasn't it listed as a work-study job? How come they didn't know what the job paid? What the heck was entomology? She wrote down all the information on the card anyway, double-checking to make sure she got the phone number right.

On her way out of the building, she spotted a student roster lying on a bench in front of the closed-up Office of

Student Activities. She found out Peter York was a freshman. He was enrolled in the architecture program and, as she knew, he lived in White Hall. He was from Greenwich, Connecticut. That's all it said about him. Mia dropped the directory, hoisted her bag onto her shoulder, and set out into an early evening that now felt full of possibility.

She left campus by the main gate and stopped on the bridge over Escadilla Gorge. This same gorge ran past her house, but up here on the hill where the bridge dangled a few hundred feet above the rocks and the roaring water, it was a rushing force of nature. Closer to her home it was nothing but a creek.

Mia walked back slowly. Halfway down the hill, she took a last look up at the college. In the distance, the windows of the buildings perched at the edge of campus caught the last rays of the sun and reflected golden light. It was beautiful, and she would have stayed longer to enjoy the view, but it was time to go back where she belonged.

Most of the shops on the Commons were shut for the night. She stopped at Jewel Moon, her favorite store, even though the closed sign was already in the window. Mia never ever wanted to steal from Jewel Moon. She'd gotten to know the owners, Janet and Margo, a couple of ex–art students from the college who stayed in town after they'd gotten their degrees. They only carried things made by local artists. Jewelry and ceramics and knitwear. All of it was beautiful. To take even one piece and hoard it for herself seemed to Mia like the worst kind of crime. Just looking was enough. Was everything, in fact. Mia was perfectly happy, right at that moment, simply to peer at some jewelry made of thin gold wire and garnet beads.

"Hey, Mia!" someone shouted out to her. She turned, her reverie broken. It was James, a boy she knew from school. With him were some older guys who hung out by the fountain to beg for change from passersby. She hated them on sight. They dressed like street people in ripped clothes, but she knew they weren't so poor that they needed other people's money. Most of them were born and raised right here in town.

James came toward her. "What's happening with you, girl? Got a quarter?" He wore his baggy pants hanging low like the rest of the group, his baseball cap turned backward.

"What do you think?" she shouted back, and walked away without waiting for him to catch up.

She heard someone whistle then, and she wanted to walk faster but didn't want them to know she was bothered by it. Turning around, she saw that three of them were following. Then they called out to her.

"Oh, miss! Can you spare a blow job?"

"In your dreams, jerkoff," Mia said under her breath.

"Where ya going?"

"Can we come?"

"All over your tits?" They erupted with laughter.

Mia spun around and faced off against them.

"That made her mad!" one of them shouted gleefully.

She saw how big they were, that they had nothing better to do than follow her. It was a lot darker on the street. Up ahead was a music store, Johnny's Guitar Works. Mia knew someone who worked there. She turned away and walked even faster. Mia didn't say another word, but she was filled with anger, and shame, because these jerks felt familiar enough to talk to her like this.

She quickly slipped into the store. The guy she knew smiled when he saw her. His name was Robbie and they'd met at a concert on the Commons last summer. He'd been trying to get her to go on a date with him ever since. He was tall and slim, and he was no kid. His face was pock-marked, and his hair was greased back like someone who learned how to style it in prison. He'd scare those gutless idiots if they followed her in here. "Hey, princess, what's brings you here?"

"Some guys on the Commons were trailing me."

"You want me to go get them? I'll kick their skinny asses so hard they'll have to wear diapers again."

Mia laughed. "That sounds good."

"I'd walk you home but I'm stuck here. Why don't you hang out for a little while?" He gestured toward a stool in front of the counter. "Want to hear a song I'm working on?"

"Sure."

Robbie pulled a guitar out of a black case that was covered in stickers from different bars in different cities. It was a twelve-string acoustic that looked as if he polished it every day. Laying it across his lap so it fit into place like a lover, Robbie gave her a sly smile, as if he'd wanted to give her these thoughts and enjoyed knowing that he had. Mia caught the flash of a gold tooth.

"There's no words yet. Just the tune." He began to play, strumming the strings and fingering the frets with an intensity that made the instrument howl with longing. The sound struck her straight in the heart. When he was done, she realized she was holding her breath. Two other guys in the store applauded. Mia said, "That was so great. What do you call it?"

Robbie looked at her through a lock of hair that had fallen over his unattractive face. "I'm thinking about . . . don't laugh now . . . 'Wasting My Way to You.'"

Mia was silent for second. "How'd you come up with that title?"

"Well . . . sometimes a guy feels he could just waste away, wondering if he's ever going to get the girl. Or if there'll be anything left of him by the time he does."

Mia just nodded. "It's really good."

Robbie was strumming again. "So how about that date, Mia?" he said as he played. The truth was, there was something scary about Robbie, though he'd never done anything to alarm her. "Why would you want to date a girl with a curfew?" she said, trying to joke him out of it.

"Because she's the sweetest girl in town. And the prettiest, too."

"Can't be me you're talking about."

"Look, why don't you come to the Common Ground Saturday night? My band is playing there. Then it won't be like a date. Just come down to hear some music."

"Robbie, I'll get carded. I can't get in there."

"Don't worry, I'll leave your name at the door. You won't have any trouble. Bring a friend. A *girlfriend*, I mean."

Mia laughed. "Can I bring two?"

"Absolutely. So I'll see you then?"

"Okay. I'll do it."

"There you go. It'll be fun. So . . . how are you getting home? You want me to call a taxi?"

Mia didn't have the money for a cab but didn't want to admit it. "Nah, I'm fine. Those jerks are probably back hanging at the fountain."

Walking home fast as she could and keeping to the shadows, Mia thought about how Robbie wasn't even close to what she wanted in a boyfriend. Peter York was more like it. But what was the harm in having someone want you? She was planning what to wear when it occurred to her she'd never even get out of the house on Saturday night because she'd been grounded. Unless she could find some way around that.

By the time Mia got back to her house, it was almost completely dark. But the flickering light from the TV shone through Grandpa Andy's front window, welcoming her home. She let herself into his apartment and found him sitting in his worn red chair in front of a silent television. He'd forgotten to turn the sound on. He stared into it like he was looking into a fire and had gotten lost in the glow.

Mia turned it off. "Hey, G.A. I'm here."

He turned to look up at her with a blank face. She wasn't sure he recognized her. Only a year ago he'd crashed his car into a tree, then he'd had a heart attack in the hospital. Even though he wasn't old, only in his late sixties, his body had grown weak, and he wasn't thinking too clearly most days, either.

Mia went over and stood by his chair so he could see her better. As she reached out to touch his shoulder, his smile appeared. "Hello there, little darling," he said. He was the only person who called her that. Mia liked it.

"How are you today, G.A.?"

"Not too bad for a sick man. And you?"

Mia sighed. "Just okay. Well, not so good, actually."

Grandpa Andy gave her a sideways glance. "What are you complaining for? You're not sick, little girl."

She rolled her eyes at him in mock exasperation. "I've got problems, mister. A person doesn't have to be falling apart like you are to have problems, you know."

"Well, I guess it's a good thing to have problems. No problems would mean you were dead."

"Don't talk like that, G.A.," Mia said. "How about some tea?"

"Thank you, please."

Mia walked to the kitchen, turning on lamps as she went, and put the kettle on to boil. She hated when he talked about dying. She didn't know how she'd be able to stand it when he was gone. He was the only good guy she knew in the whole wide world.

The place smelled a bit stuffy after the warm day, so she opened the back door to air things out a bit. He had a pretty garden that she liked to sit in during the summer months. Inside, she tidied up around the apartment. She restacked his collection of science magazines and swatted some dust off his pictures, plaques, and awards with a dish towel.

Her grandfather had won many accolades for his teaching and grants for his work, and he'd been published in prestigious journals. There were pictures of him with visiting scientists and political appointees. She liked looking over all these mementos. These things were evidence of his brilliant mind, his rich and amazing life, so full of experiences. She was proud to be his granddaughter.

"What did you do today?" she asked him.

"I don't know. Read the paper. Wrote a letter to an editor about something. What was it? They got something wrong. Oh! I can't remember now."

Mia walked over to the old manual typewriter that sat on a desk by the window. There was still a piece of the thin onionskin paper he liked to use wound around the barrel of the machine. It looked like he'd started a letter but only got as far as "Dear Editor, I feel it is my duty to inform you . . ."

Mia thought it was so unfair that someone as smart as her grandfather was now reduced to blanking out in front of a television. The kettle whistled then, breaking her train of thought. She put a chamomile bag in the cup and slowly poured the steaming water over it. When the tea was ready, she brought it in and pulled up a chair to sit beside him. He just sipped at his tea, nodding, and once again Mia wasn't sure he was really there with her, or that he was even thinking anything at all. "So. Problems you say," he spoke up finally. "Want to tell me about them?"

Mia sat up. He remembered what they'd talked about when she first walked in. Maybe he was getting a little better. "Well, first of all, school stinks," she told him. "They're teaching us things we'll never use in real life, and we're all supposed to excel at them or face a lifetime of disgrace and mediocrity."

"Your teachers tell you that you're mediocre?"

"Let's just say it's implied."

"Hmm." Grandpa Andy nodded again, and after a minute or two Mia thought that was the end of their talk.

His two parakeets twittered in their cage in a corner of the room. Mia got up to check on them. "Their paper is getting dirty," she said. "I'd better change it." Angel was a shy bird who'd cower at the back of his cage like he was doing now, though she was only changing the paper as she'd done a hundred times before. Devil was a bold bird always up for an adventure and willing to learn new tricks. His favorite was to ride around on her shoulder while she ran around the apartment really fast. Grandpa Andy had let her name them.

He watched as she slid out the tray as gently as possible so as not to disturb the birds. After she put in a clean piece of gravel paper, Mia carefully removed the two plastic cups attached to the bars of the cage, refilled them with fresh birdseed and water, and put them back in without spilling a drop.

"Don't you listen to them," Grandpa Andy said out of the blue.

Mia looked at her grandfather, uncertain of what he was talking about.

"You're not mediocre. Those teachers are no good! You just have to find out what you like to do, and do it! That's the responsibility that falls on every one of us in this life. I told your mother this many times over. She didn't listen."

"She's stubborn, all right," Mia said, patting Grandpa Andy's shoulder. "Wonder where she gets that from?"

"Bah!" He harrumphed. "Can't blame me for her bad traits."

"She's insisting I get a job now," Mia said.

Grandpa Andy nodded again, but sadly now. "Well, maybe she knows what's best for you, after all."

Mia didn't say anything else. She was too afraid to ask if Constance had told him about her trouble at the store. And she certainly wanted to avoid having to tell him herself. The thought of lowering his opinion of her was more than she could bear. She just stood there wondering exactly what her mother had said the night before to turn him around like this. He never gave in with Constance. Ever. He looked as worn out as his chair, sitting slumped there holding an empty teacup. She took it from him and placed it on a side table. She could see he didn't have the strength to argue with anyone anymore.

"Find work that you love," he said weakly. "Don't wind up like your mother, working beneath her abilities at that . . . that cafeteria. . . ." He stopped himself, let out a disgusted grunt.

"I heard about a job. But I'm not sure if they'll want to hire me, or if I can do it."

"What do you mean if you can?" He was looking at her crossly. "That's no way to talk."

"Well, it's a job working in a laboratory."

That perked him up. "Is it really? Excellent. I like the sound of that."

"In the ento . . . entomology department at the college."

"The study of insects. How fascinating!"

Mia's heart sank. "Ew! That doesn't sound right for me."

"How would you know unless you give it a try?" Grandpa

Andy's voice croaked as he leaned forward in his chair, getting more excited by their conversation now. "Science is the only thing that can illuminate the mysteries of life or even attempt to offer a reasonable explanation for the world around us. A most worthy occupation. I miss it terribly. I would be so proud of you."

"They're not going to want me. They'll hire someone who's done lab work and who's careful, or precise. You know, scientific."

"You can be all those things. Look how you take care of the birds. And remember how you saw the difference in their behavioral traits . . . and named them Angel and Devil? That's what science is all about. Observation. Plain and simple."

"Maybe you're right." She didn't want to disappoint him, but she really wasn't so sure about this job now. "Are you hungry yet?"

"I suppose," he said. "If it's time for dinner, it's time."

Mia stood up and went into the kitchen to check the freezer. It was empty except for some leftover pasta with meat sauce. She'd have to shop for him over the weekend.

She put the Tupperware container into the microwave and zapped it. She thought about what her grandfather had said about science illuminating the mystery of life. All she could see were the more practical aspects. Science built the microwave that cooked his food. Science kept him alive after he'd had his heart attack. This was all good. But better yet, science was the thing he loved, and she loved him. Mia felt a little glimmer of inspiration percolating inside her—a desire to please him.

She brought out his food and set it up on a tray at his

knees. "I'm going to call about that job, Grandpa. Maybe I'll get it. Maybe I'll like it."

Grandpa Andy enthusiastically pounded the arm of his chair. "That's the attitude. You're a good girl. But call from here; I want to hear. And make sure they know your family name; that could help you up there with those snooty academics."

Mia dialed the number she'd written down and waited as it rang. When the person on the other end picked up, she spoke into the receiver in a voice as full of authority as she could muster. "I'm Mia Morrow and I'm calling about the entomology job." She listened for a moment then said, "I can come in tomorrow, after classes. Around three?"

Suddenly her heart lifted with anticipation. And Grandpa Andy ate quietly, watching and nodding the whole time.

*The heels of* Mia's leather flats clicked hard against the smooth stone floors in the basement of Sutton Hall, the sedate old college science building. In her hand she carried a torn slip of paper telling her where to find the lab in room B1127. But was that last number a seven or a one? She'd written this note herself and now she could hardly read it.

Maybe this interview was a mistake. Outside, the world was warm and bright, and inside the building it was dark and dreary. The air was completely still. A male student passed her in the hall, staring intently at the ground, the pockets of his shirt jammed with measuring devices and pencils. Mia turned to ask him where the lab was located, but he vanished around a corner before she got the chance.

"Weird science," she muttered to herself.

Turning down another hallway, she walked along reading the numbers on the plastic plaques to the right of each gray metal door. Finally she came to the one she was looking for, and the door was open. Inside she found a lanky guy sitting at a metal desk, studying a spiral-bound notebook filled with numbers. He was so intent on his work, he didn't notice her.

"Professor Finkelstein?" Mia asked.

With a jerk, the man looked up. He stared at her for a moment through wire-rimmed glasses perched on the end of his nose. "You're half right and half wrong!" he answered, sounding perfectly jolly.

"I'm sorry," Mia said. She read her scribbled note again and checked it against the door plaque. "Isn't this B1127?"

"No, no, you don't understand. I am Finkelstein. But a professor I am not. I'm merely a lowly doctoral candidate, struggling to make a name for himself in the field of ento-mological envirogenetics. And you are?"

"Mia. Mia Morrow? I phoned about the position for a lab assistant."

"Right. I remember now. Is it three o'clock already? Time flies when you're studying flies. Heh, heh. Just a little bug joke."

*Yuck.* Flies. Behind him on shelves that reached to the ceiling were clear plastic boxes filled with buzzing insects.

Finkelstein closed his notebooks and pushed them aside. "Please, have a seat," he said, pointing at a tiny metal chair lodged between the wall and his desk.

Mia hesitated. She didn't want to put her handbag on the floor, where it might come into contact with some gross fly gunk, and it was too big for her lap.

"May I?" he asked. He took her bag from her and laid it down delicately on the metal desk, close to where she sat. "Is it all right there?"

"That's fine," Mia said.

"I think it shows great regard for valuable things that you wouldn't put your pretty handbag just anywhere. That's a quality I look for in a lab assistant. I like your shoes, too. They match the purse."

"Thanks," Mia said again, crossing her ankles. She wished he'd stop commenting on her as if she were some kind of specimen under a microscope. She wondered if there really was a job. Maybe this geeky doctor type, or whatever he was, used the career services posting as a way to meet girls. She calculated the distance to the door.

"So tell me," Finkelstein asked, "how do you like it here?"

Mia took a look around the room. It was the most depressing place she had ever seen. Tired fluorescent lights flickered overhead. There were no windows. Everything was made of cold, hard metal: the desk, the chairs, the lamp Finkelstein was reading by, and the rows of shelves holding up the fly boxes. The best thing she could say was that there wasn't anything there she'd want to steal.

Mia lied as best she could. "I like it fine. It's only ten hours a week, right?"

"No, dear. I meant at the college. Are you a freshman?"

"No, a sophomore." It wasn't a lie. She just didn't tell him it was in high school.

Finkelstein's eyes widened with surprise. "Oh, my! Every year I get older and the undergraduates seem much younger. What's your major?"

"Communications." A field of study she'd looked up the night before on the college Web site. She hoped he wouldn't ask her anything about it, because she'd have nothing to say.

"Where did you grow up?'

Her mind went blank for a second. She hadn't expected he'd ask something like that. And now that he had, she was tempted to come up with some other place, but she didn't know anything about anywhere else. She reluctantly admitted, "I was born here."

"Ah! You're a local," he said, and then, "What's the matter?"

Mia knew she was making a face her mother would call "unpleasant." But she couldn't help it. To her, locals were the guys at the fountain. Being lumped with them made her want to gag. "Most of the locals I know are complete losers," she told him, and was instantly sorry she said it because he studied her even more closely than before, as if the truth were written on her skin.

"Well, that description certainly doesn't fit you." Finkelstein smiled a big goofy smile.

He was so odd; she wished she could just get up and leave. This was never going to work out, she never should have come here to the basement of Sutton, to the lair of this fly guy.

"Did you bring a résumé?"

"I didn't. Because, well . . . this would be my first job."

"I see." Finkelstein stood up and Mia assumed he would end their meeting now, but instead he gestured grandly to the small room they were in and said, "Let me show you around." Stepping over to the metal shelves that were stacked to the ceiling, he declared the obvious: "This is where we keep the flies."

Mia joined him, squinting into the clear plastic boxes illuminated by vigorous grow lights. The restless buzzing was overwhelming.

"You may wonder what all this is about," Finkelstein said over the noise. "I am studying the effect of the pesticide PZ841 on successive generations of the common American housefly for the purposes of determining the exact length of time that it takes for traces of the chemical to disappear from the test group."

He pulled down one of the boxes containing the flies and held it tenderly. "Take a look. They're not nearly as frightening as one might think."

Stepping closer, Mia saw that the container was the exact size of a shoebox! She peered inside. They were the smallest flies she had ever seen, a more delicate and miniature version of a fly. Their color was a limpid shade of gray.

"They're kind of pretty," she said.

"These are still babies. Just two days old," he told her, replacing that box and taking down another from a higher shelf. "See? Look at these bred two weeks earlier. The genetic characteristics mature. The eyes shift to the top of the head and wing definition grows more distinguished."

"How come so many of them are dead? Do they get sick of being stuck in this box?"

"They succumbed to the effect of the pesticide. It killed them prematurely. The deceased ones are our barometer." Finkelstein was silent then, waiting for her to say something.

"What's a barometer?" she asked.

He spoke more slowly this time. "Counting the dead flies allows us to measure the effect of the pesticide. Every day we count the number of dead in each box and record the findings. I take the data and convert it to a formula, which gives me a rate of probability for degenerative effect over a period of time. That is, the speed with which the flies are being killed off, for successive generations where the start-up group is exposed to a specific dosage of PZ841."

"Oh. This sounds very complicated."

"You're not expected to do my job. I analyze the data. Your job is to clean the boxes, feed the flies, help them to breed. And you'll count the dead and record the numbers in a book."

Feeding flies. Breeding flies. Images of nasty, dirty, creepy-crawling insects threatened to engulf her.

"So what do you say?" he asked. "Do you want the job?"

"Can I think about it?"

He turned from her abruptly and jammed the plastic box back into its place on the shelf. It made an unpleasant scraping sound, like nails on a blackboard. "Salary is quite worthwhile, I'm sure you'll find."

She doubted that. "Oh, really. . . . How much?"

"How much do you need?"

Mia let out a heavy sigh. She owed the store a lot of money, and if she didn't pay she'd go to jail. But this Finkelstein was beyond eager about her, and she didn't like that. The flies buzzed. Minimum wage wouldn't be nearly enough to serve time in this bughouse. "Ten dollars an hour?" she said, hoping he'd laugh her out of the room.

But he replied, "Okay, I can cover that in my budget. So you'll take it, then?"

"How come you don't hire a grad student?" Mia asked. "Wouldn't that be better?"

"No. I don't want an insider," Finkelstein told her. "This is a very competitive field, and I don't want someone I can't completely trust, someone who might be after my position, looking over my shoulder."

*So he's paranoid as well as weird*, Mia decided. Then she thought of something that would probably be a deal-breaker. She'd tell the truth. "I'm really sorry . . . but I lied to you before. I'm not a sophomore in college. I'm only a sophomore in high school, but I wanted a chance to get the job. I guess that you can't hire me now. Really sorry."

Finkelstein appeared to give this some thought, then said, "Well, no wonder. I thought you looked young. But it doesn't make a difference. This isn't a work-study position. As long as you prove yourself mature enough to complete the tasks, there's no reason you can't be part of my team. It's yours if you want it."

Unable to actually say yes, Mia tried to nod but was only able to dribble her head up and down.

"Excellent, excellent. A fine choice, you'll see. We'll have fun," he said. "Does your class schedule allow you to get here weekdays at three in the afternoon, every day? You must arrive at precisely the same time to take the count, otherwise the test results are thrown off."

High school let out at two-thirty. Putting two hours in, she'd be home in time to make dinner for Grandpa Andy. "Yeah, I can do that."

"Great! Let's start tomorrow. Friday afternoon at three o'clock sharp. And we'll get buzzy. Ha-ha. Another little bug joke. I mean busy. You see?"

Mia quickly grabbed for her purse and went to the door, and as she was about to say good-bye she remembered he didn't want to be called a professor. "So . . . should I call you Dr. Finkelstein?"

"Although I like the sound of that, I haven't yet earned it. But I hope to finish my dissertation at the end of this semester. And then we'll see! Until then I'm simply Jerome Finkelstein. You can call me Jerome . . . or better yet, call me Jerry. How's that?" He gave her the goofy smile again, and Mia quickly slipped from the room.

*Maybe I'll call you Fink*, Mia thought, and she ran up the stairs, through the front doors of the bug building, and out into the fresh warm air.

*Mia decided to* blow the last hours of the day on the arts quad. She needed some sun. Half an hour under Finkelstein's fluorescent grow lights and she felt as if she might go belly-up, just like one of his dried-up dead flies.

The quad bustled with student activity, like the day before. Mia settled down in her usual spot, stretching out on the grass. She closed her eyes and heard flies buzzing all around. One landed on her bare knee and she sent it skittering away with a flick of her hand. How could she possibly do this job with Finkelstein, his grow lights, and hundreds of insects? Mia sighed. The money was good. And she had no other choice.

The bell tolled from the library clock tower. Four times. Her mother would be working at Butler already. One positive thing about the fly job, Mia thought, was that Constance might finally get off her back. Perhaps even free her up for Saturday night. She decided to share the sort-of-good news.

As soon as she stepped inside Butler Hall, she knew she had made a mistake. Blond Peter York and his friends were on the end of the food line, and if he saw her there with Constance he'd be certain to form an opinion of her and her cafeteria-worker mother that she didn't want him to have. Mia panicked. She spun on her heels to take off, but it was too late.

"Mia! Are you hungry, honey?" Brenda, her mother's co-worker, shouted out to her.

Mia waved back. "No, I just uh—"

"Your mom's right here. Constance!"

And there she was. Pink starched uniform, hair caught back in a hairnet. Little pink cap. Oh, God. Constance carried a tray full of something. It was heavy and her back was bent over from the weight. She heaved it up and slapped it into place on the steam-heated counter. "What are you doing here?" she said sternly. "You're not supposed to go out after school this week. Remember?"

Mia walked over to the counter. "I came to campus for a job interview, Mom. And I got it. I wanted to tell you."

Constance's face instantly lit up. "Are you kidding me? Did you hear that, Brenda?"

Brenda nodded sagely, and Mia understood it meant her mother had already told her everything. "See?" Brenda said to her mother. "You worried for nothing."

"Come back here and tell me more." Constance gestured for Mia to join her behind the counter.

Mia nervously glanced at the line of students as it got shorter and brought Peter closer. Constance gripped her in a bear hug and wouldn't let go.

"Okay, Mom. Okay."

Constance was undeterred, still enthusiastic. "Let's hear the details. It's on campus? So where are you going to be working?"

"You're not going to believe this. It's a job working in a lab. It's in the entomology department."

"Wow. How did you get a job studying bugs?"

It took Mia by surprise that her mother knew what *entomology* meant. She said, "I'm not really sure. I won't be studying them, though. I'll be doing stuff like feeding them and counting them. I think."

"Well, your grandfather will be thrilled about that." Constance sounded bitter, but then she hugged her daughter again. "Oh, Mia. What a relief. I'm so glad you came to tell me."

Over her mother's shoulder, Mia could see Peter making his way up the line. He was only ten students away now. She could not be spotted here.

"What's the pay like?" Constance asked.

"It's good, it's good," Mia said, moving away. "I'll make ten bucks an hour."

Constance shrieked and everyone within earshot looked at them, including Peter York. Mia quickly turned her back to the line of students. "Calm down, Mom!"

"I'm just thrilled!" Constance said. "Are you eating here tonight?"

Mia turned away to look over her shoulder. Peter was only a few feet away. "No. I've got to go."

"See you at home," Constance called after her.

Mia bolted as if the person talking to her was just some crazy stranger, and she didn't look back. On the way home, Mia thought about how it made her feel to see Constance so happy. Like some kind of weight was off them both. She also thought about the one other thing she now knew about Peter York. On Thursdays he went to early dinner at Butler. But she wasn't going to look for him in there ever again.

———

The Commons was crowded for a late afternoon. People were out enjoying the last bits of daylight. There was no sign of those nasty guys she'd run into. And Jewel Moon was still open. Mia went in.

It was a small shop, intimate. The opposite of the cavernous department store. It was wild and chaotic in there, with things hanging from the ceiling and display cases made from gnarled wood. She loved how the shop was bathed in natural light coming from the front window and skylights overhead. It smelled good, too. Like a pine forest. But not fake or too sweet. Like the real thing.

There was soft music playing, and Mia felt herself relax. She usually worked her way around the store the same way every time, starting with the expensive cases up front, where the jewelry was displayed. But today she studied the necklace she'd admired in the window the other day. It was a simple choker made from stiff gold wire, with a delicate little garnet-colored pendant dangling from it. She was so lost i᷈ ᷈ooking at the thing, Mia didn't hear Margo come out ᷈ ᷈ack office. "That one certainly seems to capture you᷈ ᷈ ᷈ ᷈n, Mia. Why don't you try it on?"

"O᷈, h᷈" Mia was startled. But when she looked at Margo, who was dressed in clothes that looked like funky robes, she couldn't help but smile. The outfit suited her, Mia thought. Kind of regal. "I'm sure I can't afford this," Mia said about the necklace.

"Won't cost you anything to just see how it looks."

Mia watched Margo unlock the case with a set of keys she kept in a drawer below the register. She turned away, worried Margo might think she was casing the joint or something. But Margo didn't seem to notice or care what Mia saw, and she reached in to take the necklace out and placed it on a small black velvet board. The piece gleamed in the overhead spotlights, which seemed to strike it with precision and make it sing.

"Gosh, that's even prettier than I thought," said Mia.

"The artist is Janet Yee," Margo told her. "She teaches in the studio art program at the college."

"I love the bead." Mia touched the fiery red pendant with her finger. "Or the stone. Whatever it is."

"It's an enameled metal locket," said Margo as she delicately took hold of the pendant and clicked it open with her polished nail.

Inside was a tiny black-and-white photograph of a fly.

Mia laughed. "Oh my God, I can't believe that!"

"This artist has a sense of humor. You expected to see a pretty girl or a baby, right? Someone's loved one?"

"Yeah, I did. But the other thing is . . . I'm starting a job where I have to feed flies and breed them. I think they're really gross, but then looking at this bug, I think maybe they can be really beautiful, too. Or kind of interesting, anyway. Do you know what I mean?"

"I do. I think bugs are cool. We have a lot of pieces that are based on insects. It's a common subject for artisans, because bugs are so intricately constructed and small, too, which makes them a good basis for jewelry designs. I'll show you some."

Margo brought over a couple of pieces from other cases. Mia wondered why she'd never noticed that there were so many bugs in Jewel Moon. Gold earrings shaped like bumblebees. Spider and cricket pins. A scarf with polka dots made from tiny ladybugs. After they'd looked for a while, Margo picked up the fly locket again. "Ready to try it?"

"I'd love to."

"It suits you," Margo said as Mia bent over to look in the oval mirror on the counter.

"How much is it?" Mia asked her. It was so special. She *really*, really wanted that fly locket. To celebrate getting the job. And to spin it into something beautiful.

Margo checked the tag. "Three hundred and fifty dollars."

"Yikes." She'd never be able to get something like this. Not by any legal means, anyway. "Not in my lifetime, I guess," she said. "I wish the artist made it out of something other than gold. Then it might not be as expensive."

"Hmm . . . That's a smart idea." Margo was quiet for a moment, then said, "The piece is simple enough that if we make it in silver, the price will come down quite a bit. I'm going to find out if Janet Yee can do it. Thanks, Mia."

Mia was flattered by the praise, and a bloom burst out on her cheeks as she fumbled with the clasp to remove the necklace.

Margo said, "I'll help you with that, sweetie. Turn around."

Soon after the necklace was off, Mia made her way around the shop. She looked at other things for a few minutes, but there were no more fly pieces and Margo was back on the phone. At the door, Mia turned to say good-bye. All Margo could do was smile and wave, but that was enough.

Mia went out on the street. The door closed with a *whoosh*

and shut her off from the warm, shiny and beautiful interior spaces of Jewel Moon. As she walked home, she turned over and over in her mind what Margo had said.

Bugs were cool. Mia was smart. She hoped both things were true.

Mia told Grandpa Andy her news. But his reaction disappointed her. It was as if he'd heard her words but they had no real meaning for him. "Oh, that's good," he said, and that was all. Mia talked about Finkelstein and what she saw in the lab, hoping Grandpa Andy's love of science would be sparked once more. But it was no use. He was too out of it. Mia fed him the dinner she'd picked up, a teriyaki chicken rice bowl, and she sat doing homework while he finished his meal. After that, she put on a Mozart tape that he liked. He fell asleep before the first movement was over.

Mia didn't want to go up to her empty apartment, so she leafed through some fashion magazines looking for images she wanted to add to her wall goddess. A little after nine, she heard Constance come home. Grandpa Andy shifted abruptly in his chair. Overhead there were heavy footsteps, and Mia knew George was on the move. He clomped down the stairs to greet her mother at the front door. Mia heard him say something in a deep voice that made Constance laugh. And then he laughed, too. Mia thought this was an odd turn of events, so she got up and pressed her ear to the apartment door.

"Where would you like to go?" George was asking.

"I like the Moosewood," Constance responded. "But it's a

natural food kind of place. I don't know if you like that kind of thing."

"What's natural food?"

Constance laughed again, like he was making a joke, and Mia realized her mother was nervous. "It means the food is organic, no pesticides and no preservatives. It tastes better, and it's better for you."

At that moment, Grandpa Andy sputtered in his chair. "What's that? Who's there?"

Mia kept her ear to the door. "It's nothing, G.A.," she whispered. "Mom's home."

"Okay by me," George said. "What time do you want me to pick you up for our date?"

"I hear a man's voice!" Grandpa Andy was wide-awake now.

Mia shushed him with a finger.

"Gosh. That sounds so formal," Constance told him.

Her mother . . . going on a date!

"Well . . . I look forward to Saturday," Mia heard Constance say, and then George went out and her mother put her key in the lock to Grandpa Andy's front door. Mia leaped back to her spot on the couch, managing to pick up the magazine and turn it right side up before the door opened.

"Hi, Mom," Mia said, looking up. "Did I hear you talking to George?"

Constance came into the room in a happy rush. "George and I have a date on Saturday. Can you believe it?"

"Another good-for-nothing." Grandpa Andy shook his head.

"Grandpa! Don't say that," Mia admonished him. And then to her mother, "What made you decide he was okay?"

"Right, I know he's not a CEO or anything. . . ."

Mia backpedaled. "I didn't mean that, only you weren't interested before."

Constance's initial excitement faded. "I just figured if you could go ahead and get a good job, I could go out and have some fun for a change. That maybe it was time."

Grandpa Andy harrumphed deeply and significantly, and then he tried to get up out of his chair, but he wasn't strong enough and he fell back.

Constance was about to react to Grandpa Andy's obvious displeasure, but Mia jumped in. "Ignore him. He's tired," she said. "Way to go, Mom."

Constance flashed a sour look at her father. "Why don't you go to bed if you're so beat?" Then she turned and went out, slamming the door shut behind her.

Mia stayed to help Grandpa Andy get to his bedroom, laid his pajamas out for him, and kissed him on the forehead. "You're a good girl," he said to her in a very sleepy voice.

Walking up the stairs to her apartment, Mia decided she would do everything she could to encourage her mother to enjoy this date, despite the fact that she agreed with what Grandpa Andy had said. George certainly wasn't a prince. But the date was good news for herself as well as her mother. Now she'd be able to sneak out and meet Robbie at the Common Ground. But better than that, maybe things would finally change around there. She felt like she'd waited forever for that to happen.

Those who restrain desire,
do so because theirs is weak enough
to be restrained.

—WILLIAM BLAKE

*On Friday afternoons,* Mia and her friends played volleyball in gym class. A girl named Nicky had called out to be captain and was now choosing players. While standing around waiting to be picked for a team, Mia asked her friends, "Do you honestly think I should take this job?"

She'd started to worry as soon as she'd woken up, about the dirty flies and the Fink guy, and she hoped they would talk her out of what had to be the nastiest job ever known to man, woman, or girl.

"I think it's going to be good for you," said Gael.

"But I don't know if I can do it."

"You won't know unless you try," said Michele.

"I'll have to breed insects," Mia told them. "Can you imagine what that's like?"

"It sounds . . . kind of interesting," said Gael.

"It does not! It sounds revolting!" Mia said.

"What else can you do?" added Gael. "I mean, without any real skills like typing. It's either this or scooping ice cream at the mall. And I know you, Mia. You'd hate wearing a uniform like your mom does. Right?"

"Look on the positive side of things," Michele told her. "Now you can indulge your favorite pastime . . . checking out guys on campus."

Nicky called from the court. "Mia. Red team."

Smuggy smug smug. That's what her friends were. When

did they start acting like they had all the answers? It bugged her so much. Mia turned to Michele just before she walked on court and said, "You just reminded me . . . about that cute college boy playing Frisbee up on the arts quad the other day?"

"Which guy?" Gael asked.

"He ran over to us to catch the Frisbee. You know . . . blond hair, blue eyes, gorgeous?"

"Oh, yeah. I remember *him*!" said Gael.

"He asked me out," Mia said to her friends.

"No way!" said Michele.

"See you out there." Mia turned and headed over to the other red players. Now that the lie was out of her, she realized she'd have to make it come true somehow, and before they figured out she'd made it up. Mia looked back at her friends standing so close together that their heads touched, yakking at a frenzied speed, oblivious to all the game activities going on around them. It occurred to her that this fire she'd started had an unexpected effect. It made her the odd girl out.

Mia walked over to Nicky. She was a jock and in Mia's opinion took these gym games way too seriously. "You're going to call Michele and Gael, right?"

Nicky looked at her coldly. "You've got to be kidding. Michele ducks when the ball comes near her, and Gael isn't the most coordinated person, if you know what I mean."

Mia had to laugh. "You're probably right. But if you don't choose them, when it's my turn to serve, I'm going to launch it into the net. And I'm likely to miss the shots you set up for me."

"You do that and you're going to be sorry." Nicky called out, "Amy, red team."

The blue team captain called Gael next. Mia tried again. "C'mon, Nicky. Don't be a drag, we can win even with Michele." But Nicky picked a different girl, and then it was too late. Michele went to the blue team, and the last few girls standing around were sorted out or sent to the bench. Coach Barnes tossed a coin to determine the serve.

"Red team wins the toss," Barnes shouted out.

Mia could play this game. She was tall and she hit the ball hard. But she wished they could just volley, have fun with it and get some exercise. Instead, it was going to be played like a real game, with scoring and rules and whistle-blowing and all the rest.

"Mia, you take position one," said Nicky, full of her captain's authority.

Mia lumbered over to the back right corner to serve. Once she got in place, Barnes blew the whistle to signal the start of play. Mia tossed the ball from hand to hand, pretending to size up the other team's players.

Nicky got annoyed pretty quick, as Mia expected. "Let's go, number one. Eight seconds coming up!"

Service had to happen within eight seconds of the coach's whistle. That was a game rule. "Keep your pants on, Nick," Mia said to her captain. Just as Barnes raised the whistle to his lips to fault her, Mia tossed the ball high for a jump service, then leaped into the air and brought her right arm down like a sledgehammer, punching the ball right into the net. It dropped fast as a dead comet onto the court.

"Fault!" Barnes called out. "Point blue team."

"Oh, darn," Mia said directly to Nicky, who gave her a look as dirty as an old washcloth.

Mia played the game while breaking as many rules as she could. It was a pandemonium of missed shots, lousy returns, not following through on the setups the other players made—and all done on purpose just to get back at Nicky. As the match wore on, the red team won some points as her teammates dove for balls that fell all around her, but the blue team was firmly in the lead. After a few rotations, Mia was in a frontline position facing Michele across the net.

"So what's his name?" Michele asked.

"Who?" Mia pretended to forget all about Peter York. But she enjoyed knowing Michele had not.

"Blondy. The college guy?"

"Oh, right. Peter. Peter York." And then, because it sounded like they'd had a conversation, Mia added, "He's from Connecticut."

"So what?"

"So it's better than here."

"No it's not. They've got slums in Connecticut just like anywhere else. Don't you know Yale is in the middle of a ghetto? Probably why he decided to come to college here. Or his grades weren't good enough to get into an Ivy."

*God. What a know-it-all.* Mia felt a fire rise to her cheeks. A fresh impulse glowing there.

The whistle blew again. But for Mia, time slowed as she watched the blue team server set up a weak underhand shot. Slow and easy it headed right for her. Mia jumped up to block the ball from coming over the net. Her plan was to flush it, a fast drop shot, knowing Michele would never be able to return it. She put some muscle into the return and angled her hand. And in the next instant it was too late to take it back. White and black diamonds on a spinning orb went straight down, striking Michele in the throat. Mia heard the air rush out of her and then the ball loudly smack the wooden court, dropping out of play. When Michele looked up, there were tears in her eyes.

"Oh, shit," said Mia.

Barnes blew the whistle. "Point red team. You okay, Michele?"

She could hardly talk. "I'm okay," she managed to squeak.

"You sure?" Barnes asked.

She nodded and wiped her eyes.

"Take the bench, sweetie," Barnes said.

Mia silently mouthed the words *I'm sorry*, but Michele turned away, her face registering only pain. Another girl who hadn't been picked in the first round took her place.

"Better work on your aim, Mia," the coach said, and the game continued.

But now Mia felt miserable. She distractedly let several more points fall to the blue team until Nicky went to serve. Mia wasn't done sticking it to her captain yet. The whistle blew and Nicky tossed the ball up. Mia knew she was going to punch it; she always did. Nicky was utterly focused on that ball as it rose in the air, instinctively measuring the timing of her release.

Mia took a quick look at the opposing side. The six players were all in position. In that split second before the ball was served, Mia did something she shouldn't have— sidestepped to her right—and two blue players at the net had to shift over to see around her. But by then Nicky's shot was already coming at them fast, clearing the net by a hair. It landed behind the blue players at the net, and just out of reach of the back row as well.

Barnes blew the whistle. "Point red!"

"What the hell?" said Kelly, the blue team captain. To her girls at the net she shouted, "How could you miss that?"

"I couldn't see!" one of them yelled back.

"Yeah," said the other net player, as if it were dawning on her, too. She looked over at Mia, who was now about a foot out of position. "We were screened! By Mia!"

"Bullhonkey," Mia said. "Ball was in play. I moved."

But Nicky called it, too. "For sure, Coach. She's screening!" She looked right at Mia. "She should be replaced and expelled."

Coach Barnes sighed into his whistle, and it made a wheezing sound. He walked over. "Both teams want you out of here. Hope you're proud of yourself. Hit the bench, Mia."

Everyone watched her walk off court. A couple of the girls whispered to each other, shooting her dirty looks. Gael only looked disappointed, but somehow that was worse.

Barnes called to Michele, "Do you want back in?"

Michele shook her head and another girl got off the bench to take Mia's place.

Mia sat down next to her friend. "Are you all right?"

Michele wouldn't look at her.

"I was just trying to make a point. I didn't mean—"

"Sure you were," Michele croaked. She sounded terrible.

"No talking on the bench," Barnes called out to them.

They watched the game now being played in earnest. The girls executed proper setups and hits, digging down to catch difficult low balls. They practically flew over the court.

"So that's how the game is supposed to be played," Michele commented coolly.

Mia didn't say anything.

The players managed to get through several matches before the bell rang, signaling the end of the period. Almost immediately, Coach Barnes came over. "Where does it hurt, Michele?"

"I'm fine. It's just sore. Hurts to talk," she whispered.

Coach Barnes lightly tapped around the muscles in her neck. "Any pain here?"

"No."

"Or here?"

Michele winced.

"It's nothing major," he said. "But go see the nurse. They may want you to get an X-ray tonight to be sure. And it might swell up, so ask if you'll need a prescription for some pain medicine to help you sleep. Will someone take her over there?"

"I can do it, Coach," said Gael, joining them on the bench.

"I can go, too," Mia said.

"I want to have a word with you, young lady," he said to Mia. "Stick around."

"See you at the nurses' office," she said to her friends. Gael had her arm around Michele's shoulder, and they walked away without even looking at Mia. This was not good. She felt like she was falling into some deep empty hole that had no bottom, and no friends.

Coach Barnes turned his intense gaze on Mia. "You

could be the best player in this school if you'd stop trying to mess things up. I hope you learned a lesson today.
Breaking rules never wins the game. I should have penal-
ized you but"—he lowered his voice a bit—"I don't want to
dampen that spirit. Just hone it. You have natural skill
at the sport. Great impulses—a killer instinct. You don't
think. You just attack. I think you could go pro if you got
serious."

Mia was surprised. She never got compliments at school.
But pro volleyball wasn't something she saw herself doing.
It was just a game, not something that thrilled her, not something she wanted really badly. That's what she was looking for out of life. That feeling. But for now, all Mia really
wanted was to get out of there and join her friends.

"I guess, but I don't really care about it that much," she
told him, and saw his face drop. "Sorry, Coach. Can I go
now?"

"Yeah, go on." His voice sounded sour.

On the way to the nurse's office, Mia wondered why everyone else had ideas for her future. And why they were so
disappointed when she disagreed with them.

She found Michele and Gael still waiting to see the
nurse. Even though she apologized to Michele for hurting
her, the girls sat there without saying a word. Mia wondered
if they were going to be mad all weekend. And then she remembered Saturday night and Robbie's invitation to the
club. They'd been trying to work up the nerve to get in
there for months.

"Hey, I almost forgot . . . do you want to go to the Common Ground on Saturday? I got us passes."

"I thought you were grounded," Gael said, sounding exhausted or disgusted; Mia couldn't tell which.

"Mom's got a date. She'll never know," said Mia.

"Is that boy going to be there?" Gael asked.

Mia had much less enthusiasm for the whole Peter York thing now. "Him? No, he won't be there. At least, I don't think he will."

Michele looked at her with narrowed eyes and said, "If I'm feeling better. Maybe . . . yeah."

"I'll go if she goes," Gael said.

"Okay! Now that's the kind of teamwork I like."

Her friends still seemed like Glum and Bummed, though they agreed to meet at Mia's house at eight the next night. And then Michele got called in to see the nurse. It turned out nothing was broken, but she was badly bruised, and the nurse gave her a prescription for aspirin with codeine.

Mia whispered, "You should get that filled and bring those with you on Saturday."

"What for?" Michele asked.

"What do you think?" Mia told her. "We're going to have some fun. That's what for."

"If you say so," Gael said.

After school, Michele called her mother to pick her up, and she offered to drive Mia up to the campus for her first day of work. The girls said nothing the whole way.

Michele's mother looked back at them through the rearview mirror. "You're all so quiet."

"Just looking forward to the weekend," Mia told her.

Michele and Gael looked out the windows of the car, as if they hadn't heard.

*Mia got dropped* off at the entrance to campus. She walked slowly toward the entomology building, wishing she could join the crowds lounging in the sun instead of heading to the flies in the basement.

Finkelstein glanced at the clock as she walked through the door. "Good, good, good," he said. "I like my lab assistant to be prompt." He pointed toward a beat-up metal desk that had her name taped to it and said the obvious. "This will be your work area." She noticed his desk had been turned away from the wall and positioned to face hers. She put down her things.

"Today we'll go through the basic routine of what I need you to do," he continued. "There are quite a few steps, but once you do it a couple of times, I have no doubt it'll become like second nature."

Mia only hoped she could get through the next two hours without barfing.

Finkelstein took two white lab coats from a metal locker. He put one on and handed the other to her. "It should fit you. They don't come any smaller."

Mia stared at his outstretched hand holding the starchy garment. "I hate uniforms and I'm not wearing that," she said in a flat tone that startled her new boss.

"But everyone wears them. And there's a reason. This is messy work. You wouldn't want to soil your clothes."

Mia didn't move.

"Suit yourself," Finkelstein said. "Hey, that's a pretty good pun if I do say so myself." He put the white coat back in the locker. "It's right here if you change your mind."

Finkelstein stepped over to the shelves. Two units six feet long reached all the way to the ceiling. They were crammed top to bottom with clear plastic boxes, and the boxes were filled with flies. "The first thing I want you to notice is the way the boxes are labeled. See this one?" He pulled down one of the boxes, and the flies inside went completely insane, their light bodies zooming through that little bit of captured air. Mia drew back a bit, but Finkelstein didn't seem to notice.

"Here is group two-point-three," he said as he held the box up. "This means that these flies are part of group two and are the third generation in the group." Mia forced herself to look inside the box of angry flies. Most whizzed and banged against the sides, but a few were belly-up on the bottom. "I'm studying twenty groups in all," he said. He put the box back on the shelf, and she relaxed. "Do you have any questions about that, Mia?"

She thought hard. "Well, how do you know the flies aren't dying because they can't survive in a box?"

He had to think about that. "Because if that were true, then they'd all be deceased, you see. Not just a few." He seemed relieved to have an answer. "Almost had me stumped there. Well done. Tell me now, the next time group four breeds, which generation will it produce?"

Mia looked at the shelf holding group four boxes and read the labels on those boxes. They went up as high as 4.5. "Are there any other group four boxes on other shelves?"

"No, I like to keep them together. They're all here."

"Then . . . I think . . . the next box will be labeled four-point-six. So that's the sixth generation?"

"Excellent!" he exclaimed, and Mia realized for the first time Finkelstein wasn't sure she could do this job at all.

"Now it's time to get them feeding and breeding," he told her. "There's three easy steps. Follow me," he said over his shoulder. She forced herself to stand beside him at a long black counter. It had a sink built into the top and a small refrigerator tucked beneath it. He opened up a cabinet that was full of clean Pyrex vials and took a bunch of them out.

"Each fly box gets one vial of food and one vial of breeding material every day. As I like to say, one for feeding, and one for breeding! Makes it easy to remember, right?"

How hard can it be to remember to put two vials in a box? Mia had to bite her tongue to keep from saying so out loud.

"We label these first," he instructed, numbering the vials with a black marker. "Box four-point-one for these two vials . . . four-point-two is next. Two vials for each box. You see? You do the rest." He handed her the pen.

When she was finished with that, he led her over to a plastic drum in the corner of the lab and lifted the lid, revealing what looked like dry sawdust. "Dip in one of those empty vials from each group. Fill them up with that breeding material." She did it, and he took a plastic honey jar from the small lab refrigerator. He squeezed some of the amber liquid into the first sawdust-filled vial. "The scent of the honey will attract the flies to lay their eggs in the sawdust. You do it now."

"Does it matter how much honey they get?" Mia asked.

"A little is enough to draw them in."

Mia carefully squeezed out a few drops one by one.

"Okay, I like to do the next step of the procedure at the last possible minute. And even then it's best not to breathe deep when you spoon this stuff into the vials." Finkelstein pulled a clouded Tupperware canister out of the fridge. As he cracked the lid on the container, a disgusting smell was released that had to be some combination of excrement and rotting food. Mia nearly gagged. It was the most horrible thing she'd ever smelled in her life. Finkelstein put on a pair of rubber gloves. He quickly dug in with a tiny spoon, scraped the contents into the glass vial, and then handed the spoon to her. "Your turn," he said.

She put on some rubber gloves, but what she really needed was a nose plug. She worked as fast as she could. Some of the food spilled on the counter, but Finkelstein quickly wiped it into the sink.

"Okay. You'll get better at that as you go along." He closed the lid on the container and placed it back into the fridge. "Now we put the new vials into the boxes."

Back beside the fly shelves, he reached for a box from group four. As he tried to hand it to her, the frenzied flies ricocheted inside the box and she wouldn't take it from him. He put it on her desk instead.

"Now we count the dead," he said, ignoring her obvious resistance to interact with the flies. He pulled out his spiral-bound notebooks and placed the one for group four on her desk.

Mia still hadn't moved. "They can't hurt you, you know," Finkelstein told her.

She shivered involuntarily.

"All you need to do, Mia, is count the dead ones there on the bottom of each box. And then write the number down in the column under today's date. Okay?"

Mia glanced at the book. There were columns of numbers, pages and pages of them, marching across the paper in precise formation. Looking at the box, she noticed the flies had settled down. And then she looked closer. Some of them were dead. Two, to be exact.

Pointing to a cup of pens he'd placed on her desk, Finkelstein said, "Always use a black pen in the books. It hurts my eyes to have to read a column of numbers written in different colored inks." He came in to look over her shoulder as she got ready to make a mark in the book.

Mia neatly wrote the date and the time in the right-hand column, ran her finger down to the row for box 4.1. "Put a two here?"

"That's right. Nice handwriting, too. I commend you. Keep going." He watched closely as she finished the count for group four. She closed the book.

"Is that it?" Mia asked.

"No. We harvest the eggs next."

"Oh, I see." *Ew.*

In the corner of the room near the shelves was a tank like the kind used at kids' birthday parties to blow up balloons. Finkelstein reached for a tube that hung off the tank and put the hose to the mesh lid of the box. The flies buzzed madly again and he had to speak up to be heard. "This is $CO_2$. Carbon dioxide. It immobilizes them." He turned the knob on the tank, and five seconds later all the flies in the box were motionless at the bottom of the box.

"Wow, that knocked them out."

"Yes, entirely."

Mia stared. "I wonder if they're dreaming."

"About what?"

"Flying, I'd guess," Mia said.

Finkelstein laughed as he removed the lid from the box. "Let's do the switch now. Make sure you put the right vials in the right box, according to the way they're labeled. Take out the used vials and put them on that tray."

Mia reached into the box of blown-down flies as if she were sticking her hand into hot wax, but then she just did it, forced herself to pull the dirty vials out. Some unidentified juice had spilled over the sides, and one of the vials had a dead fly stuck to it. "Oh, yuck," Mia said. But by the fourth box she realized this was a lot like taking care of Grandpa Andy's parakeets. Dirty water cups and poo on paper wasn't any less gross than this. She finished the rest of the boxes quickly, filling the tray with used vials.

"Now what?" she said.

"We must harvest the breeding material."

She pointed to the used vials on the tray. "Are you talking about all those really dirty ones?"

"Well, yes . . ." He sounded almost confused as she was. "That's where the eggs have been laid."

Finkelstein pulled five gray cardboard boxes out of a closet. They, too, were the exact size of a shoebox. Watching as Finkelstein filled them with sawdust, she wondered amusedly, if flies wore shoes, what would they choose to wear? Perhaps rubber boots. For all the muck they walk about in.

Finkelstein called her over. "Let's get these vials changed," he said. Using a metal tool that looked like a thin putty knife, he showed her how to scrape out the contents of the used vial into the box with fresh sawdust. "And like so, we transfer the eggs along with the used breeding material into this breeding box. Label them with the group number, today's date, and my name. Okay? You finish up the rest."

Mia picked up one of the vials. It stuck to her glove. "These vials are completely vile," Mia said.

Finkelstein laughed. "That's the spirit. You've got to keep up your sense of humor."

Mia hadn't been joking, but she didn't say that, either.

When she'd emptied the last vial, he said, "Now you're done. With group four. Nineteen more to go."

"What? We're doing all those fly boxes today?"

"Actually, that's your job. But I'll help you. Should only take a few days before you get up to speed and can do it all yourself." He walked back to the sink area. "Ten more vials . . ."

Mia didn't follow him right away. She just stood there among the shelves full of breeding flies that towered over her head. Mia checked her watch. They'd managed to kill about twelve minutes total. She sighed. *It's only two hours a day*, Mia said to herself. Only two hours. Only two till she could fly away.

*Mia thought Saturday* night would never arrive. She spent the day doing things Constance had asked her to do for months. She cleaned up her room, did laundry, and hung up all her clothes. Surely her mother would see she was on her best behavior—no need to worry she might be sneaking out to clubs or about to blow off her grounding, which was supposed to last the whole weekend.

Late that afternoon, Mia found her mother trying on different outfits in front of the mirrored closet door in her bedroom. A pile of rejected clothes lay on the bed. Mia pushed them aside and sat to watch Constance attempt to squeeze into black pants that were too small. She was trying hard to pull up on the zipper but couldn't budge it the last couple of inches.

"That's never going to close, Mom."

"Guess it's been a while since I've worn these," she said, yanking them down and flinging them onto the pile. She took a big gulp from the drink on her dresser. She sighed. "I never should have agreed to go out with him. I've got nothing to wear."

Mia stood up. "Why don't you let me help? I'm pretty good at picking out clothes, you know."

Constance gestured grandly with a sweep of her arm. "Be my guest. But I don't think there's anything in there that looks right."

"Well . . . that depends on what kind of a look you're trying to create."

"A look?"

"Right. Sexy or sweet. Sophisticated or playful. You know?"

Constance looked panicked. "I don't know. I guess I want something that makes me look like I'm . . . somewhat . . . I don't know. Someone fun-loving but not frivolous. Nothing too revealing."

"Okay, that's helpful." Mia riffled through the hangers. This wasn't going to be easy, she could tell right away. The closet was filled with a lot of boring clothes that were either old and faded or just too casual. It was sad how little Constance had. "You really should have done this earlier, Mom. You could have bought something new."

"I'm not spending money just so I can go out to dinner. That's silly."

"No, it's not. You want to look nice, don't you?"

"It's just George. I don't even like him that much."

"Well, I suppose in that case you should just wear any old thing." Constance looked ready to argue some more, but Mia saw her change her mind. Searching deeper, Mia pulled out a striped blouse in a silky material. "This is okay. You could wear it tucked into jeans with a belt."

"Not very feminine, though."

"Didn't you just say you didn't like him that much?"

"I didn't mean that. I'm just not going to marry him or anything."

Mia smirked at her mother. "Right. I doubt there's a wedding dress in here, anyway."

"Very funny."

Mia stuck her head back in the closet. Way at the back,

Mia saw a sleeveless black garment; it looked kind of racy. She grabbed it, but it wasn't until she had it out of the closet that she saw it was a black leather vest decorated with fringe across the back.

"Wow! Mom! What the heck is this?"

Constance bit her lip. "Oh, that. I forgot that was in there."

"How could you forget? It's great!"

"I used to wear it all the time. When I was your age."

"Grandpa Andy let you out of the house in this?"

"No. I'd sneak out after he went to bed." Constance reached for the vest, like it was equally repellent and attractive to her. "But don't you try that!"

"No, never."

"And he did catch me once."

"Wow. He must have been mad as hell. What happened?"

"Let's just say the fact that I was wearing this vest was the least of my problems with him at that point."

"What do you mean?"

"Well, it was around that time he found out I was no longer the good little girl he thought I was."

"Oh, you mean me." Mia's arrival in Constance's teens had been a difficult Morrow family moment for sure.

"No, no. That's not what I'm talking about." Constance threw the vest on the pile of unfit clothing. "Listen, forget it. Eventually I outgrew this. Thank God."

"But, Mom, I think you should wear it tonight."

"I would look utterly foolish. And half naked."

"Not if you put a blouse on under it." Mia handed her the striped silky one. "Here, try this."

Constance gave her a doubtful look but did as she was told. She stood up straighter and sucked in her stomach but still couldn't button up the leather piece. "Guess I'm a lot broader in the shoulders than I use to be."

"You can wear the vest unbuttoned." Mia pulled the blouse to hang loose, straightening the collar. Together they looked at Constance's image in the mirror. It was rare for them to have a moment of closeness, and it felt nice. Neither of them seemed to want to end it. But Mia wasn't sure how to tell Constance she didn't look good in the vest—not because it was too small, but because it made her mother look old to wear something that belonged to a young person. She realized she wanted her mother to feel good about herself for a change.

Constance broke away first. "This isn't going to work." She took the vest off. "Back in the closet, I guess," she said, putting it on the hanger.

"Can I have it?"

"You want this old thing?"

"Well, yeah! It's cool."

Mia could tell Constance was not in favor of this for some reason. "I don't think it's a good idea," she said.

"You're not going to wear it."

"Mia, I don't think so."

"Come on! Why not?"

Constance's face twisted into sudden anger. "What is it with you? You're always pushing. Can't you take no for an answer? I said no and I meant it!"

Mia felt like she'd just been slapped. Mia decided their intimate moment was over. "What's wrong with *you*? Why's it so hard for you to give me something good? You don't even want the thing, but you don't want me to have it, either. How messed up is that?"

As Mia walked out, she heard her mother say, "Damn it!" But she didn't see the rush of hot tears that spilled down Constance's face, because her mother quickly shut the door.

Mia spent the rest of the afternoon checking through magazines for more images to use on the goddess. She didn't come out of her room, because she heard her mother banging around out there and didn't want to see her again. Around seven o'clock Mia realized she hadn't heard from her friends all day. She decided to give Gael a call, since Michele was probably studying and wouldn't want to be disturbed.

The phone rang a few times, and her friend's mother picked up.

"Hello, Mrs. Baum. Is Gael home?"

"Hi, Mia. Sure. She and Michele are upstairs."

"Oh." That was a surprise. She didn't know they were getting together before they came over. But then she remembered they'd said they were going to study history. Mia heard Mrs. Baum call up to her daughter. "Pick up, honey! It's for you." Mia heard the clunk of the receiver being placed on a table.

And then she waited some more. It was taking Gael a long time to come to the phone. She could picture her friends hanging out in Gael's perfect girly bedroom with the white canopy bed and long wicker chaise in the corner.

Mia found herself getting irritated. Why were they making her wait? When she came on the line, Gael sounded as annoyed as Mia felt.

"Hey, Mia. What's up?"

"Are you still coming over at eight?"

"What time is it now?"

"It's already seven."

"I guess we'll be a little late. I think."

"You don't sound very sure."

"Well, my mom's still cooking . . . and I don't know when dinner's going to be ready."

She didn't say anything else, and the silence sounded to Mia as if plans were shifting, just like subterranean plates during an earthquake, but she wasn't sure what to do about it. "Are you still coming over so we can get ready together?" she whispered into the phone, so her mother wouldn't hear.

"You better not wait for us."

"Oh. Okay."

"Okay. We'll see you. Later."

"Like when?"

"Probably around eight-thirty or nine."

"But I need to be home before my mother gets back. So that won't give us much time at the club."

"We shouldn't be later than that."

"Don't forget to bring those pills."

"What?"

"The painkillers," Mia whispered. "Remember?"

Gael grunted, and Mia knew trouble was brewing. "I don't know about that," Gael said. "Bye, Mia."

Mia stayed on the phone after Gael got off. And then she

heard the recorded voice of the phone company: "If you'd like to place a call, hang up and try again." Mia considered calling right back to tell them she would go to the club without them because they were being so weird. But that wasn't really what she wanted.

Mia ran a bath and stepped in. She sat in the steaming water, worrying about the friendship for the umpteenth time. Usually there would be a bunch of calls back and forth among them over the weekend. Mia didn't know when she'd stopped trusting Michele and Gael, but now she couldn't even remember the last time they really talked. It had to be way before that volleyball game. And why didn't they believe she was sorry about that?

Mia heard a knock on the door.

"Can I come in?" Constance entered without waiting for an answer and posed in the doorway, a fresh drink in her hand. She was wearing a pair of tight jeans she'd managed to get zipped and the striped shirt with a belt that cinched in her waist and made her look curvy. "What do you think?" she asked, twirling around like a beauty contestant. She was obviously a little looped from that second drink. Mia had to hand it to her mother. She was transformed. Her long blond hair hung down, silky and fine. Her face glowed and her large blue eyes were hopeful, shining orbs.

"Not bad. For an old lady," Mia said sourly.

Constance took a swallow of her drink. "Maybe George'll have a better reaction." She bent toward the mirror to apply some makeup. Mia watched her pat concealer under her eyes. Constance talked to the mirror while she worked on her face. "Look. I don't think you should get so upset about the vest. It's just that I barely want to remember what I was like in it, much less see it on you. Can you understand that?"

"You mean when you were young and did crazy things?"

"Exactly."

"Like getting knocked up when you were seventeen?"

Constance turned around to face Mia. "Don't talk like that."

Mia didn't say anything more. She wondered why her mother never stopped to think about how it would hurt to hear that Mia's arrival on the scene was something that never should have happened. That it was the mistake of a wild and crazy girl. And how stupid to think the vest had something to do with it. Like if Mia wore it, she'd get pregnant, too.

"So what's your plan for tonight?" Constance said. "You're still grounded until Sunday, remember?"

"I'm getting together with Michele and Gael. They're coming over with a movie."

"Good. What is it?"

"I don't know." Mia felt as if her nerves were grating against the inside of her flesh. "What time do you think you'll be back?" she asked.

"I don't know. Ten or eleven."

Just then there was a knock on the front door. Constance swallowed the rest of her drink and ran out of the bathroom. Mia heard her mother open the door. "Wow. You look really good" was the first thing George said. Her mother laughed warmly.

"Don't wait up," Constance called to Mia, who didn't answer. She heard them go out, and their footsteps tromping down the stairs. Then the front door was shut and locked.

Mia jumped up out of the bathtub and dried off. She'd already decided what she'd wear. She went straight into her mother's closet and pulled out the fringed leather vest.

Back in her room, she shimmied into it naked. Buttoned up the front, it fit her like a glove, pushed her breasts up high. She added her favorite jeans and a pair of high-heeled boots. Swinging around in front of the mirror, she watched the fringe sway with her.

It wasn't really stealing. More like anonymous borrowing. She'd have it back on the hanger and hidden away again before her mother knew it was missing. Better yet, it was payback for her mother's meanness, as far as Mia was concerned. Was she being too impulsive? Maybe. But who cared about that? It felt good. Looked good, too. On *her*.

She blow-dried her hair, brushed her eyelids with lavender eye shadow and lined them with black eyeliner, and then sat on the couch to wait for her friends.

At nine o'clock she was still waiting.

# 10

*The line outside* the Common Ground ran all the way to the end of the block. Although she still hoped Michele and Gael would show up, she also knew they weren't coming.

Mia was so distressed, she wasn't sure what to think. Not only had they stood her up, they'd also lied and made her wait like an idiot. Why didn't they call? They must have done it because they wanted her to know they didn't like her anymore.

So the hell with them! She was done with waiting. Mia stomped up to the front of the line and spoke to a big bouncer guy with an armload of tattoos. "The name's Morrow. I'm a guest of the band," she said, indicating with a glance that he should check the clipboard he held.

He took a good look at her first, then ran his finger down the names. Mia read them upside down. Robbie, at least, hadn't let her down. "I should check your ID."

Mia leaned in to whisper in his ear, giving him a good view of those parts that were popping up out of the vest. "You can check whatever you want as long as you let me in," she said in a husky voice, and felt a dangerous thrill shiver along her skin.

The bouncer snorted and unhooked the velvet rope. Mia felt his hot eyes follow her in. "No charge for that one," he called to the guy collecting bills just inside the doors, and Mia entered without paying.

She was immediately assaulted by pulsing strobe lights

and the pounding beat of loud music. The dance floor was crowded. College kids mostly, moving under a glittering disco ball. No one she recognized. The bar was packed, too, and the bartenders speedily swept back and forth in what seemed like an effort to get everyone drinks as fast as possible. She made her way around the room, walking past tables loaded with beer bottles and surrounded by bulky guys who shouted to one another to be heard as they glanced her way.

In the back corner was a seating area a few steps up from the main floor. A low, round table was surrounded by some mismatched lounge chairs, and a few hipster adults sat there. Mia wandered toward the group, thinking perhaps Robbie would be among them.

But when she got close, she saw he wasn't. There was an older guy with a girl on each side of him. He had his arms around them both. They giggled with each other while he talked to two other men at the table. His silvery white hair, thick as a broom, was cut short and stuck up from his head. His face was lined and craggy and mysterious, in a good way, and she couldn't look away.

Someone grabbed her from behind, both hands tight on her waist. It was Robbie. He pulled her in. "You made a strong impression on Roddy the bouncer. And now I see why," he said. "Let's go backstage. The band is there."

Mia couldn't help taking a last look at the guy at his table, as if he were some kind of magnet and she, a metallic object as thin as a dime. He'd seen her now and was looking at her, distracted from his conversation. She smiled at him, but his expression did not change. And it was definitely not friendly. Then Robbie threw his arm around her shoulder, and she couldn't see that older guy anymore.

They passed through a doorway, went down a long dingy hall, and entered a windowless room. One wall was covered in mirrors framed by round lightbulbs. Four older guys in black clothes had slung themselves on the dingy furniture. Their hair was coated with something that made it shine.

"Oh, cool!" Mia said. "This is your dressing room, right?"

"Sure is. Guys, say hello to Mia." Robbie said it like he was introducing her onstage, and she felt like she was glowing, but nobody got up to greet her. He gestured to a bar set up on a counter near the mirrors. "What's your pleasure?"

Mia looked at the drink choices but was unsure. She'd tried Constance's gin before and thought it tasted like medicine. There was cold bottled beer in a tub of ice, but she wanted something stronger, to really make a night of it. She decided to have a dark liquid. "Jack Daniel's," she said.

"Good choice."

"I love it," she lied, having never tasted it before.

He poured two shots. "To you, lovely," he said, and they clinked glasses, the amber liquid spilling over the edge and wetting her fingers. Robbie slammed his back, emptying the glass in one long slurp. Mia did the same. It burned her throat, strong but not bitter. Like a little fire going down, it took her breath away for a second.

"Ready for more?" Robbie asked.

Mia gulped and found her voice. "Oh, yeah. More than ready."

Robbie smiled and the gold tooth in front seemed to twinkle a little. She liked it now. Thought it made him look like a pirate. Shot two went down a lot easier.

"Have a beer," he said, twisting the top on a bottle for her. "I've got to talk to the guys about the set list. Come sit with us."

The band made room for the two of them on the couch. They were passing a cigarette back and forth and Mia knew it wasn't tobacco. It smelled sweet, more dangerous. She tried to act like there was nothing new here. But every nerve ending in her body felt lit now.

Robbie took a toke and passed it to her. "Do you smoke?" he asked.

It was fat and loosely wrapped and smoke billowed out of the burned end. As she put it to her lips, she tasted the tar and spit left there by the band. Mia inhaled, and a rush of smoke entered her lungs, cutting off her air. She blew it out almost immediately, but it was too late. She was coughing so hard, she didn't think she'd ever stop.

"Oh! You're gonna get *really* high now," one of the guys said.

"Drink some beer," Robbie suggested, handing her the bottle. "It'll put out the fire."

Once she got herself under control, they passed the joint back to her.

She wasn't feeling any different, so she tried again. She kept her lips pursed tight and barely inhaled, but a stream of smoke flew down her throat. This time she felt the smoke, or whatever it was that the smoke delivered, getting absorbed into her bloodstream.

As she sat there while the guys talked, she started to lose the feeling in her feet and hands, as if they no longer belonged to her. Her body went rubbery. Then her brain got set loose with the rest of her. She could barely concentrate on what was being said. The guys were laughing, at her maybe, or maybe not. Robbie pulled her close on the couch, and she sank in deep. He stroked her leg over and over, and looked down at her like he was watching her get lost.

"Did you lace this?" Robbie asked, and she thought he was asking about her vest.

She laughed. "No, there's buttons, silly," she said, poking her chest out so he could see, and the guys cracked up like she'd made a joke that was the funniest thing they'd ever heard.

One guy said something that sounded like, "Yeah, there's a little T on it."

"That's nasty," said Robbie. He shook his head, looking at her.

"I like it," she said. "It's really working." She knew she might have been slurring her words now, but she didn't know why they all thought that was so funny, too.

"Just wait till you hear us play," said another. "It's going to sound like music from another planet."

An hour passed. Or maybe it was only five minutes. There was a knock on the door and someone entered who talked in a barking voice, and then everyone stood up. Mia tried to get to her feet but didn't quite make it.

"Easy does it," Robbie was saying, and she felt his arm steadying her at the elbow.

"I'm fine," she said, but she knew she wasn't. "Is there any water?" she asked, and her own voice sounded like a foreigner's, hard to understand.

"What the hell?" said the barking man, who could be heard clearly.

Someone handed her a full glass, and she drank it down fast. That helped a bit. The rest she'd have to pretend. "I can do this," she said.

"See you out there," she heard Robbie say, and all the men left the room now, their dark hair and dark clothes moving away.

Robbie led her down the corridor and out to the sound of people clapping, whistling and stamping. She could feel all the pulsing vibrations of the eager and ready audience. They climbed three steps, and Robbie said in her ear, "You can watch from here," and then he went away into bright light. It hurt her eyes to look out there, so she closed them and soon she heard the show start with a long slow wail of guitar and everyone shouting out in the dark. The rest of the band came in with a loud burst, and they were off.

Mia swayed to the music. Her body had a rhythm and she was inside it, watching it go. A few songs were played, one melting into the next, and then the band played a slow one and she slowed down, too, just moving her hips, her feet in place.

She felt someone come in close behind her, and then closer. Whoever it was, he just stood there and held her up. She didn't realize how drowsy she was, and she relaxed against this body, this friendly stranger. Her eyes were still closed. She barely felt it as his hand skittered down her arm. Just enough to know it was happening. She thought they were traveling backward, but still he held her up.

Then all of a sudden the music changed. The band was playing a fast song. What was happening? Maybe she'd fallen asleep standing, or maybe she'd simply lost consciousness, but now she was awake and aware that this stranger had one hand down her pants and was fumbling to go deeper, while the other had crashed into the front of her vest. He was rubbing at her nipple, and when she tried to buck him off, he pinched it. She pushed back harder.

"You like that, don't you? Horny girl." She heard him clearly, but still she couldn't see him, even though her eyes were open now.

She had been dragged into darkness, a black space with no one else around. He stuck his tongue deep into her ear and his hot, panting breath stank like cigarettes. Mia reached out in front and felt a velvety fabric between her fingers. She pushed on it and it gave way. And then the light cracked through and she could see the backstage area of the club. A guy dressed all in black and wearing head-phones was staring into the space where she stood. He pulled apart the curtains that surrounded her.

"Roddy, you sick dog!" he said, and she knew the bark-ing man had come to her rescue.

At that moment, she was let go. Mia fell to her hands and knees. Looking up, she saw the bouncer and the barking man standing over her, arguing, oblivious to her. She got up as quickly as she could and ran. She wanted out of there altogether, but she was back in the long corridor, feeling terribly light-headed, and the lights above seemed to be flickering as if they would go out. She found her way to the dressing room and managed to make it all the way to the couch. She flung herself onto it, facedown, and felt she was falling deeper, as if the cushions were miles below.

## 11

*Mia woke to* silence, a crush of dirty velvet beneath her cheek. Lying in the stillness for a moment, she soon remembered where she was and sat up with a groan.

There was no one in the dressing room with her, and her purse was on the table. Mia grabbed it and checked the contents. Her wallet and her money were still there. She breathed a sigh of relief.

As she stood up, her head started to pound. Her clothes had spun round on her body, and she tugged to straighten them out. She walked over to the makeup mirrors to check herself, found her hair plastered to her head and her mascara all smeared. She took a tissue from her purse and was wiping at the black smudges around her eyes when it occurred to her that it was too quiet.

Shouldn't there be some kind of noise? The band playing or drunk people hollering at one another? She didn't remember this dressing room being soundproof.

Mia opened the door and stepped out into the empty hall. There was nothing but total silence coming from the club. Walking down the corridor, she found the stairs she'd climbed to what she now understood was the backstage area. She peeked through the curtains that cut it off from the hallway, those same curtains the stupid bouncer had used to trap her. There wasn't a soul to be found. No barking man with headphones. No equipment, either. It was just a big black nothing.

Rushing down the hall now, she told herself there had to be some people still straggling out of the club, and if she hurried she'd get out the door with them. But when she stepped out into the main room, there was no one there.

The night was over. Done. Finished. Mia stood for a moment in the dim light and wondered if she'd been locked inside and if things could be any worse.

And then someone spoke. A man. "Didn't think I'd see you for a while yet. You were gone, gone, gone." He was behind the bar on the other side of the room and she couldn't see who it was. Frightened that it might be that horrible bouncer, Mia backed up.

"No need to panic. You'll get no trouble from me," the man said. "Then again, from what I've seen tonight, I'd say you're pretty good at making trouble for yourself."

"Do I know you?" Mia asked, and moved closer to the bar.

He flipped a switch, and the overhead lights came up. Mia saw that she was talking to the older guy from earlier that night. The silver hair, the chiseled face. He looked tired now. He was drying bar glasses with a rag.

"Where is everyone?"

"Last call was a while ago, and they all went home. It's much later than you think." He looked up and smiled at her. Kind of a gentle, sad smile. Not like he was sorry for her, but like he was sorry for everyone he ever knew. It put her at ease.

"Are you the bartender?" she asked.

"Nope. I own this place."

Mia walked up to the bar and sat on one of the stools. "I can't believe I passed out."

"Yup. Those boys are in big trouble."

Mia started to object. "It was my fault. I just had a little too much—"

He interrupted her. "You're fifteen. There's no way you should have gotten in here, and no good reason they could have had for making sure you did." He filled a glass with water and put it down in front of her.

"Hey, how did you know I was fifteen?"

"Honey, I know a fifteen-year-old when I see one. That's one reason. And I found your school ID."

He reached into his back pocket and handed it over. Mia drank the water, and it put out the fire in her parched throat.

"So. Mia *Morrow*," he said, emphasizing her last name like it was the name of an enemy, "what do you say we call your mom to come get you?"

Mia jumped off the barstool. "Please don't do that. Please."

"What's your plan for getting home?" he asked.

Mia leaned over the bar. "Could you drive me? If it's not out of your way, I mean." She pursed her lips at him in what she hoped was a pretty pout.

"Kid, don't flirt with me," he said. "I'm an inch away from having the police be your escort."

Mia stood up straight. "That would be bad. Very bad. My mother will freak. She already thinks I'm a hopeless case."

"I'm guessing your mother has her hands full," he said.

Mia looked him in the eyes. "Isn't there any way you can take me home?"

He groaned. "I really shouldn't get involved here."

"Please. I'll never come back again. I'll never ask you for anything else again. Ever. Come on! You've been so nice already."

"I haven't been nice," he said, turning away. "Just let you sleep it off is all."

"Why can't you just do this last thing?"

"How come you're willing to just get in a car with a stranger?" he asked sternly.

Mia thought about it for a second. "Well . . . you seem angry and worried. I can't imagine you'd ever hurt me."

"All right. Well, at least you're not as dumb as I thought."

"Gee, thanks for the compliment."

"But you've got to learn how to take better care of yourself."

For once she couldn't argue.

"You live close, right?"

She nodded.

He walked her out to his car, a beat-up old black muscle car. "So what's your name?" she asked, once she was sitting in the front seat.

He didn't answer right away. And then, with a shrug, as if he'd decided it was okay to tell her, he said, "Clancy." She gave him directions to her house, a left on Mayfair and then right on Seneca, down the hill to the first light, and then over the gorge bridge. She took her eyes off the road to look at him. His nose was a bit too big, but she liked that. A deep dimple in his chin like some kind of hero.

"What are *you* looking at?" he said, like he meant it to be funny.

"*Sor-ry,*" she said, exaggerating it. "Didn't mean to bug you."

"Uh-huh."

When they got to her street, she told him it was the third house on the right, but he pulled the car over to the curb on the corner. "My turn's here. You can walk, right?" he said.

Mia looked down the street. There were no lights on at her house. "Sure. Thanks. I'll see you. I guess."

"Not if I see you first," he said, and again there was that sad smile and he chucked her on the chin. Normally she'd hate that kind of gesture, if anybody else had tried it. "Keep your guard up, kiddo."

Mia reached for the handle, but now she didn't want to get out. "Bye," she said, but he was already looking away. She got out, and he pulled the black car slowly around and left her standing there. With nowhere else to go, Mia walked up the street toward her dark house—and the trouble she knew had to be waiting for her.

Constance had never hit her, but Mia could imagine how she might tonight. Her stomach turned. She wasn't sure if it was the drugs she'd done earlier or the fear of what was about to happen. Mia slowly put her key in the lock and turned it. She winced as it clicked open. But the building was silent after that, and Mia crept up the stairs.

Inside her apartment, the hallway was pitch-black. Her mother didn't call out to her. Feeling her way down the narrow and uneven corridor, Mia made it to her room, softly closed the door behind her, and stood there in a cold sweat, waiting. Surely Constance would come in now. Their rooms shared a wall, and there was no way she wouldn't have heard her return. But several minutes passed, and Mia was still alone. She crept to her bed, pulled back the covers, and got under, fully dressed. The soft sheets and comforter pushed her down, and Mia disappeared in a matter of seconds.

She didn't wake until she heard the front door close downstairs and the unmistakable sound of her mother's feet coming up the stairs. Quickly Mia unbuttoned the leather vest constricting her and kicked that, along with her jeans, to the bottom of the bed. Then she lay back down and threw the covers over her head.

Her mother was taking care to keep quiet, gently dropping her keys into the dish by the door and tiptoeing down the hall. She stopped outside of Mia's room, and ever so slowly the doorknob turned. Mia couldn't see anything, buried beneath the cotton daisies of her quilt. She held still as a rock, and Constance closed the door as quietly as she'd opened it.

It was hot in her room, the sunlight pouring through the sheer curtains as if it were a summer day. It was past eleven, according to her clock. Constance must have really been worried, Mia thought, or she would have come barging in by now. As she sat up, little pulses of blood throbbed at her temples.

Mia threw on a pair of shorts and a T-shirt and stepped into the hall to meet her fate. She was going to tell a half-truth—she was forming it as she walked down the hall. Her friends had brought over some booze. Jack Daniel's is what it was, and they'd drunk the whole bottle, and then she forgot she wasn't supposed to stay home and she went wandering off and got sick and passed out under a tree in a neighbor's yard—and when she woke up at four in the morning, she came home and fell asleep. And she was sorry. Very.

Mia heard the tap turn on in the shower and the water pipes banging to life. There was the screech of the shower curtain pulled open and then closed.

Mia stood there in the hall for a few minutes, wondering what she should do. Constance was not likely to get crazy angry, Mia thought, while she was naked and wet, so Mia pushed at the bathroom door and peeked in. Steam clouded the mirror and clothes were heaped on the bathroom floor—the same striped shirt, belt and jeans that Constance had been wearing the night before. Mia stood contemplating that, when Constance peeked out from the stiff old shower curtain. Her eyes were wide as saucers. In a cheery voice she said, "Did I wake you? Sorry about that. I went out for bagels; they're in the kitchen. Why don't you toast some up for us?" And then quick as a rabbit she disappeared back behind the curtain.

"Sure thing, Mom. Will do." Stunned to be faced with the opposite of what she'd expected, Mia retreated.

Constance took a very long shower. Her bagel was cold by the time she got to the table. She sat down, took a bite, and then pushed the plate aside and lit a cigarette.

"Want me to microwave that for you?" Mia offered.

"Nah. Guess I'm not that hungry," Constance said.

They both sat there quietly after that, Mia chewing her bagel thoroughly and Constance inhaling smoke. But there was something thick in the air between them. She had no idea what her mother was thinking, but Mia guessed it had to do with her date clothes on the floor and her mother's ultraquiet arrival that morning. Constance hadn't spent the night at home. It made sense. That's why she wasn't mad—she had no idea Mia had gotten in late. Because she was even later. Or earlier, really.

Mia was dying to know the truth, but she wasn't going to ask. This was a terrific bit of luck. There would be no revelations at the breakfast table that morning. A desire to restore some normalcy to the day made Mia say, "Um . . . did you have fun last night?"

A smile broke out on Constance's face. Like she couldn't help it. "Yeah, it was good. . . . We had fun. I, uh . . . well, he's a fun guy, as it turns out." Constance stubbed out her cigarette forcefully, in a way that people do when they are telling themselves it's time to quit. She got up from the table. "I'm tired. I'm going to take a nap. What's your plan for the day?"

Mia could tell from the way her mother was wafting out of the room already that she didn't really care what Mia did. This, too, was unusual, that her mother wasn't all hyped up about what Mia was planning to accomplish with her day off from school. She must be beyond tired, Mia thought.

"Think I'll go to the reservoir. Go swimming."

"That's good."

"Hey, Mom," she shouted down the hall after her mother. "It's Sunday. . . ."

"Yeah, so?"

"I'm not grounded anymore, right?"

"Yup. Don't do anything foolish," Constance called from the bedroom door, "and try to keep it down, okay?" And the house was dead silent once more.

## 12

*Mia pedaled her* bike hard to get past the worst part of the ride along Route 29. Normally she'd have called up Michele and Gael, and most likely one of their mothers would have driven them, but there was no way that was going to happen now. Not after last night.

Riding under an unusually hot sun for early spring, the sweat pouring off her, Mia angrily went over what she'd say to her friends when she saw them at school on Monday: "You guys are pathetic. Did you sit down in your bunny slippers with Mummy and Daddy for a night of TV?" They'd know she was pissed. Or maybe they'd have some kind of legit excuse that would smooth the whole thing over: "Our parents found out and wouldn't let us go. We tried calling but you were already gone."

Maybe then Mia would admit to them the night wasn't really so great. And it was all her fault. Because that's how she saw it now. After the department store. After getting assaulted. And most of all, after the sad way Clancy smiled at her as she got out of his car, like she was some lost soul without a chance in this world.

Mia rode to the top of a small hill and found the turn she was looking for. She locked her bike to a tree and took the dirt trail that led into the woods. Scrubby bushes reached out, leaving tiny scrapes on her legs as she rapidly made her way down. At the end was a gathering of boulders, and she stood there, overlooking the reservoir. It was green as the trees and shaped like a serpent's twisting body. Sunlight glistened on the surface of the water. So bright. So clear.

She thought about Clancy again. And the reason it bugged her what he thought. It was because he didn't know her, didn't have any history to draw on. He saw her exactly for what she was, and he didn't want to know more. That moment she said good-bye in the car felt like looking into a mirror, and she didn't like what he'd seen.

She knew she was going to have to change. Somehow. But for now, all Mia could do was swim. She hoped the cold water would clear her head, get her ready for a fresh start.

Brightly colored beach towels peppered the shallow gravel beach, which the local kids claimed. Closer to where she stood were some flat rocks, mostly taken up by college kids already. The two groups never mingled, for obvious reasons. Nothing in common and all that, but there was something else. The college kids preferred to sunbathe in the nude.

Mia took a quick look at the fleshy mounds, boys and girls both, splayed out below her. It all looked like walrus flesh to her. Floppy and sweaty in places she really didn't want to see. Mia quickly made her way down to the water's edge and let the gentle surf lap at her feet and ankles. She sighed with relief, and almost immediately after scanning the beach for a place to put out her towel, she spotted Michele and Gael gathering their things to leave.

Mia froze, unsure. But then she saw them turn her way and share a look, steeling themselves for the unpleasant reality of having to speak with her, and her anger spiked.

Even as she walked toward them, she wanted to stop herself, but she couldn't. "Hey! Michele! Gael! What happened to you guys last night?" she shouted out.

"Hey," Gael said, looking at her with eyes that were like glass, clear and blank. "We've got to go. My mom's picking us up."

"Aren't you going to answer my question?"

"We got hung up at my house, and then it was too late," Gael told her.

"And you didn't call . . . because why? What's your excuse for that?"

"Don't you get it? We can't help you anymore," Michele told her. She stuffed the rest of her belongings into her knapsack and stood up. "We're through."

Mia could see how much Michele hated her at that moment, and it was shocking enough, but what she'd said made no sense. Mia's mind was reeling. "What do you mean, help me? Are you talking about math class? You're still mad about that?"

Gael answered her in a voice that sounded firm and purposeful. "Mia, we're going in different directions. We like to do different things. We never even wanted to go to the club with you, but we didn't really think you'd ever get in there, so we just went along pretending like someday we'd all go. But after the game on Friday we just—"

"I knew you were still mad about the volleyball thing," Mia interrupted. "But I didn't mean to hurt her." She was talking just to Gael. It seemed like her only chance. "I told you that was an accident."

Michele harrumphed. "Your whole life is an accident.

You don't think through any of the things you do . . . you just do them. And then everyone else has to deal with it."

"Like what?"

"Like everything!" Michele shot back. "Shoplifting, the math quiz, the volleyball game, and then when you wanted us to bring drugs and sneak into the club . . ."

"You could have just said you didn't want to go."

"You're not getting it. We don't want to do *anything* with you anymore!"

"Mia, we grew up different from you," Gael added.

"Why don't you tell her the truth? Mia, you're a liar and a thief."

Mia thought she might throw up. She looked at Gael, not believing she thought this, too.

"Listen, I'm sorry." Gael did look sorry. But she also looked decided. "The things you're interested in . . . college boys, doing drugs, stealing stuff . . . that's just not who we are."

"You make me sound like a loser. I'm not like that. I'm not!"

Gael kept going. "All I know is you're not thinking about anything other than how to have some fun on the weekend. And we want our lives to be about something more important."

"Forget it." Michele hoisted her bag to her shoulder, ready to go. "She can't possibly understand."

Gael looked pained. "We've tried to be there for you . . . we tried to pull you along with us, but it didn't do any good."

Mia tried once more. "So you don't want to be friends anymore . . . and that's it?"

Gael didn't answer her.

"Who am I going to hang out with?"

Michele laughed meanly. "Well, your boyfriend is here today. Why don't you go be with him?"

Mia couldn't imagine what Michele was talking about. She didn't have a boyfriend and they knew it. "Over there," Michele said, pointing to the rocks where a group of buck-naked college boys were lined up to dive into the water from a rope swing. Peter York was among them, his white-blond hair shining in the sunlight.

Mia felt her face turn red. She'd totally forgotten about the Yorkman. And that she was supposed to be dating him. That it was another lie she'd told.

"So don't let us keep you," Michele taunted some more. "Funny, though, he acts like he doesn't even know you're here."

Mia didn't care what was true anymore. She wasn't going to let Michele get away with talking to her like that if it was the last thing she ever did. "You're just jealous because I'm going out with someone older."

Gael laughed this time. "Going out or getting laid?"

"Neither!" Michele practically yelped. "She made the whole thing up."

"You think you know everything. But you don't." Mia spun on her heels and marched off on a straight path for the rope swing. Down the beach, she turned and was glad to see Michele and Gael hadn't moved an inch, riveted to find out what she was going to do next.

Maybe she didn't think through all the things that she did. *But at least I do things, don't I?* Mia walked even faster toward the nude beach.

Most of the flat and comfortable spots on the rocks were already occupied, but there was one that was free, way back from the water. Mia made her way to it, trying not to stare at the naked people she passed, but she couldn't avert her eyes completely. A couple of the kids there looked up to see who had arrived and then looked away because she wasn't anyone any of them knew. A few of the girls had armpit hair and wore it proudly, lying back with their arms crossed behind their heads.

There was no sign of Peter York. Maybe he'd left while she'd walked over, which was good because she couldn't imagine taking off her clothes in front of him. Or any of them, for that matter. But as she lay down on her towel, a burst of shouts came from the water and then a couple of swimmers emerged. It was three boys. No, correct that . . . it was three men, water dripping from their bodies and their wrinkly penises as they clambered up the rocks. She noticed that detail before she noticed that one of them was Peter York. He moved past her in a flash of glistening brown skin and abdominal muscles and flung himself facedown on a towel only a few feet away. His buddies lay out near him.

Mia turned to look. A quick glance. Secretly. And then she wanted to look again. She flipped over fast onto her stomach like a flapjack on the griddle. Now she had a clear view of Peter. He had his back to her as he talked to his friends.

His buttocks were a shocking white. He'd obviously gotten

a tan in a place where swimsuits were not optional. So this scene was new for him, too. Mia smiled at the thought that he wasn't so different from her after all.

One of the guys noticed her at that exact moment. "Hey, that girl's checking you out," she heard one of them say to Peter. "Over there. Behind you." And Peter turned. A half-smile came to his lips, but Mia was mortified and turned away, her entire being burning ten times hotter than before. She closed her eyes and tried to disappear. All she could think was *Oh my God, oh my God, oh my God!* She wished it were possible to burrow her way into the rock.

"Go on over," she heard his friend say.

"Yeah, she's into you."

They were goading him to act. Mia had to do something or she was going to have to talk to him. The thought was suddenly unbearable. This wasn't how she imagined they'd meet, him bare-skinned as a baby with his friends sitting there like an audience. Even though she'd engineered this entire moment, now she had to do something to change it.

*Get up. Stand up. Now!*

In one swift move, Mia got to her feet. It felt like it took forever to get to the water's edge, as she carefully stepped around all the bodies, her the strange one in shorts and a T-shirt. When finally her toes gripped the last boulder, she had a moment's regret about swimming in her clothes, but she wasn't going back to her towel near his. No way! Mia pressed her hands in a prayer at her chest, took a deep breath, and dove dramatically down into the cool greenness.

She swam away from shore. Treading in the glistening water, she wiped her eyes clear and saw Peter was getting ready to dive in, too. He pushed off the rock, disappeared for several seconds. Mia spun around to see where he'd come up. With a hard flick of his platinum head, he emerged directly in front of her and then swam toward her, stopping only a few feet away.

"Hi," he said. There was that great white smile.

"Hi." Mia felt like she could barely talk.

"I'm Peter."

"Mia."

"Awesome day for a swim."

"It is."

He swam a little closer. "Have I seen you before?"

"You tell me."

"On campus?"

Mia just smiled.

They spun around and around in the still water, unable to take their eyes off each other. The sunlight seemed to shoot through his, like they were made of blue crystal. He was quietly studying her, his chin low in the water and his lips just touching the surface.

"So, Mia . . . how come you've still got your clothes on?"

And he was flirting!

"I think most people look better with their clothes on. Don't you?"

He laughed now. "Yeah, you might be right about that. So, Mia . . . what's your favorite thing to do in all the world?"

"I suppose this would be high on the list."

"Oh, yeah, lazy Sundays are the best, right?"

"Absolutely."

The circle they swam in was getting smaller and smaller

as the water drew them together. Mia could feel the ripples his feet made, and then his fingers brushed hers. She pushed back in the water, not wanting that closeness, not yet.

"Okay, so what else do you do for fun?" he asked, trying to make it sound meaningful.

She never expected he'd like her so quickly. That it would be so easy. And now that it was, she wasn't sure what she wanted to happen. But he was waiting for an answer, and she didn't have one, except to say that she liked to shoplift. Damn it! What else could she tell him? What else?

Over his shoulder, the swing was blowing in the breeze.

"I like to jump," she told him, pointing at the hanging rope.

"You do?" He was honestly surprised. "I've never seen a girl do it before."

"Want to?"

"You bet."

Mia didn't hesitate. She swam away from him fast. It was almost too much . . . the intensity of his gaze and the fact that she wanted his attention so bad but now had to go on lying if she wanted to keep it. Had to hide her true self. She turned to see if he was still following. He kept up easily, his kicks barely cutting the water.

He got out first. "You're fast," he said, offering a hand to help her climb up over the slippery rocks. As long as she kept her eyes averted from the obvious thing dangling between them, it felt like a very romantic moment. Peter seemed to sense her tension about his nakedness, and he didn't seem to care. And Mia stood there for a moment, feeling how cooling air and wet rock could not dispel the heat of a naked boy. He leaned in toward her. But he didn't kiss her. He wanted to, she was sure of it. His face was all dreamy. But did she? The accusations of her friends were still stinging. *All you want to do is chase boys. . . .*

"You want to go first?" She put her hand on the rope swing, breaking the mood.

"You're not really going to do it, are you?"

"Yeah, did you think I was making it up?"

He picked up the challenge in her voice. "Can you jump from the platform up there?"

Up the slope, a makeshift jump had been built out of some spare lumber. It made swinging out more dangerous, a much bigger and longer leap. Mia hadn't tried it before. It always seemed too high. "Yeah, of course."

"Okay, this I want to see."

Mia toed her way up the muddy rise, past the rock she usually jumped from, and crawled up onto the platform. She felt like a trapeze artist, except there was no one to catch her when she fell from the sky. What if she couldn't make it? Peter was down below, looking worried for her. "Want me to show you how?" he called out.

"I got it," Mia called back. No way was she going to back down. No reason she couldn't do this. She'd watched scrawny, skinny boys half as strong as her take that running jump and fly. Mia stepped back, mentally running through what she'd seen them do. They'd run out with both hands on the rope, but at the last moment, the apex of the pendulum's swing, they would reach up for the highest knot. That jerked the body out more, gave it a little extra momentum to clear the rocks.

And then the buzzing *zap* hit her, the one that felt so good it made her want to do crazy things.

"Come on down, babe." It was Peter. She hardly heard him.

She exploded forward, both hands on the rope, kicking off at the platform's edge. She was airborne then, and instinct took over. When she reached for the knot above her head, she felt her body take on a new momentum and was whipped higher into the air. That's when she let go. Peter yelped in approval. And Mia felt herself drop. It happened in slow motion. The light from the water glowed up at her, and she plummeted down with ease, in a free-flying fall.

When she resurfaced, Peter looked astounded. "You got major air on that. Wow. Really cool."

Mia calmly climbed out of the water, as if it were nothing and she'd done it a million times. "Yeah, that was a good one," she said. But inside she felt like she could burst. She had to do it again.

She made her way up toward the platform.

Peter said, "Hold up. I'm going have to get geared up if I'm going to match that." He ran off and came back wearing his trunks.

"One, two, three . . ." On her count, he ran for it. But he went out backward, and his fall was not nearly as elegant. She jumped out, tried to show him how to do it. Again and again he tried, but finally Peter had to admit he couldn't match her jump. After a while she told him the secret of how she'd done it, but he shrugged his shoulders as if it wasn't important, and Mia realized maybe she shouldn't have shown off.

But he offered her a ride back, and she let him load her bike into the trunk of his friend's car even though she could have easily done it herself. Then the whole way home he kept his warm wet thigh with its golden blond fur plastered to hers in the back. And when they got to campus, he asked her, "Maybe we can grab some food this week? Are you up for that?"

Was he asking her for a date? Was that what "grab food" meant?

"That'd be grcat. Yes."

"How's Wednesday?"

Mia was so excited and trying so hard to control it, she could barely think. Wednesday, she knew, was a day of the week. Whether she was busy or not, she had no idea. She just nodded.

"Should I pick you up at your dorm?" Peter asked.

Mia brewed up a quick lie about why that was a bad idea. "Oh, no. My roommate is really weird," she said. And then she topped that one off by adding, "I'm trying to transfer into another room, but so far no good. I'll just meet you at yours?" Her nerves were practically on fire now. She felt the lies churning inside her like she'd eaten some bad food.

"It's White Hall," hc told her.

Mia blushed bccause she knew that already.

"Seven o'clock?" he shouted to her, as Mia was already on her bike.

"See you Wednesday!" she answered over her shoulder, and she blew out of there, trying to get away fast before he asked anything else she had to lie about. It had turned into such a perfect day, she wanted nothing about her old self to spoil it.

We shelter in ourselves
an angel whom we
constantly shock.

—JEAN COCTEAU

## 13

*Mia discovered that* Mondays were even harder when you had no friends. Michele and Gael weren't waiting at the bus stop. She got on by herself and listened to her schoolmates chatter and laugh while an ominous feeling settled on her like stone. This was only the beginning of the snubbing she would have to deal with, she knew.

She stared out the window but didn't even see the town go clattering by. Warm memories of swimming with Peter had followed her home on Sunday afternoon, but this morning they were gone, replaced by nightmares of three girls breaking up on the beach. Like you would in a serious relationship. Michele saying horrible things, calling her names. Ugly dirty names you would only call your worst enemy. Thief. Liar. And Gael doing nothing to stop her or disagree.

The bus arrived at school.

Mia went straight to math class that morning, even before the bell rang. She knew her ex-friends were probably in the room somewhere, but she didn't look around for them. She took the first empty seat she could find. She heard some whispering, and it felt as if the lowered voices were talking about her.

That's when she started to build her cocoon. Inside of it, Mia would try to survive. She might hear people say bad things about her, but she would not listen, and she would not look at anything other than what was in front her. She would have to make the cocoon thick to be safe, to stay calm. And then maybe when she saw her old friends, the cocoon would be so thick they'd never be able to hurt her again. At least there was the hope.

Soon Mr. Sabatelli came in and started to run through problems on the board. She took notes, but the beat of her own heart was the only thing of any consequence, and she felt it fluttering in her chest, struggling to keep on.

When the bell rang, Mia stood and gathered her books and left the room quickly before the two girls who used to be her entire world turned their hateful faces on her, before they got the chance to be so horrible again.

It felt like the morning was a hundred years long. The breakup had changed everything. It seemed as if all her schoolmates were avoiding her. Mia asked a girl she'd known since kindergarten if she wanted to run through math problems that afternoon. The girl gave her a blank stare and then made some excuse about having a doctor's appointment as she melted away down the hall. Mia said hi to a boy she knew had a crush on her the previous year, and all he did was nod his head at her and keep on talking to his friends. It was as if everyone had heard what happened with Michele and Gael and now wanted nothing to do with her, either.

And then the worst was at lunch.

Mia filled her cafeteria tray and had to find a table to sit at. Not the cheerleaders' or the jocks' table, obviously. Not the rich kids or the bad students, because those were all boys.

She was shocked to realize how few real friends she had

in school. Or anywhere. She knew people, of course, kids she'd grown up around, but they didn't count. They didn't really know her. Because she'd never let them get to know her. She hadn't needed them. And now that she did, she couldn't help but wonder, what was the point of having friends if they were only going to abandon you?

She saw the two of them then, as they entered the cafeteria and got on line. Michele and Gael. Talking to each other. A closed circle of two. They'd managed to erase her in the course of a weekend. She didn't think they were pretending. For them, she no longer existed.

And she decided right then that there was no way she was going to sit at an empty table. Mia spotted a girl she knew from English class, Katie Bartlett, eating with a girl who was a grade ahead.

"Hey, guys," she said, taking a seat next to them without asking or even checking to see if they minded, because she didn't know what she'd do if they did.

"Hey, Mia," Katie and the girl said back, friendly enough. They kept on talking to each other. The subject was clothes and what they wanted to buy and what they thought didn't look good unless you were really skinny, and Mia joined in for a while, but she found herself faking her interest. This was odd. Mia loved clothes, but today it all seemed so unimportant. She forced herself to add her opinion here and there. "I think wide-legged jeans could be fun to wear once in a while, you know?" but when the girls got up to bus their trays, she was relieved.

She finished up her food fast, put her brownie in a napkin, and got up to go. She went out to sit by herself on the sloped lawn overlooking the soccer field and waited for fourth period to begin. Only twenty minutes more, and then she had two more classes. Gael was in chemistry with her, and after that was composition, where she had no friends, ex or otherwise. Then it would be time to get up to the college, to the bugs that needed to be fed. She could hardly wait.


Mia was running by the time she got to Sutton Hall. Finkelstein was at his desk when she walked in at five minutes past the hour. He stood up abruptly. "Good afternoon, Mia. Let's not waste any more time. I'll watch you work through a group and if it seems like you've got the hang of it, you can do the rest on your own."

Mia stood in front of the tower of flies and realized she wasn't quite sure where to begin. What did they do last time? Group four first? Then she remembered the columns of numbers. "I think I'll get the notebooks out," she said, still unsure of herself.

"Good, good," Finkelstein responded.

She spread them out on her desk and took a quick look down at the black ink marks marching like a line of soldiers down the page. Numbers, numbers. Two dead. Four dead. And so on. The columns gave away nothing to help her.

"Let's start with the vials, shall we?" Finkelstein gestured to the cabinets that hung over the lab sink. The instructions he'd given on the first day started to come back to her. First label the vials, then fill them with sawdust, then the honey. The last thing was the yucky fly food.

*Right. Here goes.*

Mia walked over and pulled the glass vessels down, one by one, filling a tray that was sitting on the counter. She worked steadily and easily, with Finkelstein offering a correction or helping hand here and there. She felt like she was on an assembly line, but the product was flies in all their various stages, from eggs to babies to mature buzzers. After she'd finished the first round of sawdust and honey, squeezing out perfect dollops of the amber liquid, she looked up at Finkelstein with a little hint of a smile, proud of her efficiency.

Next came the fly food. She bent to retrieve it from the fridge, then remembered the need for rubber gloves. There was a pair drying on a rack near the sink. She put them on.

"Good move," Finkelstein said.

There was no holding back now. She took out the Tupperware container and was about to pull back the lid, when Finkelstein said, "That reminds me of a joke. What did the judge say when the stinkbug walked into the room?"

"I don't know. What did he say?"

"Odor! Odor in the court!"

Mia laughed despite herself. "That's a terrible joke."

"I know," Finkelstein said.

She dipped a teaspoon into the food mix and started to fill the empty vials. The gloves made her hands clumsy, and the mixture spilled onto the tray, counter, and floor. When she finished, all Finkelstein said was, "I'll have to find an easier way to do that. There's got to be a tool we can use. Clean up the spills, all right? Use paper towels. I don't want that stench on the sponge."

When she was done, Mia ripped off the gloves and threw them in the sink. "Time for gas, right?" she asked.

He nodded, encouraging her with a smile.

Standing beside the fly shelves, she could actually feel the vibration of their buzzing. It set her teeth on edge. She had to force herself to pull the first box for group one from the shelf. And suddenly it was as if the clear box didn't exist and a raft of buzzing insects, angry at being moved, lofted up into her face. Mia flinched and dropped the box.

"Oh, no!' Finkelstein cried out as it hit the ground and the lid flew off. The flies came zooming out. There was nothing for Mia to do but stand there and feel terrible while Finkelstein went after them with a swatter. In a few minutes he finished them off and collapsed in a chair.

Mia braced for the worst. "Did I ruin the experiment?" she said.

"Well . . . we lost a part of group one," he said. "And that's not good. There's going to be a hole in the data. But there's nothing to be done about it now, I suppose. You'll have to be more careful, Mia."

"You're not going to fire me?"

Finkelstein looked up. "You're doing your best, aren't you?"

Mia nodded. "I can do better. I think."

"I think you can, too. Ready to try again?"

"Yes. I am." Mia stepped up to the shelves once more, determined not to let the flies surprise her this time. She pulled out a fly box slowly and held it tight. She made herself go stone cold to the buzzing as she placed it next to the tank of $CO_2$.

"Not many people can do this work. It's not for the timid," Finkelstein said.

Mia smiled ever so slightly. "Yeah, I'm not definitely not the timid type."

"That's good, believe me," Finkelstein told her.

Mia shrugged off the compliment, because she really wasn't sure it was true. Not being timid had cost her a lot so far.

After they finished with group one, Finkelstein led her down the hall to a room that looked like a warehouse. Rows of metal shelves were filled with those neat gray cardboard shoeboxes. "This is the breeding area. It's where we store all the breeding boxes until the eggs hatch, because it's temperature-controlled," he told her. Lab assistants glided about the room in white lab coats.

"Do all these lab people breed flies for you?"

"Goodness, no!" Finkelstein laughed a little too loudly, and several of the lab assistants turned to look their way, as if they knew Mia had asked a stupid question. She slouched against the shelves.

"Don't worry. It's an easy misunderstanding to have, with all these boxes. But I'm only one of many doctoral candidates using this room, you see. We all work under different professors in the program. You can put today's boxes on the shelves labeled 'Finkelstein' and that's all there is to it."

She liked the breeding room. It was quiet, like a church. And there were lots of students, who were closer to her age than Finkelstein, though there wasn't a girl among them. Maybe she'd make some new friends here. It wouldn't hurt to try.

She went straight home after work, looking forward to telling Grandpa Andy all about her job, hoping that perhaps today he'd enjoy hearing details of the lab procedures. But as soon as she unlocked his door and let herself in, she could tell something was wrong.

He wasn't in the living room, and the television was dark. As she crept quietly down the hall to check if he was napping, she noticed all the pictures in the hallway had been pulled off the wall, leaving squares and rectangles of richly colored wallpaper behind. It looked like he was in the middle of moving out. Continuing to his bedroom, she found his bed made. He wasn't there.

"Grandpa?" she called out, heading for the bathroom. It looked neat as a hospital, nothing out of place. A clean towel on the rack was dry as a bone. She ran for the kitchen next. It was empty except for the sink full of dishes. She'd have to wash them. But first she had to find him.

There was one last place to look. The backyard. The kitchen door had been left open, and stepping out onto the stoop, she felt her heart lurch when she saw him lying flat on his back on the ground, in that grassy area where she liked to sit in the summertime. He wasn't moving. She flew to him, calling his name. But she found he was just lying there quietly with his eyes wide open. "Mia? Hello, my girl," he said as if they were sitting down to tea. "Good to see you."

"G.A.? Are you okay? What's going on?"

"I got tired. Very tired. After all my work." He vaguely gestured toward the rear of the yard. There was a huge hole dug in the back corner beneath the crab apple tree that still had a swing hanging on it from when she was little. A shovel had been sunk into the ground. It stood there, poking up like a marker. "And so I lay down here for a rest. It was so nice I didn't want to get up. Then after a while it occurred to me I should go back in the house, because I'd been down here too long. But my legs . . . they gave out on me." A tear trickled out of his eye, and Mia wiped it away before it slipped into his hairy ear.

Mia wasn't sure what to do. His doctor had told both her and her mother that it wasn't a good idea to question Grandpa Andy about the things he said and did. That it might confuse him more than he already was, mess up what was left of his reason. But what was he doing out there?

"Nice hole, Grandpa," she said.

"It needs to be deeper. There's so much to bury."

"So it's meant to be a grave?" Mia voice faltered and she realized she was nervous now. This might be more than she could handle. And how was she going to get him back in the house if his legs didn't work?

"That's right. I want to be buried here. No churchyard for me, you hear? I'm a man of science. I am."

"You are. That's right."

She looked up at the house wishing her mother was around, but Mia would have to solve this problem alone. The dark of the upstairs apartment told her Constance was definitely at work. She wondered how long Grandpa Andy had been out there.

"What made you take all your things off the wall?" Mia asked him.

"The past is all over and done, I say. No point in think-ing about it anymore. Or being reminded of it every time I turn around."

"Mind if I take a closer look?" she asked, gesturing at the place he'd been digging.

"Be my guest."

Mia stood up and peered inside the hole. It was quite deep. So deep that he could have broken a leg if he tripped and fell into it. At the bottom was a pile of framed pictures and awards. All his belongings that she liked so much. She came back to his side and took his hand. "Grandpa. I'm sorry to have to tell you this, but I don't think you should throw away your things like that."

"Give me one good reason why not!" he demanded.

Mia thought for a moment. "Well . . . did you ever think that I might like to have them?" Grandpa Andy's eyes opened wide, and she continued. "Because I love to look at all your things. I know most of them by heart. I could tell you the name of the president of the university who signed your degree. Or the name of the newspaper where you're shaking the governor's hand."

"I didn't realize . . ."

"They're part of my past now," she told him. "And I want to keep them. If you don't want to look at them anymore I'll put them in a box and take them upstairs. But don't throw them in the dirt. That's wrong. Someday they'll be the only things I have to remind me of you." A lump rose in her throat.

"Oh, oh . . ." Grandpa Andy said as her first tear fell, and he pulled a dirty tissue from his breast pocket. "Don't be sad. I'm giving it all to you. Everything. The pictures. The furniture. The house. It will all be yours."

He was talking nonsense again. "Okay, G.A."

"I mean it! It's all for you. Not your mother. She's no good!"

Mia didn't know what to say to that. She'd never heard G.A. speak so harshly of Constance. Maybe he thought this made sense at the moment, or they'd had another fight, but how could he even think about not leaving things to her mother, like the house? Though Mia had learned recently that sometimes people who are supposed to care about you simply don't. No matter how much you want them to. Make a couple of mistakes and that's the end.

But what had Constance done to make G.A. completely give up on her like this?

The sky darkened over their heads. His skin looked blue in the rising twilight, and her jeans were cold and wet from the dusky moisture growing in the grass. She had to help him. "Well, Grandpa, you don't think I'm going to let you sleep out here tonight, do you? We've got to get inside."

"Yes, yes. But how to do it? That is the question, right?"

"Try sitting up. Can you get that far?" Mia got behind him and helped lift his upper body off the ground. "Now wiggle your feet. Can you do that?"

They both turned to look down at his large black shoes. Grandpa Andy was studying them with the intensity of a mind reader, as if he could will them to move. "C'mon, feet!" he said. "Give us a wag."

Mia laughed. And his feet jerked to life.

"All right! Way to go, Grandpa!" Mia cheered.

Next she had him bend his knees and roll over onto all fours, then she grabbed him under both arms and managed to pull him up. He was unsteady, but he was able to put one foot in front of the other. She wrapped her arms around his waist, and slowly they went toward the house.

Once she had him settled in the kitchen with a slab of microwaved meat loaf and some canned corn, she went out into the yard and retrieved the things he'd thrown in the hole. The glass was broken on a few of the pieces, and they were wet with dirt from the grave he'd dug.

His grave. Mia shuddered. To think about burying him here. What a crazy thing to say.

She stayed with him while he finished his dinner, and then she put him in front of the television. A news program was on, and he usually enjoyed them. "You sit there for a little while. I'll be back to help you into bed. Okay, Grandpa?"

He nodded but didn't take his eyes off the flickering screen. Mia picked up an armload of the mementos she'd rescued from the backyard and climbed the stairs to her apartment. A streetlight lent a glow to the darkened living room upstairs.

She went to her room and sat there wondering what she should do. She was pretty sure Grandpa Andy needed to see a doctor, but was he sick enough to call an ambulance? Was this an emergency? Should she do it anyway? Should she call her mother, even though Constance wasn't supported to receive calls at work?

Mia killed time doing homework for a while and after that flipped through a magazine looking for images to add to the wall goddess, but she was too distracted. Although the pages were filled with all sorts of desirables, nothing truly appealed to her. At ten o'clock, Constance still wasn't home and Mia went back down to check on Grandpa Andy

She found it very hard to rouse him from his chair. He didn't seem to fully wake up, and she couldn't get him out of his clothes on her own. She tucked him in wearing his shirt and pants, kissed him on the forehead. He was already asleep and snoring, so she went back upstairs and went to bed herself.

Mia hoped that everything would be okay. But she really wasn't sure that it would. Not at all.

# 14

*Late that night,* Mia was awoken by the downstairs doorbell. It took her a second to realize that's what it was. The first ring happened in her sleep, and it wasn't until the second one buzzed, insistently, that she broke through to the surface. She checked her clock. It was two in the morning.

The doorbell rang again, but this time it was coming from Grandpa Andy's apartment. Mia could hear it through the floor of her room. And then it rang in George LeRoy's place upstairs. Whoever was down there was set on waking everybody up. She got out of bed.

Her doorbell rang again. Mia couldn't believe it didn't wake her mother. From the top of the stairs she could hear the cackling of the pranksters on the other side of the front door, laughing their heads off. Obviously it was hilarious to them to wake people up in the middle of the night. She picked up the phone and dialed 911 as she crept down the stairs.

A voice on the other side of the door was saying, "Where is the lock? I mean, the key?" and Mia recognized it immediately. It was Constance. Mia hung up the phone and yanked open the door. Her mother came crashing into the dim foyer, along with a heavy-footed George LeRoy, who stepped on Mia's toes by accident.

"Ouch!" Mia cried, and shoved him away. He fell into her mother, and both of them dropped onto the carpet like overpacked luggage, howling with laughter.

"I couldn't find my keys!" Constance said, too loudly, handing her bag over to Mia. "Look. See? They're not in there."

"You lose your keys, too, George?" Mia asked.

Constance and George looked at each other and cracked up again. "Oh my God . . . you live here also, don't you!" Constance shrieked.

"I don't know." George snickered. "I was just following you."

Mia was stunned. "Mom! Are you nuts? I almost called the police!"

Constance roared with laughter. "She was going to call the cops! Can you believe that, George? My daughter the shoplifter wanted to call the police!"

"Quiet, Mom. You'll wake Grandpa."

"Oh, shush yourself," Constance said.

Mia gave her mother a disgusted look, then turned and went back up the stairs. She heard Constance and George clomp up behind her and say their sloppy good-nights, and then her mother came stumbling down the hall. Mia followed her into her bedroom.

Constance wasn't just a little tipsy. She was drunk. But *really* drunk. She blabbered on about what a good time she'd had with George and how great it was to forget about life for a while. She was stripping out of her clothes at the same time. She nearly fell over kicking her legs out of her pants, and that cracked her up, too. She seemed to like being drunk.

And Mia was frightened. Who was this person? Mia didn't know her all of a sudden, but it was the happiest she'd ever seen Constance, who was practically reveling in her drunkenness.

"You were right," Constance said. "I should get out more."

Mia picked up the clothes her mother had shoved against the closet door and folded them neatly onto hangers, something her mother would usually have done without thinking about it. Constance finally noticed that Mia hadn't said a word. "Youallright?" she asked, slurring her words together.

"Yeah, I guess. Except . . . I wish you'd come home earlier."

"You do?" Constance's look of surprise cut through her stupor, but only for a second.

"Yeah, because I'm worried about Grandpa Andy. He isn't feeling so well. I think we should take him to the emergency room."

"Oh. I saw him before I went out. . . ." Constance was pulling down the sheet and crawling into bed now. ". . . He seemed the same to me." She flopped across the bed like a rag doll.

"Did you guys argue again?"

"Don't remember. Don't want to. I've got the spins."

Looking at her lying there, Mia remembered what G.A. had said about Constance. *She's no good.* At that moment, Mia found herself agreeing, then pushed the ugly thought away. Because she wasn't going to judge. Not when she'd made her own mistakes. That was for sure.

But she had seen enough. "I'm going to check on him."

"Good," Constance murmured into her pillow.

Mia crept back downstairs. Grandpa Andy was snoring lightly, so she quietly exited his apartment. She was glad at least the drunken ruckus hadn't woken him. And her reentry into the apartment upstairs didn't wake Constance, either, even when Mia reached across her mother's bed to turn off the light.

In the morning, Mia grabbed two Pop-Tarts from the pantry and headed down to share them with Grandpa Andy before school. Everything in his apartment was just as she'd left it the night before. She loaded the toaster and went into his room. He filled up the double bed, like a hibernating bear in a den too small for his bulk. He wasn't snoring anymore.

She leaned over him, saying, "Rise and shine, G.A. Want some breakfast?" He didn't answer, so she shook his shoulder once, then again even harder. When he didn't even stir, she ran out of the apartment and up the stairs, taking them two at a time. "Mom!" she shouted. "I can't wake Grandpa Andy!"

"Oh, crap," she heard her mother say from under the covers.

The ambulance team arrived with sirens blaring and tried everything they could to revive him, and then they quickly strapped him to a gurney and flew out of the apartment. Mia and her mother got in the ambulance with Grandpa Andy and the paramedics.

At the hospital, the doctors asked her a lot of questions about the previous night. Did he eat all his dinner? What time did he fall asleep? Did you check on him later in the evening? They made Mia feel like there was something she could have done to save him.

Mia waited alone in the emergency intake room while her mother watched the doctor examine her grandfather. They'd been in there for over an hour, and it was getting harder for Mia to sit still. All she had were unanswered questions. Why did G.A. say such horrible things about Constance? Did he know she was out getting drunk? Why did Constance get so trashed? As much as she always saw her family as messed up, this new vision was worse. Much worse. And to top it off, the hospital reminded her of the fly lab with its linoleum floors, sterile white walls, and long hallways. She looked over to a set of glass doors that led to a grassy courtyard.

"Excuse me," she said to the attendant behind the admittance desk. "If my mother and grandfather come looking for me, will you tell them I went outside, just over there?"

"Sure thing. What's your name, sweetie?"

Mia told her and stepped out of the stuffy room. Outside, bright daylight shone down on the courtyard, warming her up. A few people smoked cigarettes, and she sat on a bench away from them, but there wasn't much to look at except for the smokers. Right away she spotted someone she knew but never expected to see again. It was the older guy from the Common Ground. Clancy. He was looking right back at her, same as the first time she saw him in the club, except this time he was smiling. She waved and he gestured her over.

"Shouldn't smoke, you know. It's bad for your health," she said as she approached.

"Yeah, but it's my only vice."

"That's what my mother says."

He chuckled. "How are you, kid? Staying out of trouble?"

"Yup. Pretty much. No one's invited me back to the Common Ground, anyway."

"Yeah. I made sure of that."

"You did? How?"

"Fired Roddy."

Mia felt a secret thrill. That animal had gotten what he deserved. "Thanks," she said.

"For what?"

"Well . . . I guess I thought you did it for me."

"After what happened to you, it had to be done."

Mia didn't try to hide her disappointment. "I just hoped you'd decided to be my knight in shining . . ." She looked him up and down; he was definitely dressed casually. "Wearing whatever. My knight in torn jeans."

"I did warn Robbie to stay away from you. Told him he'd be out of a gig if he didn't. Guy's no fool. He makes about five hundred a month off the club."

"No wonder I haven't heard from him."

"Glad to hear it."

They smiled at each other. "So what are you doing here?" Mia asked.

He gestured toward an open door across the courtyard. "I'm here for an AA meeting," he said.

"Alcoholics Anonymous? You?"

"Ten years sober and proud of it."

"Huh. You never drink at all? Not even once in a while?"

"Nope. It's bad for me. Or I'm bad for it. One of the two. Anyway . . . I didn't like myself anymore and I knew I had to stop."

"Yeah. I've definitely felt that way."

Clancy smiled one of those sad ones again. "So what bad news brought you here today?"

"My grandfather got sick. He's still in with the doctor. I've been waiting awhile now."

"That's too bad," Clancy said in his heartbroken way. "But maybe he'll be okay."

"I doubt it." As soon as Mia said that, she realized it was true. She didn't expect Grandpa Andy to get better. She looked up into Clancy's eyes. "He's really so sick. And there's nothing the doctors can do for him because I think he's given up. Do you know what I mean?"

"I do," he said. She couldn't read him, what he was thinking, but he made her feel like he knew exactly what she was talking about just by how he was listening.

Right about then, Clancy glanced at something over her shoulder. It held his gaze. Mia turned to see what had caught his attention and spotted Constance stepping through the glass doors. So he found Constance attractive. Just like George.

Mia gasped. "That's my mother. I don't want her to see me with you. She'll start asking all kinds of questions."

"Let's not have that. I have to get back to my meeting, anyway. Good to see you again, Mia." He turned and quickly became invisible, blending into the group of smokers who went back inside.

Constance came to her side. She wore a completely blank expression, like someone had vacuumed out the inside of her head.

"How's Grandpa Andy? What did the doctor say?" Mia questioned her nervously. "Is he coming home with us?"

"No, he's not. And they're not sure what's wrong yet. They want to keep him here for observation."

"Oh, no!" Mia cried out. "That sounds bad."

"It's just for a few days. I'm sorry, Mia. They told me we have to prepare ourselves for the worst. As if there's any way to do that."

"Can we visit him?" Mia said.

"He's sleeping now, and they don't know when he'll wake up. We'll call later to see when he can have visitors." The two of them just stood there in the courtyard, unsure of what to do next. "This is just too much," Constance said then, as if she were talking to herself.

"Are you going to work tonight?" Mia asked.

"No. I'm taking the night off."

That sounded like a terrible idea to Mia. Especially after last night. "How come?" Mia wished she didn't sound so nervous.

Constance sighed heavily. "I'm not in the mood."

"What does that mean?"

"I found out Butler Hall is going to hire a twenty-one-year-old graduate of the hotel school to be the new administrator in training."

"You're not getting the job you wanted?"

"That's right. They passed me over for the promotion. And everyone else on the staff, for that matter. There's no one there who hasn't been on the line for at least two years."

"So what are you going to do?"

"I don't know. But I don't feel like working now. I really don't."

"Wow. That sucks, Mom. I'm sorry."

"What do you care?" Constance said dryly. "It's just a stupid cafeteria, right?"

Mia didn't know what to say. She couldn't take back her insult from a few days before, and telling Constance that maybe this was all for the best didn't seem like it would cheer her up, either.

Constance looked at Mia, and her face softened. "Don't look so worried," she said. "There's nothing you can do for Grandpa Andy. Okay?"

But Grandpa Andy wasn't the only person Mia was worried about.

*Mia gingerly lifted* the fly boxes from the bottom
shelf. She treated them gently after the trouble she'd had
the day before. She didn't want to drop one again. But she
easily remembered how to do the job, and she changed out
five fly boxes at a time without any help from Finkelstein,
who worked quietly at his desk.

The job helped take her mind off her worries, but little
bits would creep back in. Why was her mother drinking so
much all of a sudden? Was she going to stop? Was G.A. going to get out of the hospital? Would she ever have any
friends again? Why were things flying so out of control?

When it was time to put a batch of bugs to sleep, Mia un-
wound the rubber tube from the tank of $CO_2$ gas and
placed the tip against the wire mesh lid of the plastic box.
She must have left it on too long, because she looked up to
find Finkelstein getting concerned.

"Sorry," she said to him. "Got a little lost in thought."

"Well, they're fine, but do pay attention."

"I am. I will."

Mia refocused, delivering the latest offspring in groups
five and six into their sawdust cribs. She carefully and thoroughly scraped out the contents of each used vial into a
breeding box. The work was easy. It was a relief, actually.
Mia felt her mind settling down, and for the first time, looking more closely at what she was doing, she saw some teeny
tiny white dots buried in the sawdust. These were fly eggs,

she realized. Nothing more than white specks. Kind of cool.

"I'm going to bring these boxes to the breeding room," she said when she had finished and put all the used Pyrex vials in the sink.

Finkelstein gave a wave of his hand, too busy with his calculator to look up.

"So what happens when they're done breeding?" Mia asked.

"I'll tell you when we get to it," he said, still studying his books. "It'll be in about a week or so."

"Why wait till then?"

Finkelstein put down his pen. "I don't want to upset you. It's a bit gross to the uninitiated."

"What could be grosser than scraping fly eggs out of a vial?"

Finkelstein was regarding her with that funny smile once again, as if she'd asked directions to the moon. "Are you sure you want me to tell you now?"

"What difference does it make? I have to face it someday."

"Right you are. Well, after the seven-day mark, we check the boxes every day. You'll know immediately if the maggots have hatched. And then a few days later, after passing through the pupae stage, they turn into flies."

"Maggots?"

"Yes."

"I have to deal with . . . maggots?" Mia looked down at the tray she was holding in her hands. It was full of boxes containing fly eggs, all waiting to be born into their grossness with her help.

"I'm sure you can handle it," Finkelstein said.

Mia left the lab and went into the breeding room. With a black marker she dated and labeled the five new boxes with an abbreviated form of her boss's last name, FINK. She hoped he didn't mind, but she had bigger worries.

Just about everything in her life was falling apart and now there was going to be a big steaming pile of maggots on top of it all. It was too much. And what if Finkelstein was wrong? What if she couldn't handle it? Any of it?

Mia stayed in the breeding room longer than she needed to, counting up the boxes she had made since she started working there. Twenty-five in all. She felt herself grow calm in the white space, watching the other lab assistants as they performed their duties like age-old rituals, their heads bowed in silence. One of them came up the aisle toward her. Mia saw him mark up all his breeding boxes for Professor Deacon, the same person Finkelstein was working for, and put them up on the shelf. When he was done, he turned to her. "Are you all right?" he asked.

She wasn't sure how to answer. She wasn't. Not really.

"You look a little confused, just standing there," he added.

"I'm just taking a break," she said, slightly peeved. "If that's okay with you."

"It's fine. I know this place can be overwhelming at first. So if you're feeling lost . . ."

"Well, that's not the word I'd use."

"What would you call it?"

"I don't know. Maybe unsure of things, a little."

"About what?"

Mia wasn't going to tell him what was really going on.

But she liked his face. It was open and relaxed. And he seemed to be completely present and with her, at that moment. Really paying attention. It was a nice feeling. "I don't know . . . I just wonder why everyone is bothering with all these flies, that's all," she confessed.

"Did you know this is the only program in the country doing work like this? Our research will affect the way pesticides are formulated and applied in the future."

"Who cares how some bugs die?"

"You don't understand. Pesticides are sprayed over us as well, over our vegetables and fruits and the ground those plants grow in. These chemicals go right into your cells and affect your body chemistry. They can make you sick. And they may kill you prematurely." Mia could see he was getting all worked up now. His eyes were bright and animated. "No one knows the effect at all," he continued. "Or how long the pesticides last once they've been released into the environment. The government approves them to protect crops and keep the farmers happy, but there could be consequences. We're collecting the proof that could save the planet."

Mia got what he was saying but wasn't sure how to respond. The lab guy looked embarrassed. "Sorry," he said. "I didn't mean to go off on you like that."

"It's okay. Actually . . . this is the longest conversation I've had with anyone for a week."

He laughed. "Me, too, I think. My friends are all sick of me talking about this stuff."

"It's good you have so much interest in science." She was thinking of Grandpa Andy now. "It makes some people feel alive."

"Yeah. That applies to me for sure. So what's your name?" he asked. She noticed for the first time how he stood up straight and tall in his white lab coat.

"I'm Mia."

He stuck out his hand. "Glad to meet you. I'm Graham Stoddard."

Realizing that she hadn't given him her full name, she added, "And my last name is Morrow." Then she shook his hand.

"Well, Mia, it's great to work alongside a girl for a change. Nice break from all the boring dudes in lab coats. You must be the only female assistant in the whole program. You're either incredibly brave or incredibly foolish."

"Probably both," she told him.

He laughed again. And then things got awkward between them. She didn't know how to end it, and neither did he. "I'll see you around, Mia," he said, taking a step backward like a polite intruder.

"I'll be here."

He gave her a little wave before he left the breeding room. People in this program sure could be weird, she thought. But Graham struck her as a kind of good-weird, if there were such a thing. She took the long way back to the lab, feeling grateful to him for helping her forget things, even if it was only for a little while.

Mia changed her clothes in the ladies' restroom of Sutton Hall after work. She was having dinner with Peter and had packed an outfit to wear—a floaty top with ruffles around the low neck, and a slim miniskirt. But checking herself out under the fluorescent lights in the dull lavatory mirror, she had to admit that she didn't look as good as she thought she would. Worry had made itself a mask on her face. Her brows seemed permanently knit; the corners of her mouth fell as soon as she stopped forcing herself to smile.

Once she arrived at White Hall, she wasn't sure where to go, but as it turned out, Peter's room was easy to find. He'd taped up a bunch of photographs of himself on the door. Lots of party shots. Him with a table full of people at a restaurant. Him and some guys with their arms around one another's shoulders, clutching plastic cups of beer. She almost changed her mind about knocking on the door but then decided she shouldn't judge him without getting to know more.

"It's open!" someone inside the room shouted. She couldn't be sure it was Peter.

She entered, walking into a scene not unlike the one she'd seen in the photos on the door. Guys were hanging about the room holding cans of beer in cozies just like the locals used all summer to keep their drinks cold. Two guys lay across the twin beds, and there was a guy sitting on top of Peter's desk. He let out a low wolfish whistle, and Mia tensed. It all reminded her a little too much of backstage at the Common Ground, but almost in the next second, Peter dragged himself out of a beanbag chair. "You made it," he said, draping his arm across her shoulder. "You remember Henry and Dan, right?" The guys from the reservoir. Mia made a mental note to remember their names this time. "Ignore Greg," Peter said about the guy on the desk, who was grinning as if baring his fangs and who looked strong enough to push apart the walls of the tiny room.

"You took off so fast on Sunday," said Peter, "and I wasn't sure we were still on for tonight, so the guys came over and I kind of invited them, too. You don't mind, do you? Just Henry and Dan. It'll be fun."

Since they were sitting right there, gauging her reaction, Mia lied. "Sounds great."

"Want a beer?" Peter offered, and Greg threw him a can from the minifridge.

"Oh, no, thanks," Mia said. She wasn't curious about alcohol anymore. Not after her night out. Or her mother's new consumption habits.

Peter looked surprised. He tossed the beer back. "Let's head out, then. Ready, guys?"

They left campus and walked down College Avenue, the main street leading away from the school. Mia was disappointed that Peter didn't stay by her side. Instead, it was like they were like a foursome, and she was just one of the boys. Except none of them asked her what she wanted to do. The boys decided to grab pizza and then attempt to pick up a couple of six-packs. None of them had fake ID, but the Quick Mart downtown didn't always check. They'd head for the park after that.


The grass was cold and so was the pizza by the time they got settled in Stuart Park. It was only a patch as big as a city block with a playground at one end, but the moon was out and they had it to themselves, and Mia felt better about things because Peter sat close to her. The guys talked about their architecture program and which teachers were the toughest and how much work they had to do that weekend. Mia listened and watched the stars overhead, trying to feel that she was a part of things. But it was a lot like hanging out with Michele and Gael.

After a while, Peter asked her, "So what year are you, Mia?"

"I'm a sophomore," she told him, dreading how much more lying she'd have to do that night.

"What's your major?" asked Dan.

She said the first thing to pop into her head. "Entomology."

"What?" Henry said.

"Are you kidding?" Dan said.

They were shocked and looking at her in a new way now, as if seeing her for the first time. Their reaction annoyed her. "Why so surprised?" she said.

"It's an unusual choice of major, that's all," said Peter.

"I guess. Mostly I work in the lab, doing the stuff the grad students and professors don't want to do. But I'm learning a lot."

"So you work with bugs?" said Henry. He seemed dazed by this information.

"Just flies," she told him, noticing a group of shaggy-looking guys had entered the park and went over to sit on the playground equipment. "Right now I'm studying the effects of a certain pesticide by monitoring how fast it kills off the common housefly. The whole point of the research is to prove that this stuff they spread on our food has real dangers to all life-forms on the planet." She was stealing lines from Graham Stoddard as best she could.

"She's a Fly Girl. That's F-L-Y," Dan said, pretending to rap.

She was ready to change the subject now, before she gave herself away. And almost in the same moment, she wanted to leave the park altogether, because those guys had gotten bored with the swings and were making their way over. Mia recognized them. They were part of the same pack that had harassed her on the Commons. Little James and his older brother, what's-his-name, plus a few other idiots.

"We should go," she said, but it was too late. The gang was circling now. Dirty and disheveled, they looked like they made the park home base every night. She felt a tightening in her stomach. She was scared of them, but worse than that, she didn't want to be outed as another local in front of her new friends. "Hey there!" one of them shouted out. "You guys got a cigarette we can bum?"

"Sorry, no," Peter called back.

"That's probably wise," said a greasy-haired guy in an army jacket. He led the gang closer. "When you've got your health, you've got everything. I'm sure your daddy told you that."

This was going to go badly. Mia knew it immediately. Henry seemed to get it, too. "Oh, great," he said.

"Very funny," Peter said to the guy who'd just insulted them. "But at least I know my father."

"He just ranked on you!" said one of the guys to the leader, adding a huge fake laugh. "Hardy, har, har!"

"Hey, that's Mia Morrow!" said the little twerp, James,

peering at her through the dark. "What are you doing with these assholes?" he said.

"I could ask you the same thing," she answered back.

Peter turned to look at her, confused. But he didn't say anything. He seemed to be waiting to find out whose ground he was standing on. His or theirs.

The guys fanned out now, surrounding them. "Mind if I have a beer?" asked the ugly one, and without waiting for an answer, he took what was left of their last six-pack. He kept one for himself, then threw the rest to the others. He gulped it down and let out an overly satisfied belch.

Peter got to his feet. Henry and Dan jumped up after him and Mia saw the looks on their faces. They were frightened as rabbits. She wished Peter was, too, because he seemed to have no idea that these guys weren't kidding around. The circle tightened around them.

"Let's *go*, guys," she said for the second time, but Peter didn't seem to be listening. The date and the evening and the hope for a happy future felt as if it was all evaporating like smoke in the air. Mia could tell from the determined look on Peter's face, and his hands that had already curled into fists, that he wasn't going to back down.

"I didn't hear a bell," said the ugly guy. "Can't be time for class."

"Listen, jerkoffs," Peter said, his voice going hard and cold. "You've got two choices. You can get out of my way or get ready to hurt. I'll start with you because you look especially stupid." He pointed to the one closest to him, James's older brother.

Mia could see what the real problem was, even in the

dark of the park. Peter was not about to back down to a bunch of guys he considered to be his inferiors. And the guys were really looking forward to beating on him for that alone.

The first punch came out of the black air and careened right into Peter's temple, knocking him sideways. But he stood back up fast.

There was no time to think. Mia lunged at little James. She took hold of him, yelling in his face. "Wait till I tell your mother about this, you moron!" Gripping the kid by the back of his shirt, she pulled him out of the park. He wasn't going easily, but since she was taller by almost a foot, he couldn't stop her, either. Without looking back, Mia knew all the guys were watching her drag the boy away. She could hear the townie guys laughing, their focus shifted. The joke was now on James. By the time she got to the edge of the park, the kid was nearly crying.

"C'mon, Mia. Don't! Please!"

Some of the guys taunted him now. "No! Oh! Please!"

Peter and Henry and Dan caught up. Mia took the kid as far as the first set of streetlights and then spun him around and shoved him hard. He fell down, and she yelled, "Run!" to Peter and his friends, and they did, even though no one bothered to follow them, as if the dark boundary of the park kept the gang in its grip. When they'd gotten as far as the Commons, they slowed down and caught their breath.

"How the hell do you know those guys?" Peter asked Mia, his anger just as alive as before. She looked at his flushed face, his swollen temple.

There was no way out of this, not that she could think of.

"I grew up here. Just like those assholes in the park that you didn't have the good sense to be afraid of."

"Yeah! What were you trying to do?" Henry said to him. "We could have wound up in the hospital."

"If it weren't for Mia, things could have gone much worse," said Dan.

"Right," Henry seconded. "That was quick thinking."

"I didn't think. I just did it. You know?" and as soon as she said it, she realized it was true. Not all her impulses were bad. Sometimes they made her do the right thing.

Peter sighed. "I hate this Podunk town," he said. "I can't wait to get out of here."

His friends agreed. Dan said, "I can't imagine what it would be like to have to grow up here."

Mia wanted to put the place down. She'd felt the same way for so long. It was too small, too old, too boring. But now, hearing it coming from them, she found that she couldn't.

It was all over after that. Peter and his friends wanted to go back up the hill even though it was only nine o'clock, and Mia made an excuse for why she wasn't going back with them. "I'm going to stop in and see someone before I go back to campus."

Peter said, "Another friendly local?" and then didn't wait to hear her answer, which meant he didn't care whom she was going to see, or assumed it wasn't somebody worth talking about. They made no plans for another date, if that's what this had been. There was no kiss good night.

Once she turned the corner and the light from the streetlamps on the Commons starting fading away, she started to pick up her pace, turning around several times to make sure no one followed her down the street. But she was alone with the rows of parked cars and sheltering trees thick with leaves.

She walked past the guitar shop. It wasn't open. The neon sign hanging over the door was dark, but she stopped to peer in the window anyway. Looking at the row of brand-new, shiny guitars hanging on the wall behind the cash register, illuminated in the glow of some security lights, Mia thought of Clancy and how he'd protected her from Roddy. Even though he wouldn't admit it. She wished the owner of the Common Ground were right there beside her. Then, she thought, she'd feel really safe.

At the bridge that crossed the gorge near her house, Mia slowed down. She heard a car coming, and when it got close to her, the driver flashed his brights. It troubled her, but only for a moment. She watched as it passed her by like a boat on a slow current. When it was gone, it felt darker than before. She paused to listen to the water work its way down the rocky pass and flow under the stone bridge.

She knew that all her hopes for some kind of a relationship with Peter had been a big fantasy and nothing more. It seemed so painfully foolish now, all the things she'd wished for . . . a fancy restaurant with white tablecloths, his warm and affectionate glance, the candlelight. Boy, she sure had been in dreamland about him!

Mia was also sorry about all the lies she'd told. But it didn't seem to matter, because he didn't like the parts of her he'd seen. That she could high-dive better than him, that she could take care of herself. He had no respect for who she really was, or he wouldn't have been so quick to dismiss her.

And despite how that stung, it was nothing in comparison to what Michele and Gael had done, or to any of the other real troubles in her life. She could get over one bad date.

Mia continued on toward her house. It was dark, top to bottom. George was out, her mother was out, and her Grandfather—gone. The big, dark, looming Victorian was hers alone.

The pure and simple truth
is rarely pure and never simple.

—OSCAR WILDE

*Monday marked the* end of the second week since Mia started to work at the fly lab. It was the only thing she'd ever done for two weeks straight, other than go to school. It also marked the day that she was to begin checking for the hatchlings. The spawn. The offspring. Those she did not wish to name. Or even see. *Maggots.*

She arrived at the lab sporting a baggy old sweater and a pair of carpenter jeans, because today of all days she didn't want to worry about spilling food or dropping bugs. Not to mention gagging or barfing, which she feared were distinct possibilities.

When she got to the lab she found a white envelope placed on her desk. It looked like some sort of official notice, with her name showing through a small sheet of plastic on the front. She was confused, temporarily, until she realized it was payday. Her first ever in her life. She tore the envelope open. And gasped.

Finkelstein looked up from his computer screen. "I know. The taxes are so high, aren't they?" he said. "You'll probably get some of that back at the end of the year."

"But this is more than my grandfather gave me for my fifteenth birthday."

It was a good chunk of what she owed the department store. And she'd only been working two hours a day for two weeks. In another month or so, she'd be out of debt and everything else she earned would go straight into her pocket.

"Glad you're pleased," Finkelstein said.

"I'm so happy I could scream!"

Finkelstein looked alarmed. "Don't. I'm sure to hear about it from others on this floor if you do."

"Don't worry, I'm just saying it's great!" Mia got ready to go to work, putting away her things, pulling out the data notebooks. "So . . ." she said, turning to Finkelstein with a ghoulish grin. "Have you seen them?"

He nodded gravely. "Want to hear a bug joke before you have to get started with all that?"

"When have I ever not wanted to hear one of your jokes?"

"When you started working here."

"That was then."

"Okay, what do you call a nervous insect?" Finkelstein looked ready to burst at the seams to tell her the answer.

"Hmm . . . I don't know," she said.

"Mia, you didn't even think about it. Try to guess."

"A nervous insect . . . nervous. Edgy . . . jumpy . . . jittery. Wait a second. I think I got it. A jitterbug?"

"That's it!"

"Finally! I never thought I'd get one."

"That's because you never tried."

"I always knew you'd tell me the answer."

They were silent for a moment. Mia didn't move. Finkelstein said, "Why don't you start with the count instead?"

"No. I want to get this gross business over with."

She led the way to the breeding room and then walked down the aisle until she was standing with nearly a hundred of her boss's boxes towering over her head like wobbly gray skyscrapers.

Mia sighed. She had to start lifting lids.

"I can open the first one if you're scared," he told her.

"I'll have to do it myself eventually, right?" Steeling herself, Mia pulled down a box dated April 16, her first day of work, and placed it on the counter. "Here goes," she said, and lifted the lid with the very edges of her fingertips.

And then she froze.

Because what she saw surprised her in a way she never would have expected. Peering into the box, she saw fleshy white worm forms barely bigger than a grain of rice, glistening against the tawny brown of the damp sawdust. They lay curled around one another like sweet little noodles, having burrowed a bowl-shaped nest for themselves.

"Are you okay, Mia?" Finkelstein asked.

Mia stood staring into the box. She watched the maggots feel their way around, their clean whiteness intensified in the harsh overhead light of the breeding room. And she saw that the ugliest thing in the world was surprisingly beautiful. It was as if the whole world had been turned upside down.

"Do you want me to take them?"

Mia looked at Finkelstein and could tell he didn't know how she was feeling at all. She imagined she'd be having a whole different reaction right then, too. "No, they're really *cool*," she emphasized, looking into the box again.

Finkelstein beamed. "I think so. Why don't you check on the others?"

Mia gently closed the box and placed it back on the shelf. She opened up all the boxes with the same date. Each one had its own pile of tiny maggots writhing around in reaction to the blast of light. She flipped through boxes dated after the sixteenth. They showed no signs of life.

"Every box bred," Finkelstein said. "You had an unusually high success rate."

"Really? It's good?"

He put his hand on her shoulder to make sure she heard the compliment. "It's very good," he said.

A hundred questions filled her mind. "How does a maggot turn into a fly?"

"Well, in the next cycle of life it'll form a cocoon."

"What's the cocoon made of?"

"It uses its own saliva. Very strong stuff, strong as silk." Finkelstein peered at her nervously. "Are you sure you're not getting grossed out?"

"Go on. I'm listening," she said.

"At this point, most of the larva's tissues disintegrate all at once, into a kind of cellular soup. New adult tissue forms out of the soup, while a few body structures such as the breathing apparatus and circulatory system remain unchanged. After about a week of this activity, the transformation is complete. The maggot metamorphoses into the tiny fly."

"Wow. It's so fast. Only a week to become an adult? And it forms a new creature out of its own cells . . . is that what you said?"

"It's not so unusual. Humans change form as well by discarding cells as fast as they grow new ones. Just not as quickly or dramatically."

Mia thought about that. "Change can happen really fast for people, too."

"I suppose that's true, in certain cases," Finkelstein said, and paused. "I can't believe how interested you are in all this. It's really wonderful."

For the first time ever, Mia felt like she understood why Grandpa Andy was so in love with science. It did more than illuminate the mysteries of life. It was the window itself. She felt a little more alive just by looking through.

"What happens next?" she said to Finkelstein, about the flies.

"The wings of an immature fly aren't sufficient for flight. So we simply transfer it to the clear plastic boxes." He pointed to a few empties stacked away on a nearby shelf. "And it begins its cycle of eating and laying eggs."

Graham Stoddard was walking down the aisle toward them, probably to check on Professor Deacon's other brood. She smiled at him, but as Graham got closer, he started to do a pretty good Finkelstein imitation, which involved wearing a kind of google-eyed look and sweeping his hands back and forth, as though conducting an orchestra.

Finkelstein quickly realized they were no longer alone. "Oh, it's Graham," Finkelstein said, sounding dour at being interrupted.

"Not trying to eavesdrop on us, are you?" Mia said, with a quick wink to her boss.

Graham was flustered for a second. "No. Of course not. I came to check on—"

"A likely story," Mia interrupted him, enjoying herself. That ought to teach Graham not to make fun of her helpless boss.

Finkelstein cleared his throat as if changing the subject. "Mia's first batch of larvae hatched."

"You must be so proud," Graham said to Mia.

"Indeed," Finkelstein replied.

"Can I see?"

Mia pulled one of the April 16 boxes to show him, and they huddled together over it. Mia could smell the soap Graham had used to wash his shirt, a fresh scent like the outdoors. As Graham reached out to stick his finger into the box, Finkelstein restrained him. "Don't do that. You could hurt them!"

"Nonsense," Graham said. He gave the worms a stir and they swam around. "They're all doing well," he said to Finkelstein. "That's a little trick Deacon taught me. You can see if there are weak ones from the start."

"Huh. Well, we've got to get back to the office," Finkelstein said. "Come along, Mia."

"I'll be right there," she told him. "Five minutes."

Finkelstein looked confused, and then realized she meant for him to go on his own. He strode quickly up the aisle then, as if late for an appointment, though Mia knew there was no one there waiting for him.

"I didn't mean to embarrass him," Graham said. "We all learn from each other around here. He's a bit unwilling when it comes to sharing our findings."

"He's odd, I know. The other day he gave me some books on flies that were so simplistic. The type was large and so were the pictures. They were books for someone in sixth grade. They made bugs boring."

"But they're not!"

"I know that. At first I thought it was because he didn't think I was smart enough, and then I realized, it's more a reflection of how he thinks. But I like him."

"Sorry. I didn't realize. I wouldn't have imitated him like that."

"It's okay. Now you know."

"Hey, you just gave me an idea. I have some bug books I think you'd find interesting. Want to have a look?" He sounded nervous. Or excited. Mia couldn't tell which. A jitterbug. "They're back in my office."

As they left the breeding room together, she spotted Finkelstein at the vending machine down the hall. He'd obviously been standing there waiting for her to come out.

Mia turned to Graham. "You know what . . . I'll stop by your office tomorrow, if that's okay."

He looked disappointed but said, "That would be great. Room 1141. It's around the corner."

They parted, and as she walked up to the soda machine, Finkelstein put some coins in and bought a Coke. Together they went back toward the lab. She knew that he was unaware that he was muttering to himself. When finally he spoke to her, he said, "Listen, Mia. I need to tell you something . . . about working in this department. You know we're all very competitive with one another, and though I don't want to squelch your enthusiasm for being here, the thing is . . . if you become friends with Graham, or something more than that, then . . ."

"So you're upset I didn't come back with you?"

"Don't misunderstand me. I simply need you to be careful of what you say. Because whoever turns their research in before the others will receive some very definite benefits."

"We don't talk about your work."

"Good."

"And he hasn't asked me out."

"Would you go if he did?"

"Finkelstein! What's with all the interest in my dating life?"

"Nothing . . . nothing at all. Honestly, Graham is one of the best students in the program. Industrious. And well liked. All I ask is for you to be careful what you say around him, all right? He works for Deacon just like we do."

"I know that. But you know you can trust me, right? I'd like to think I've earned that."

Finkelstein seemed to relax. "Yes, of course. I do. I couldn't be more pleased with our partnership. And I'm not one bit surprised, either, I'll have you know."

Mia seemed to relax then, too.


After the fly lab, Mia walked home from campus. She didn't want to go home. With Grandpa Andy still in the hospital and her mother out all night and every night, it wasn't a good place to be. Mia's mood usually hit bottom as soon as she got anywhere near the old house.

When she got to the bottom of the hill, she went into the bodega on the corner of Fifth and Carmine. Checks were cashed at a window in the back. They took a percentage, Mia found out, and so she decided she'd open a bank account with her next paycheck.

When she was done with that, she walked to the Commons and stopped to peer in the window at Jewel Moon. Something there caught her eye: a grouping of objects she'd never seen before. They were boxes of different sizes and shapes, and just like her goddess on the wall at home, they were covered with images from magazines. Nothing she found interesting, just pictures of things like flowers and little children. But Mia had never thought of wrapping her work around something that had a shape of its own. Something that didn't have to be on the wall. She wanted to see these boxes up close.

Janet didn't seem to be around again, and Margo was working behind the cash register. She was examining a book that looked a lot like the notebooks Finkelstein kept. Columns of numbers covered the page, and Margo peered intently through glasses perched on the end of her nose as she read through the rows, keeping place with a finger.

"Hiya, Margo!"

The shopkeeper looked up. "Oh, hi, Mia." She put the notebook down and rubbed her eyes.

"Looks like you're working hard."

"We're having trouble keeping on top of inventory changes. I guess when we set this business up, we weren't really thinking about what we'd need for the long run. So our bookkeeping isn't matching our new computer tracking system."

Mia peered down at the open book on the counter. "My boss up at the lab uses the same color pen for all his data entries. Now I know why. That page is hard to read."

"Yeah, that's why we decided to switch over and put everything on an inventory program. Wish it were easier to figure out than it is, though."

"Wish I could help."

"Oh, that's sweet. Thanks. I'll get it figured out. I hope.

So how are you? Haven't seen you here in a while. More than a week, I think."

Mia laughed. "I guess I'm in here a lot, aren't I?"

"Fine with me. Hey . . . guess what? Remember the fly locket you liked so much . . . Janet Yee did a less pricey version for us. Want to see?"

"You bet."

Margo went into the back office and came out with several necklaces in plastic ziplock bags. She pulled them out on the counter. "I have to clean up the inventory before I start adding more to it. That's why I haven't put these out yet."

Mia picked up one of the lockets and flipped it open. This one had a picture of a beetle inside. It seemed to be encased in a clear, amber coating. "It looks like a bug caught in tree sap," Mia said.

Margo nodded. "I think so, too. Did you notice that Janet Yee decided not to enamel the outside of the locket? She constructed it out of silver clay and then had it kiln-fired. Has a very handmade look now. The price point is excellent."

"How much?" Mia asked, certain it wouldn't matter, because it was sure to be out of her reach.

"The small bugs go for fifty-five dollars," Margo said as she pointed to the one in Mia's hand. "And the larger version is eighty."

Mia felt herself flush all of a sudden. She had cashed her check and was carrying one hundred and twenty dollars. The money practically pulsed; it was hot in her pocket. She could afford the smaller locket and still have a decent

173

amount left over to start paying back the department store. That buzzing *zap* came back, and suddenly Mia understood. It wasn't stealing that gave her a charge, made her do crazy things. It was wanting. Feeling the thing had to be hers. The necklace was so beautiful. She pictured which shirt she'd wear to show it off. How it would sparkle at her throat. How it might make Michele and Gael see she was someone special.

So that was the heart of it. Wanting things went much deeper than the object itself. And now she could buy the necklace. She had the money.

"Want to try it on?" Margo offered.

Mia took a final look. As much as she wanted it, she knew it wouldn't bring her friends back. And she wanted to get out of trouble even more. The sooner she was done with the department store, the better she'd feel. She put the piece down. "Not today. Maybe once I've earned a bit more at work I can think about it. It's very cool."

"Well, we have you to thank for it. Your idea after all. And Janet Yee did a great job."

"Definitely." It was a great relief for Mia. All that temptation was hard to handle. But she'd done it. It was a first. "Hey, Margo, I actually came in to look at those boxes you have in the window." Mia quickly moved away from the jewelry cases.

"You mean the decoupage?"

"I'm talking about the ones with all the pictures pasted on."

"Right. It's a classic technique. . . ." She reached to pull one out of the window. "The artist layers on multiple images and then seals the pieces with a clear coat. See how it shines?"

Mia held one in her hands. There was something intriguing about it, the way it made you want to look at all the pictures pasted there. Mia handed it back. "It's interesting. I like to make things that are kind of like it."

"You do? You never told me that."

"I take magazine images, cut them, and repaste them together. It's very simple, really. But I make new images out of them."

"Very cool. You'll have to show me sometime."

"I guess I could do that." If she could find some way to get the goddess off the wall. Or maybe she'd make something new. It would have to be something really special. Something no one would have thought of before. Something she'd never thought of before. She wanted to run home, just to try to figure it out.

Mia said good-bye then and headed for the door.

"Come back soon," Margo said.

"Soon as I can," Mia told her.

*It was nearly* six o'clock that night when Mia got home. She was surprised to find Constance there, and she looked terrible, still in her old bathrobe with dirty hair. The apartment looked a wreck, too, with used glasses everywhere, clothing strewn about, and big old dust balls in the corners.

Just as she expected, all those feelings Mia had earlier in the day, feelings of being on top of things, began to slip away, and she became her old self again. All snappish, she said to her mother, "Nice of you to stay home for a change."

"I won't be around long," Constance answered in turn.

"Where you going this time?"

"Nowhere special. Just out."

"Yeah, right," Mia said flatly, then turned and headed for the kitchen/dining room, where she threw her book bag on the counter and sat down at the table. Her mother came in a few moments later.

Constance sat down and lit a Marlboro, her hand shaking a bit. They both noticed at the same time. Her mother took a deep drag on the cigarette, and blew the smoke out with an even deeper sigh.

"What's the matter, Mom?"

Constance waved her hand as if she were brushing the question away. "There's nothing . . . I'm just having a hard time."

Mia took a deep breath and tried to get un-mad. "Maybe this will cheer you up. Look what I've got." Mia pulled out her wallet and showed Constance the wad of cash she was carrying. "Today was payday. Now I finally understand why you like work so much."

Constance took a look at the money in her hand. "How much?"

"Enough to start paying back Roger Brady at the department store. It's not going to take me very long at all."

"Oh, that's good."

Mia thought her mother sounded like she didn't really care one way or the other whether Mia got out of debt. And from the way Constance's eyes were swimming and unfocused, she also realized that her mother was drunk. But this wasn't a fun buzz like the night she'd lost her keys.

They were silent for several seconds, during which Mia looked closely at Constance, and what she saw was something like a pollution covering her mother. But it wasn't just surrounding her, it was as if she were possessed by it.

Then Mia said, "You still mad at the people at Butler?"

"Yeah, that's part of it, of course."

"I know you liked it there, up till now, anyway. But if they're not treating you well, you could look for another job."

"It's going to be hard to find something that pays as well as the school."

Mia thought about it for a moment, about what her mother should do. "Well . . . if it's better for you to be at the school, why don't you try a different dining hall, where they might appreciate you more?"

Constance looked up then. "This is a change, you telling me to find a job."

Mia heaved a sigh at her mother.

"It's not easy. That's all I'm saying," Constance told her. "I don't think you understand that."

"Jeez, Mom! I understand you need to find a solution. That's all you have to do . . . instead of getting all depressed and then going out and getting drunk." Mia could have censored that comment—she almost did—but then decided it should be said. Constance just sat there with her mouth hanging open. "I'm sorry, but it's the truth, isn't it?"

Constance stood up, wobbling a bit. "Since we're being all truthful with each other, there's something I want to tell you. You are just like your grandfather. No goddamned heart. You think I liked it there? That stupid cafeteria. I only worked at that place to take care of you!" A little bit of spittle escaped Constance's mouth. "That ever occur to you . . . either of you?"

Constance pushed back from the table. "And what did I get for it?" As if she knew she was being too ugly, not even wanting to hear herself, Constance fled down the hall. Mia heard the bedroom door slam shut. It banged so hard it actually stopped Mia's heart for a beat.

Her mind was racing with fear and anger. *She did it for me?* Mia thought bitterly as she sat there. *Did I ever ask her to? I never asked her to do that lousy job. Just the opposite! I told her I thought she shouldn't work at such a crappy place. . . .*

And that's when Mia understood. For the first time. No wonder it made Constance so mad whenever Mia put the Butler job down, because the person for whom her mother had made such a sacrifice didn't respect it.

And neither did Grandpa Andy.

It really wasn't so complicated. And it wasn't so bad hearing the truth, either. Mia thought about whether she should go into her mother's room. Could she fix things? Since they couldn't talk to each other before all this stuff started happening, it wasn't a surprise that they couldn't talk to each other now that her mother was such a mess. But everything was turned upside down. Her mother was angry and acting out, and Mia was the one trying to reason with her.

She wished she knew how.


About an hour later, the hospital called. Constance knocked on her door and told Mia her grandfather was awake and they could go see him.

They didn't say a word to each other on the cab ride over. Mia's stomach was doing flip-flops as she sat there beside her mother. When she'd asked about G.A.'s condition, all her mother would say was he was having a momentary reprieve and the doctors didn't know how long it would last.

At the hospital Mia found herself glancing down corridors, hopeful that she might see Clancy there. But he was sure to be working at the bar this late.

Her grandfather was on the fourth floor. Riding up in the elevator, Constance said, "I have to look over some paperwork with the doctor, so you can go in to see him without me." Mia left her mother at the nurses' station and followed their directions down the hall toward his room. G.A. seemed to be sleeping as she entered, but as the door clicked shut behind her, he woke. Seeing her, he smiled in that way that always made her glad, but now with only the right half of his face. The other side sagged, unresponsive.

"How are you feeling, Grandpa?" she asked as she came up to his bedside.

"Hmm. Yesterday was bad." He talked out of the good side of his mouth, like some kind of sleepy gangster. But she supposed it was a miracle he could talk at all. "Today better." He lifted his good arm to show off his IV taped there. "Nice cocktail they gave me."

Mia had to laugh. "Glad it's helping."

"No pain."

Mia nodded. No pain. She hoped that was true. "Mom is here, too. She'll be in, in a minute."

With that, Grandpa Andy turned his face to the wall.

"I want you to be nice to her, Grandpa." Mia's voice trembled.

"What's the matter?"

"She's been away from home a lot."

"Drinking?"

"How'd you know?"

"She's no good," he said again, slurring his words like he was drunk, too. Mia didn't know what to say or how to defend her mother, especially given how Constance was acting. And G.A. was in no condition to hear it, either. "Don't talk 'bout her now," he said, coughing. "I love you. You've been"—more coughing—"everything to me. Your mother never . . ." He couldn't finish.

Mia felt the time had come to tell him the truth and set him straight. "Grandpa, I'm not the good little girl you think I am."

"Of course not," he barked. "You're not perfect." He coughed some more; it took him a minute to get it under control. "But you make choices. You can do good. Or bad."

Mia thought about it. "Except sometimes you don't know what the right choice is until you've already made the mistake."

Grandpa Andy reached out with some difficulty to take her hand. "Yes! You can see that. She can't. She can't stop herself . . . the drinking . . . will get worse."

Mia realized that might be very true. She didn't see an end to it, either. There was so much she wanted to ask her grandfather. About the past and why he thought her mother was drinking so much now, and how come no one told her this had happened sometime before. But there was one question that she wanted to ask most of all.

"G.A., do you love Mom?"

He didn't get the chance to answer. As if on cue, Constance opened the door. Mia and Grandpa Andy looked up guiltily, their conversation coming to an abrupt halt, while Constance stood in the doorway, unwilling to enter their shared space. And then she switched over, strode into the room all brisk and confident. Mia observed this shift her mother made—a transformation into that other person she used to be, the tough one. The get-it-done one. Was it always an act? Did her mother only pretend to be strong, as she was now also pretending not to be drunk, though Mia could smell her breath across her grandfather's bed.

Constance spoke to Grandpa Andy. "The hospital needs you to sign these papers." She handed him a pen. "Can you sit up? Help him, Mia."

"What are they?" Grandpa Andy asked, while Mia propped up some pillows behind his back.

"They pertain to your medical care," she said. "About what you're willing to endure. At the end."

Grandpa Andy looked through the documents. Then he took the pen from Constance. "You want me to sign?"

"I think it's best."

"What do they say, Grandpa?" Mia asked.

"You tell her," he said to Constance.

"It's called a DNR, which stands for Do Not Resuscitate."

Mia didn't like the sound of that. "What does it mean?"

"It means if he can't function on his own, can't breathe, can't swallow, or his heart stops beating . . ." Constance looked hard at her father. "The hospital will not take any action to bring him back."

"So he'll die?" Mia took hold of his good hand, the one ready to sign his life away. "How can you give up like this, Grandpa? It goes against everything you believe in. What about science? What if the doctors can find a way to make you better? What if they can heal you?"

"Shh . . . shh . . . I'm dying anyway, little darling." G.A. squeezed her hand, and then he signed the papers.

"Have you given thought to your will?" Constance asked. Her whole face seemed to quiver with the question.

He leveled a harsh glance at Constance. "I hear you've been up to no good. Staying out all the time. I remember when—"

Constance interrupted him. "Mia must have filled you in. Thanks for that, Mia."

Mia hung her head. She had tattled. She wasn't proud of

it. She only wanted G.A. to fix things with her mother. Make her stop what she was doing. But Mia saw how it only revved her mother up. Constance paced the room, like an animal desperate to escape. "Terrific. Now you two have something else you can agree on about me." She looked ready to spit. "You're so cozy together . . . aren't you? I should have taken off long ago."

"Stop talking nonsense," Grandpa Andy said weakly. "I don't want to hear." He coughed again. "You asked about my will. I'll tell you . . . I have a lawyer handling things," he told Constance. "You'll get what's best for you. Nothing you can do about it. Not now."

Mia saw the tears start to well up in her mother's eyes, and she saw how angry it made her mother that G.A. didn't care. "No reason for me to stick around then, I guess . . ." Constance trailed off.

"Mom! Don't . . ."

"Let her go," Grandpa Andy said.

But Constance had turned away. "You can carry on with your conversation. I'll only be in the way." The door shut behind her, making a whooshing noise that sounded exactly like the end of things.

Mia sat there quietly with her grandfather because she wasn't sure what to say. The fight seemed to have taken everything out of him, and in a short while he was sleeping, his breathing uneven but deep. She took him in, trying to memorize his face. She thought he didn't look sick, just tired. Like he couldn't give anyone a bit of trouble. But he had. And he still did.

A nurse came breezing in without a knock to check the

flow on the clear plastic bag hanging from a pole by the bed. She tapped it with her finger, opened a drawer with no attempt to muffle the noise for his sake, unwrapped a plastic nozzle of some sort. She replaced it on the bag and tossed the old one into a nearby metal can. It hit the bottom with a clunk. Grandpa Andy didn't stir.

"Want me to close the door?" the nurse said on her way out.

Mia nodded.

As soon as it clicked shut, Grandpa Andy slowly opened one eye. His voice sounded weak and dry. "I get no peace in this life."

Mia stood and poured some water into a plastic cup for him. He could barely lean forward off the pillow to take a sip. Lying back, he said, "I was dreaming. You were there."

"What were we doing in the dream?"

"We were at the lake." His voice was only a rasp. "There was a playground, and you were swinging, going higher and higher. Laughing." His eyes were closed and he was half-smiling.

"That happened. I remember it. We had a picnic. You, me, and Mom. I was probably six or seven. We didn't do stuff like that often."

Grandpa Andy shook his head now.

"G.A.?"

"Yes, my dear."

"Why did she say she should have taken off? Was it when I was born? Was it because she didn't want me?"

"No. Not at all."

"So what then? What was she talking about?"

"She wanted to go away . . . with you . . . but she didn't know what was best." He was coughing again. "She couldn't raise you without my help. And I couldn't let you turn out like her."

"But Mom has only ever tried to do the right thing. It may not have been what you wanted for her—"

"SHE'S A DRUNK!" her grandfather bellowed. "A sot. An inebriate. My daughter . . . my beautiful daughter. Ack, pathetic! I don't want—" he pounded his weak fist on the bed. "I won't think about the past. Not now." He reached for her hand absently, like he was trying to get hold of air. "I have such high hopes for you. Tell me about you. Anything."

"All right, Grandpa. I can do that," Mia said, pressing his hand down to rest on the blanket, trying to think of something good that she could say to calm him. And then it came to her. "Do you remember when I called the entomology department from your apartment?"

"Yes! Much better." Grandpa Andy closed his eyes again.

"Well, I hated the job at first. I had to work with flies, changing their food and harvesting their eggs. It was messy and I couldn't remember how to do everything I was supposed to do—"

His right eye opened wide. "But you picked it up. Right? Just like the birds!"

"Yes, very much like the birds. I did learn how to do it. And I've learned so much. I've seen things that should be ugly and it turned out they weren't. In fact, it was just the opposite. And it all seemed natural. Just a side of life I hadn't seen before."

"So you had a real eye-opener then?"

"Exactly."

"Smart girl."

For the first time since he fell sick and went into the hospital, Mia felt like they got their old relationship back. Her cheerleader, her number one supporter, her Grandpa Andy. She had a part of him her mother never got. "I love you, Grandpa, you know that, right?" she said, and broke down crying, the tears pouring out of her.

After a minute or two, he lifted her chin and quieted her with his steely gaze. "Death's a fact of life. No point in crying about it."

Mia sniffed. It made sense. In G.A.'s tough-love kind of way, he was taking care of her. Another thing her mother never seemed to understand about him. "I'll try."

"Tell me more about work, won't you?"

Mia wiped her face dry, then spent the next hour dredging up every detail about the lab, wanting to create as full a picture for him as she possibly could. She talked about how the bugs were so strange and interesting. She talked about Finkelstein and about Graham and how much she liked them. And she kept on talking, even when she knew Grandpa Andy had slipped away from her, smiling his way into sleep, or somewhere else.

## 18

*The next morning* came too quickly. Mia woke on the living room couch feeling wiped out. She'd stayed at the hospital a long time. Then spent the rest of the night fitfully waiting for Constance to walk through the front door. Which didn't happen. And hadn't happened by the time she left for school that morning.

Mia could barely keep her eyes open through her morning classes. A nap at lunchtime helped, but it made her late to chemistry class. Slipping into the room just as the final bell quit ringing, Mia took the first available seat she found, then looked up and realized she was sitting next to her ex-friend Gael. They hadn't spoken since that day at the reservoir.

Gael looked at her once, then returned her attention to the front of the room. That was it. Gael wasn't friendly, but she didn't seem mad, either. Mia was relieved. The lecture began.

The teacher, Ms. Barton, wrote a long chemical equation across the blackboard, which Mia copied down in her notebook, taking care to get the complicated formula right.

$$6CO_2 + 12H_2O \longrightarrow C_6H_{12}O_6 + 6H_2O + 6O_2$$

Mia knew a question was coming from the way her teacher was staring down the class now. "Who can tell me what chemical reaction is indicated by the equation on the board?"

No one raised a hand.

"Let's take a closer look at it, break it down." Pointing to the left side of the equation, Ms. Barton said, "The compound element $H_2O$ is . . . ?"

Several students in the room answered together, "Water."

"And this is . . . ?" She was pointing to the $CO_2$ part of the equation.

"Carbon dioxide," the class listlessly parroted back, Gael included.

Mia felt on familiar ground all of a sudden. Carbon dioxide. Letter *C*, letter *O*, number *2*. It was what they used to gas the flies. She sat up in her chair.

"And what is this third element on the right-hand side of the equation?" Ms. Barton was pointing again. "Anyone? We need to move on, so I'll tell you it's sugar. Does anyone know what the name for this process might be?" She waited again. "No one? It's photosynthesis."

A couple of students groaned, as if they should have known the answer.

"And who can tell me what the catalysts are for photosynthesis?"

Several hands shot up in the air, including Gael's. The teacher picked her.

"The catalysts are light and chlorophyll," she answered smartly. Mia knew it, too; they'd learned that in biology last year.

Ms. Barton went back to the board. "Excellent. Chlorophyll and light will be our catalysts. So . . . photosynthesis is the production of sugar, oxygen, and water," she said, writing out the names of the compounds, first on the right-hand side of the equation and then on the left, "from the catalysts called carbon dioxide and water." Mia wrote this down, too, though it wasn't making much sense. "Today we are going to conduct experiments that illustrate the photosynthetic process . . . the process whereby green plants manufacture food and store radiant energy from the sun. Does anybody have any questions before we start?"

Mia thought of one and raised her hand.

"Miss Morrow?"

"Can carbon dioxide be a dangerous element?"

The two students at the desk in front of her, Brad and Parke, turned around and gave Mia a look like she was some kind of idiot. "Why would they give out a lab experiment that wasn't safe?" Parke said.

"Actually, Mr. Parke, carbon dioxide can be a safety hazard," Ms. Barton informed him. "When concentrations rise, it can make people start to feel dizzy or very tired, and very high concentrations can lead to unconsciousness or even death."

This was something Mia hadn't known, until now. Funny, she hadn't even thought to ask why the flies lost consciousness but not the person administering the gas. She guessed it took less to knock out bugs. She'd have to ask Finkelstein about it. Mia was enjoying this now. They were learning something to do with the real world, finally.

Ms. Barton said, "I've set up a supply station where you can pick up the things you'll need to conduct the experiment. Form teams of two with the person sitting next to you. One of you can collect these items for your team."

"I'll go," Gael said, and was out of her seat before Mia could agree.

Mia sat there waiting, nervously. This class experiment was

going to be a lesson in slow torture unless she could think of something to break the tension between her and Gael. It had to be something light, no big deal, maybe funny. A joke.

Gael returned with the supplies and took her seat, and Mia turned to her. "So, Gael, do you know why bees hum?"

"What?"

"I said, do you know why bees hum?"

Gael shrugged her shoulders but wouldn't look at her. "No, I don't. Why do bees hum?"

"Because they forgot the words," she told her.

"Very funny," Gael said, deadpan. But Mia could tell from the way her eyebrows raised that she couldn't help being amused, despite herself. Just as Mia had been when Finkelstein told it to her.

"Want to hear another?"

"Sure." Slightly more enthusiastic this time.

"What did one firefly say to the other?"

Gael met Mia's eyes as she thought about this one. "Hmm, light my fire?"

"Got to glow now."

"God! That's so awful."

"I know. That's why it's funny." Mia pointed to the supplies Gael had neatly arranged on the table. "So what have you got there?"

"Not sure."

Mia recognized some of the items from work. "Here's two petri dishes, two vials, a pipette, and a Magic Marker. And what are these?" She picked up two leaves, each wrapped with a thin strip of colored paper. One in green, the other blue. "Aren't these curious?"

"Indeed." Mia caught the look with which Gael now regarded her. It was one of clear surprise.

Most of the class had taken their seats now, and Ms. Barton said, "Okay, students. As you can see, you have two leaves to work with. The leaf wrapped in green was grown in light, and the leaf in blue was grown in darkness."

"Simple enough," Mia said, and Gael nodded in agreement.

"Mark one petri dish with an *L* for light, and mark the other with a *D* for dark. Then unwrap the leaves and put them in their corresponding dishes."

Mia picked the green leaf, the light one. She had hers in the dish when she heard Gael curse under her breath. "What's wrong?" Mia asked her.

"I tore the paper in half."

"It doesn't matter. We're conducting the experiment on the leaf, not the paper."

"Are you sure?" Gael asked. "I thought the paper had the chemicals on it."

"I don't think so."

Ms. Barton overheard. "You can toss out the paper once you've unwrapped the leaf, people."

"See?" Mia said.

Gael nodded and quickly plopped her leaf into place.

"Now pour a thin layer of water in the petri dish," Ms. Barton continued, "and carefully unfold the leaf so it lies flat in the water."

Gael watched Mia do hers first. She poured the water from the glass slowly and then used the tip of her finger to gently press the edges of the leaf into the water, which seemed to relax and grow as it absorbed water into its cells. "It looks like it's expanding," Mia said.

"Or spreading its wings," Gael said, and then she did her own.

"Now pour the water out," the teacher said. "Carefully, everyone. Don't lose the leaf as you do this."

Mia held the leaf in place with two fingers as she slightly tilted the petri dish and let the water drip back into the glass.

"You're good at this," Gael said, draining her petri dish just as Mia had done.

"Yeah, well, because of the flies, I guess."

Gael looked confused again.

"I've gotten used to working in a lab," Mia explained.

"Oh, right. You're still doing that job? That's great."

"Now observe the distribution of green and yellow-white areas in the leaves," said their teacher. "Make a rough sketch in your student guides of these different areas. Don't try to make it perfect. I'll give you a minute or two for this."

Mia looked at the leaf and put the tip of her pencil on the blank page. Her hand just drew what she saw, all the sharp edges of the jagged-edged leaf. She liked how it turned out. Gael was still working hard at her drawing and using the eraser quite a bit. She used her arm to hide it from Mia.

"Everyone should be finishing up now," the teacher announced. "So put the pencils down."

Gael threw her pencil onto the desk. Mia peeked at her drawing, which looked more like a pockmarked hand than a leaf. "It's not so bad," Mia said. "You can see the spots really clearly."

"Thanks," Gael said. "But it sucks."

"She said just do a rough sketch. It's fine."

"I guess so."

"Here's the tricky part," Ms. Barton continued. "I want you to expose one half of the leaf to the iodine solution. So fill up the pipette and use it as a dropper to stain half the leaf."

Gael let Mia do it and watched as she carefully released the iodine onto her leaf like she was feeding a delicate creature. Then her leaf started turning black on one side. "That's cool," Mia said.

"Yeah. I better do mine now," Gael said. Mia handed her the pipette.

Ms. Barton spoke again. "So, class, I'd like you to note this difference on the sketch you just made," the teacher said. "Mark the dark sections with diagonal lines, like so." She demonstrated on the board.

Mia got busy marking her sketch as the teacher had directed. She heard Gael say, "C'mon, c'mon," but Mia didn't look up from her work. When she was finished with her sketch, she saw that Gael looked miserable. "Shoot! I screwed mine up," she said, and let her petri dish clatter on the tabletop.

"What do you mean?" Mia looked at Gael's leaf, which looked exactly the same as when the experiment started.

"Look. It didn't turn black," Gael said, clearly frustrated. "I don't know what I did wrong."

For a moment, Mia couldn't understand what the problem was, and then all of a sudden, she realized there was no problem. "It's because you have the *D* leaf. Grown in darkness, remember?"

"Oh, right, because it wasn't exposed to sunlight, it didn't experience photosynthesis."

"You got it."

"I thought I just messed up."

"But you didn't." Mia smiled.

"Right. The Morrow and Baum team figured it out," Ms. Barton said as she walked past their table. "Good work, ladies. Now, what the catalyst did . . ."

Their teacher went on to talk about how molecules move during photosynthesis, referring back to the original equation on the blackboard. And Mia could read it now, understand it. Oxygen, carbon, and hydrogen re-formed and rebonded as part of this growth process normal to plants. Rebonded. What was the human equivalent? Mia wondered. Could it happen between her and Gael? Did Gael want that? Mia felt like maybe she did.

The bell rang, but Gael seemed to take her time packing up. As they walked out of the classroom together, Gael seemed lost in thought. In the hall, she turned to Mia with a wary look and said, "So, how's everything going for you these days?"

Mia knew Gael didn't want to hear anything bad. "The job is good. My mom is leaving me alone these days," she told her, trying to put a positive spin on Constance's absence. "I'm staying out of trouble, you know?"

"You seem better," Gael said. "I'm glad."

"I am better," Mia said, and it was true. Everything else was messed up, but not her.

"Well, gotta glow now," Gael said, smiling at her.

To Mia it felt like a big change had taken place between

them. But then Gael met up with Michele, who was waiting at the end of the hall for her. So everything was still the same as on the day their friendship fell apart. Mia was about to walk away when suddenly she saw Michele get furious. It was almost as bad as that day on the beach. She wasn't yelling at Gael, but Mia could tell she was saying something mean. Her gaze was pointed and narrow. Gael had actually taken a step back, and looked at a loss as to how to respond.

Mia remembered how this felt.

Michele was a yucky person.

Poor Gael.

And now Mia understood Michele had bullied Gael then, and she was doing it today. As she watched Michele turn to go and saw Gael follow her, Mia realized that hard as she might try, she didn't think she could be the catalyst that rebonded the friendship. The whole equation was way too volatile.

Likc Finkelstein, Graham had an office that was only a few doors down from the breeding room. He shared it with two other students who didn't seem to be around at the moment. As Mia got closer to his workspace, she saw that he'd decorated the wall above his desk with illustrations of birds and bugs. They looked like old-fashioned etchings where the marks of the pen and pencil were still visible. "Where did these come from?" she asked.

"Aren't they great? They're from a few different books. But most are just photocopies from *Audubon's Buttterflies, Moths and Other Studies.*"

Mia looked at him. "I've never heard of it. Who's Auto Bond?"

Graham chuckled.

"What's so funny?"

"Nothing, nothing. I just love how honest you are."

"Oh." First time anyone had called her that.

He pulled a thick old book off the shelf and handed it to her. Mia silently took in the illustrated cover and the correct spelling of the artist's name. "Audubon was one of the first naturalists," he told her. "Spent most of his career . . . actually most of his life out in nature, studying the details of all these amazing creatures. He was the first to draw them from life, and in such incredible detail in their natural environment."

"They're amazing. Was this what you wanted to show me?" she asked, holding up the book.

"This one among others. You said insect books were boring. I wanted to change your mind."

"Yeah, Finkelstein's books are nothing like this." Mia pointed to a drawing on the wall. "Look at the wings on the dragonfly. It's as beautiful as a piece of jewelry."

"More, I think," he said.

Mia and Graham looked at each other, smiled awkwardly. She looked back at the wall. "That's a fly!" she said, pointing to a tiny drawing in black and white. "But look how he's drawn it."

"What do you mean?" he asked.

She was looking hard at the drawing. "I never noticed that. . . ." she said.

"Noticed what?" Graham pressed in for a closer look at the drawing, trying to see what she saw.

"A fly's body is shaped like a heart." Mia picked up a pencil from Graham's desk. "Do you have a blank sheet of paper I can use?" she asked.

He rushed to tear one out of a notebook for her. Mia drew then, copying the fly on the wall, starting with a perfectly rounded heart. Her hand moved smoothly and lightly against the rough surface of the paper. With ease she attached legs, wings, and a head. And when she was done, it didn't look like Audubon's fly. It looked like her own. Her very first good drawing. She showed it to Graham.

"Very cool. How did you do that?" he asked.

"I'll show you." She reached for his hand. "Here, take this," she said, making him hold the pencil. Graham stiffened for a second when she touched him, and Mia hesitated, too. Should she not have grabbed him that way? She wasn't thinking. But Mia started to guide his hand, making good lines. Graham watched how the fly took shape at the point of the pencil. It came out perfect again, just like the first.

"I've never been able to draw anything before," she told him.

"You're kidding me, right? I can't believe you could see an image and then draw your own version of it like that."

"That was my first time." She looked down at the drawing, amazed by it still. "Here. You can have it," she said, and handed it to him.

"Are you sure?"

"Yes. I want to give it to you."

"But it's your first, you said."

"And now I know I can draw another anytime I want."

"You can borrow the book. Draw some more."

She thanked him, and then they were just standing there. "Guess I should go," Mia said.

"Guess so." He sounded a bit sad about it. "But there's lots more books here, so come back anytime. Okay?"

Mia took a good look at him. He was such a goofball. Eager smile just like Fink. She felt like doing something meaningful before she said good-bye, but the only thing that came to her was to chuck him on the chin. She knew she shouldn't do that. He might think it was weird. "See you soon," she said, and scooted out the door.

On the way back to Finkelstein's lab, she remembered how Clancy had given her a chin chuck that night he'd driven her home. No wonder she wanted to do it to Graham, because it was actually a good thing to do to people you liked. To somebody who already felt like a friend.

## 19

*Mia didn't go* home after work that day. She went to Butler Dining Hall. It was close to the time her mother's shift was supposed to start. Grandpa Andy had been really hard on her at the hospital, and Mia was sure her mother was still feeling it, along with all the alcohol she'd probably drunk because of it. Mia didn't know what she'd say, but maybe just showing up would make her mother feel better. Like it did last time. Maybe it would make Mia feel better, too.

Students were lined up with their trays in hand, and Mia could see Brenda working behind the counter, serving up chicken cutlets and the usual vegetables. She waited for her mother's friend to acknowledge her, but the steam rising from the stainless steel trays had fogged Brenda's glasses. Mia stood there a long time. Long enough to realize her mother wasn't going to walk through the double doors from the kitchen to work on the serving line. Mia knew without having to be told that Constance wasn't there at all that day.

She rapped on her side of the glass separating students from the servers. Brenda looked up with a frown, ready to reprimand whoever was rude enough to signal her that way. But when she saw it was Mia, her face softened. "Hey there, girl. Never expected to see you here, with your mother fired and everything."

Mia felt her pulse start to race. Constance hadn't taken

the day off. She'd lost her job. "What happened?" She tried to keep the panic out of her voice.

"Didn't she tell you?"

Mia shook her head.

Brenda kept doling out food while she talked. "Didn't show up for her shift for a few days in a row. Didn't even call in sick. Just didn't show. The boss got all huffy about it and fired her. I tried to warn her." Brenda shook her head.

"Is she all right?"

"I don't think so."

"Poor Constance. You tell her to call me, okay?"

Mia just nodded. She wasn't sure what to say. It had been a mistake to tell Grandpa Andy about Constance's drinking, and now she felt even more protective of her mother. It was almost raw, this feeling. But wasn't hiding the truth just another lie?

Brenda said, "I wish her the best. I really do. She's a good egg. Didn't deserve what happened. That promotion should have been hers." Brenda stopped working and looked at Mia with sympathy. "How about you? Everything okay with you? You want some slop? Sure look like you could use it."

"I don't want to get you in trouble. I mean since Mom's not working here anymore."

"The boss isn't around today. He'll never know. Get a tray. Then come back; don't stand in the line."

Mia sat down by herself, watching as the hall filled up with students. Soon she was surrounded, and she took some small comfort from their cheerful noise before she had to return to what she expected would be the quiet of the apartment she shared with her absent mother.

She couldn't help but feel that some of this mess was her

fault. It made her feel lower than a bug. All the times she put her mother down for working at Butler. Every time she took sides with Grandpa Andy against her. It added up. It sent Constance over the edge. No wonder her mother had kept getting fired to herself.

But Mia was mad, too. For starters, why should she feel like a bad person when her mother was the one messing up? And how could Constance lose it so completely? It was unforgivable. Horrible. Disgusting. *God, Mom.*

She got up and dumped her half-finished meal in the trash. She wanted to put a stop to what was happening, or what was going to happen, because she believed Grandpa Andy when he'd said things would only get worse. And now, if Mia didn't try to fix it, no one would.

Passing through the doors to leave Butler, she noted it would probably be for the last time. Good riddance. If anything, she hated the place more than before.

As the revolving doors swallowed her up, Mia didn't even think about waltzing around in there. She was at the department store for a reason. And it wasn't to steal.

She'd pictured this moment often, wondering how it would feel to go back to all that temptation, where everything was fresh and new, pure and clean. Mia considered putting her return visit off. Wait until things weren't so crazy in her life. But who knew when that would be? Besides, maybe Constance didn't care anymore whether Mia paid her debt, but instinctively Mia knew she needed to shed her old skin in order to move on. It was time.

As soon as she entered the gleaming store, she realized

that the girl who enjoyed taking things was long gone. The one who thought it was fun to do something bad, or who thought the best way to satisfy a craving was to give in to it, or who believed a shoe would make everyone love her.

Nothing this store sold could do that.

Not that she didn't see stuff that called to her. She paused before a rack of summery dresses, floating flowers of all colors. She could be the new girl on the block in something like that. But now these lovely things also reminded her that she had a wanting etched so deep in her heart that it had become an addiction.

Just like Constance, then, wasn't she? They were the same in that. Both reaching for something outside themselves to cure what was wrong on the inside. And at that moment, Mia felt like she truly understood her mother. It made her want to cry. But not right now.

She took a deep breath, went straight to the elevators, and rode to the top floor, where she found Roger Brady sitting at his desk, his back to the door while he fiddled with his black-and-white monitors. He turned around when she knocked and surprised her with a genuine smile. "Hello, Ms. Morrow."

"Hi, Mr. Brady," she said. "You must have seen me come in."

"I did indeed."

"I have some of the money I owe you, and I'm sorry it's not all of it, but I thought it was best to give you what I have. So here I am."

"Take a seat," Roger Brady said. "I'll give you a receipt for payment."

"Oh, great." She handed over the cash. "It's one hundred and twenty dollars. I hope it's okay I brought cash. I don't have a checking account. Yet."

"That's fine. Is this your money?" he asked, taking it from her.

"Yeah, who else's would it be?"

"Well . . . did someone give it to you?"

"Like my mother?"

"No, not Constance. She seemed determined to teach you a lesson that day. I'm simply asking if it's yours. Did you earn it?"

"Oh! You want to know if I stole it?"

"That thought had occurred. Yes."

Mia could see that she had a lot more to do to convince Roger Brady that she had changed. "No. It's mine. I got a job up at the university. In entomology. I'm working with bugs. It's good."

Roger Brady looked a bit shocked, but said, "Terrific. I'm glad to hear that, Ms. Morrow."

"Glad you're glad."

Roger Brady stopped writing. "You are? That's a big change in attitude."

"Yeah, you might not believe this, but I really feel bad about what happened. I thought taking things was doing me some good. But it turned out stealing did the opposite, because in the end I didn't like myself anymore." *Right, Clancy?*

He looked kindly at her. "Many, many people have a problem with shoplifting. Estimates tell us that somewhere around two million people indulge this behavior. So it's a common problem. I'm relieved you understand it was wrong. But it doesn't make you a horrible person."

Mia smiled to herself because somehow, and quite unexpectedly, this Roger Brady person had just made her feel better about herself. Then she asked, "Do you remember when you said I reminded you of my mother?"

"Yep, you still do, as a matter of fact."

"Were you and my mom close, back in high school?"

"Not close." He tore the receipt from the pad and handed it to her. "Here you are. Pay the rest when you have it. Can I help you with anything else today?"

"Really? Because I thought from the way you treated my mom when I got caught you might have liked her. I mean, you didn't have to let me off."

He looked at Mia, somewhat taken aback.

"Am I getting too personal, Mr. Brady? I was just wondering."

He recovered himself and answered, "No, I just admired her. Back then. She had a wild spirit, your mother. Fearless. Very independent. I saw that in you. It's . . . it's unique."

Mia just sat there thinking about what Roger Brady had just said. The thoughts were rushing through her. The mother Mia had grown up with was the opposite of the person he'd described. Wild? Her mother was all about control. Do the right thing. Clean up your room. Dinner at eight, and set the table. Shape up, Mia, before it's too late.

"How is she, your mother?" Roger Brady seemed unable to hold Mia's gaze at that moment, and it made her wonder if he already knew the answer to that question.

"Um, I really can't say."

Roger Brady nodded his head sadly. Mia was torn between wanting to keep asking questions and wanting to run out of there without uttering another word.

"If there's anything I can do . . ." he said.

Mia stood. "I don't think so." She felt dazed, as if the ground had fallen out beneath her feet, leaving her hanging in a new reality, where Roger Brady, and maybe everyone in town, knew her mother was a mess.

"Okay, Ms. Morrow. If it makes you feel any better, I think you and your mother are both good people."

At that moment, Mia snapped out of the sad trance she'd fallen into. "Oh . . . that's . . . thanks so much, Mr. Brady."

"Listen, don't worry about what you owe the store. It seems to me that the penalty we imposed on you has had its intended effect. So we can just forget about all that."

So he knew. Of course he knew.

But if Constance were her normal self, Mia knew she wouldn't want it to be that easy. "You don't think I'd blow off my responsibilities, do you? A deal is a deal. You can count on me." She reached out to shake his hand. Roger Brady seemed surprised again, and then he took her hand and matched the pressure she offered him.

Mia left the store without even a single thought about any of the merchandise there. Because she'd gotten something else instead. More than she'd bargained for, actually.

She'd been hoping for some positive proof that she'd changed. But this was more like a total transformation. Now, for Mia, it was as if all the impossibly perfect things for sale no longer existed.

Standing outside Grandpa Andy's door, she felt knocked sideways by a strong gust of loneliness. She went into his apartment just to smell his old smell, but it only made her miss him more.

The birds seemed relieved to see her, twittering loudly in their cage while she changed the paper and cleaned out their food dish. When she'd finished, she decided she could use some company, so she lifted the birdcage and its stand and brought them upstairs, settling them in a corner of the living room. Once they relaxed and started twittering again, she wished she could climb inside the cage with them, where there was nothing in the world to worry about.

In the kitchen Mia found a mess of bottles, glasses, and ice trays. The cold coffeepot had yesterday's brew in it. She started to clean up, but as she ran the tap to make ice cubes, she realized that all she was doing was making it possible for her mother to fix another drink. Mia turned the faucet off.

She wasn't hungry and she didn't feel like doing any homework, but in her book bag she found Graham's Audubon book, and she sighed with relief. Flipping through, she got to the page with the fly illustration she'd drawn before. She took out some colored paper and all her metallic pens, and drew a whole bunch of flies very fast. And while she sketched, all of the things making her hurt like crazy simply evaporated.

Bug art.

When she'd finished her flies, about twenty of them, she

started carefully cutting them loose from the paper background, and pasted them to the wall around the goddess. Then she stood back to admire her work. It looked like a beautiful and wild creature was living in a garden with insects flying all around her.

Mia decided this artwork was done.

A moment later, she heard a car pull into the driveway and ran to the window to see if it was Constance. It was George by himself in a black SUV. It wasn't his car. He had an arrangement with her mother to work on automobiles outside the repair shop, so he could make a little extra cash. He gave them 10 percent of it. But Mia didn't care about the money.

She wanted her mother to come home. It hit her like a need. The purest kind of impulse. Maybe George would know where to find her.

Mia ran into the hall, down the stairs, and out of the house fast as she could fly. In the driveway, George was buried up to the waist inside the SUV's hood. She knocked twice. Mia said, "Have you seen my mother?" Hearing herself sound a bit desperate, like she was some kind of lost little kid, she added in a sober tone, "Because she didn't come home last night."

George wiped his hands on a rag he kept bunched up on the rim of the front fender. "Oh, really?"

"Yeah. Seen her?"

"Nope."

"Have any idea where she might have gone?"

"No, not really."

"Well, what did you do on your date the other night?"

"Went to dinner. That Moosewood place."

"They don't serve alcohol there, and you guys were pretty drunk. Where'd you go after?"

"Well, the new Marriott has a bar, the one near the airport."

Maybe her mother was there. Or maybe not. Mia decided to question George some more. "Okay. So what kind of stuff did you talk about? Did she say anything . . ." Mia wasn't sure what bothered her most. "Well, did she say anything to you about maybe wanting to leave? To go away?"

"Jeez, nothing like that. It was the usual . . . you know, about our jobs and how we got where we are." George thought for a second. "She sure drank a lot, though."

"You weren't in such great shape that night, either, from what I could tell."

He hesitated, then said, "Just trying to keep up with her. I'm telling you, she can put it away."

All of a sudden, it made Mia intensely angry to hear Constance put down. Grandpa Andy sure was right about this guy! Not nearly good enough. Where did he get off ragging on her mother like that? "When you get paid for that car," she snapped, "put the cash in our mailbox."

"Yeah, of course." George threw the dirty rag down like he thought they were both crazy and he was washing his hands of the two of them.

Back in the empty living room, Mia realized she was going to need some help finding Constance, so she picked up the phone and called the police to report her mother missing. She gave Constance's age, height, weight, and hair color to the sergeant who answered.

"How long has she been missing?" he asked.

"I'm not sure, I think it's only been a night, maybe two."

"Has she gone off before?"

"Not that I know of."

"We'll need a picture of her to put in the file."

Mia wasn't sure where to find a current photo of Constance. There were no picture frames collecting dust around the apartment, no snapshots stuck to the fridge. "I'll have to look. Can I drop it by in the next day or so?"

Before they hung up, he told her not to worry. That most missing people turn up within a few days. He gave her a number to call if that happened. Mia wrote it down, but she knew her search wasn't going to end there.

*Mia didn't bother* with any lights, just crept down the dark hall. She stepped inside her mother's darkened bedroom and flipped on a lamp. It looked like the room of a person she hardly knew it all: clothing on the floors and bed, drawers left open. A cup of coffee with curdled milk sat on the dresser. A jewelry box was upended on the bed. Mia walked over to it and turned it right side up. There were a couple of cheap fake gold pieces and beaded necklaces lying on the crumpled comforter where they'd fallen. Mia put them back in the box, then put the box in its place on the dusty dresser.

There was a reason she'd come in here. In the bottom drawer of the dresser was a photo album. Mia had seen it a million times before. She'd practically studied it when she was still a little kid, because it was full of pictures from her mother's life before Mia. Looking into it was like staring into a magic pool, dark and mysterious, and floating in the middle of it was Constance as a girl. Whenever Mia asked about the photos, Constance wouldn't say much. Mia was searching, of course, back then.

*Who's this guy with you?*

*Oh, someone I used to hang out with.*

*A lot?*

*Nah, he was just a friend of a friend.*

Never any answers about her father, no matter how many questions Mia had.

Mia knew there were no current pictures of her mother in the album, but she took a look anyway. First came the naked baby shots. On a red blanket and in a bassinet. Next she was a blond toddler in a kiddie swing, being pushed by Grandpa Andy in a tie at the playground. The pretty little girl blew out six candles on a birthday cake held by Grandma Morrow in pearls. Mia never knew her. Grandma didn't live very long. And then came Constance's early teenage years. A shot of her on horseback somewhere in the mountains. She was gorgeous. Slim and strong with blond hair gleaming in the sun.

*My daughter . . . My beautiful daughter . . .* Mia could hear Grandpa Andy's voice, in pain. He did love her. Back then, at least.

The last few pictures of Constance were from when she was a little older. There was one with a bunch of kids laughing in the park. Mia lingered over it, because she could have sworn her mother looked stoned. Kind of falling over, her face too close to the camera. There was a high school graduation picture. The bump didn't show, but Mia was already in there.

And there was another. This one caught Mia's eye. Constance sitting on the hood of a hot-looking black car. Mia studied the young man behind the windshield, behind the steering wheel. His hair in the picture was jet black. Just like hers.

A burst of heat flashed under her skin. She looked more closely at this photograph. The face in the picture was young and bright, not craggy and lined. His hair was no longer dark. But that smile, the lopsided grin that came from the heart. That was Clancy. It had to be. And it wasn't that long ago that she'd been sitting with him behind the wheel in this same car. She could have sworn it.

Her mind raced down the same old worn channel. She wondered how old her mother was in the photo. And if she were pregnant when it was taken, and if that was true, was the man in the photo her father? Was it Clancy?

*You wish.*

Mia stopped. Her mind went blank, just shut off. She couldn't look anymore.

The phone rang, tearing into the total silence of the apartment. Thinking it might be her mother calling, Mia ran to pick it up. She flopped onto the living room couch as she said hello, trying not to sound overly worried.

"This is Nurse Mary McCormick from St. Vincent's Hospital. May I speak with Constance Morrow?"

Mia was instantly filled with a fear so real it felt like her cells were made of the stuff. Paralyzing. "She's not here," she squeaked, barely able to speak.

The nurse took a moment. "Let me see here. What's on the chart . . ." Mia could hear her reading from it. "Oh, I see, you must be the granddaughter. This is Mia, then?"

"Uh-huh."

"I'm sorry, dear, but your grandfather passed away twenty minutes ago." The nurse waited, but Mia didn't manage to respond. She heard the nurse say, "He was having trouble breathing and some anxiety as well. We increased his morphine and he slipped away peacefully a few minutes later. I'm very sorry, Miss Morrow."

Mia tried to think of something to say, but felt like she was disappearing into the silence on the phone.

Nurse McCormick spoke again. "Has your family made any funeral arrangements?

"Uh . . . um . . . oh, God . . . I don't know."

"That's perfectly all right. There are several funeral homes in the area. May we contact one for you?"

"I guess, but I want to talk to my mother first, and she's . . . she's not available."

"Oh. I see. I think. In any case, don't worry, we'll take good care of him until your mother contacts us. But it should be soon. Will you be coming in the morning?"

"I have school. And then I have to work. I'll be there later on, after six, is that okay?"

"Yes, of course, that's perfectly fine. You don't have to explain to me. But no one will blame you for taking some time to grieve, dear."

Mia's voice cracked. "Okay," she said, and hung up. She buried her face in the couch, in the pitch-black darkness, and despite what G.A. had wanted, she cried and cried until she went dry.

It took quite a while for Mia to rise. But when she got up, she went and got the picture of her mother with the guy in the car. She carefully placed it in her bag and headed out the door without thinking twice about what she was going to do. She was going to follow the one clue she had.

The Marriott. She didn't have a car to get there. But she knew someone who did.


There were no crowds waiting to get in, or bouncers there to screen them, and the large black metal door was propped open with a brick. Mia walked right into the darkened front hall of the Common Ground.

There was music playing inside, a song she didn't know. It sounded old, like a band from the forties. No one manned the pay window. Mia passed through a set of black drapes and stepped into the club.

One guy was pushing a broom around, and another was placing empty glasses on a shelf behind the bar. Getting ready for the night. Mia had no desire to stick around for that. "Excuse me," she called out.

The bartender looked up. The broom guy stopped sweeping. "We're not open yet," he said sullenly. "Come back in an hour."

"I don't want a drink. I'm here to see Clancy."

"Waste of time," said the bartender, who'd already gone back to stacking glasses. "He's not hiring at the moment."

Mia walked up to the bar. "You don't understand. I need to speak with him about something—" She'd almost said "something personal" but thought better of it. Clancy might not be willing if that were the case. "Tell him that Mia Morrow wants to see him. Or should I go look for him myself?"

The bartender sighed and put down the glass. "No. Wait here." He was only gone for a moment. "He's here in his office," he called out. "Follow me." Then he smiled, friendly all of a sudden. Clancy had obviously told the guy to be nice. A good sign.

She was led up a steep staircase to a little room at the top. It looked more like a closet than an office. Or like a place to hide out. Mia saw a desk piled with loose papers and heaps of files stacked on both sides of an old computer, on the floor, and on top of cardboard boxes.

Clancy was hunched over a small safe. As he looked up at her, he smiled his sad smile and her stomach sort of lurched inside her. Now that she was there with him—after what she'd just thought about him and what the reality might actually be that bonded them—she found herself feeling unsure of how far to take things. What to push for. And how to get it.

"Surprised to see me?" she asked.

"Not really. I had a feeling we'd bump into each other somewhere."

"This isn't just a bump. I came to ask a favor."

"I see. Maybe you want to take a seat, in that case, and we can talk about it." He meant in the guest chair on the other side of his desk, but Mia took his swivel one instead.

"Great idea. Let's talk," Mia said, plopping herself down. The old metal chair squeaked on its hinges as she settled in. "This isn't very comfortable, is it? Why do you keep such a crappy old chair around?"

"Got used to it, I guess." Clancy sat in the rickety wooden guest chair. "So what's this about a favor?"

"Well, I need a ride, and you're the only person I know who has a car."

"Where to?"

"Not far. Just to the airport."

"You got a plane to catch?"

"Nope."

"When do you need this ride?" he asked.

"Tonight. Now."

"I can't leave the club."

She expected this. "You know, the more I think about you, the more mysterious you seem."

"Huh. Have you been thinking about me a lot?"

"Would you like me to be thinking about you a lot?"

"I didn't say that."

"Fine," Mia said. "Not a lot, no. But in ways you might not like."

"Whoa, hey, listen. It's been a long time since I was into dating young girls."

"Don't leap to the obvious, Clancy. Because it's not like that. It's just that we've only met a few times, but there was always something strange about it. That's what I've been thinking about. "

"Not so strange. I meet kids like you all the time. When parents aren't around or don't care, kids grow up by getting into trouble. Been there myself. I know it can be hard. I sympathize. That's all. Don't read into it."

"Right. Okay. But remember the night I passed out here in the club? You knew my age."

"I saw your ID."

"That's right, you found out who I was and then you asked if you should call my mother to pick me up. Why didn't you say my parents instead?"

"Did I?"

"You did. I remember it. Because the thought of my mother coming to get me was unbearable."

"Chalk it up to a lucky guess, kid."

"And you fired the bouncer and told Robbie to stay away from me."

"That's because I could get sued by an irate parent if they found out that kind of thing was going on in my club. I'd lose my license."

Mia felt a heat rise in her face. She was looking at Clancy, and it was like a dam inside of her was about to burst, and everything about her life that wasn't okay and seemed like it never would be was going to gush out and hit the floor. They'd be swimming in it. And it felt right to get mad at him.

"So why didn't you just tell Robbie he couldn't bring me here, then? Why tell him to leave me alone altogether if you didn't care about me?"

Clancy met her gaze without wilting. He simply looked right back. "I didn't say I didn't care."

Mia felt herself settle down. It was his words, or his voice. Or just him. "Okay." She took a breath and continued. She could do this. "And then, when I saw you at the hospital and my mother showed up, you practically ran away. I realized you didn't want to see her, even more than I didn't. And I started thinking, why would Clancy feel that way?"

"Why do you need to get to the airport?"

"Well, I'm pretty sure my mom is sitting in a bar at the Marriott getting drunk off her ass and I need to get her home because—"

"Hold on. Wait a second."

Mia was unstoppable now. "—I need her to help me bury my grandfather. The man who was her father died tonight."

A deep sigh escaped Clancy. "I really can't get involved here. . . . I shouldn't . . ." He trailed off.

And again, she knew it was time. Mia couldn't go back to the way it was, even if she wanted to. She'd seen things for what they were now. Her mom was a drunk; her grandfather was beyond help. And what about the man in front of her? What part might he play in the family drama? The blood rushed through her veins as she reached into her purse. She took out the photo. Her ace of spades.

"Is that what you said back then, too? After you got my mom pregnant?"

It had the reaction she was hoping for. He took hold of the picture, studied it. Almost a minute passed, and he couldn't look away. And Mia knew something she didn't know before. It was plain for anyone to see. He had feelings for Constance then, and in some sort of faded or faraway way, he still might. When he looked up at Mia, he didn't have to say anything.

"I kind of look like you. Don't you think?"

Clancy pushed the picture back to her side of the desk but still didn't seem willing to admit anything. He stood up then and gathered his wallet and keys and put them in the pocket of his leather jacket. She thought he was going to leave, but he waited for her to join him at the door to his office.

He said, "Come on. We can talk in the car."

When she got beside him, he threw his arm around her shoulder and she didn't pull away because it felt like it belonged there, the weight and the width of it a kind of shelter she'd never experienced before. They went out together, just like that.

It was chilly that night. Mia shivered as Clancy turned the engine over, and the car heater blew cold air across her bare knees. "Sorry. Takes a little bit to warm this old horse up," he said.

"Brr. I can't wait for it to be summer. I hate cold weather."

"Well, you could've worn a bit more clothing." Clancy glanced over at her as he pulled out of the parking lot, and she could see he was only half kidding.

"I didn't know it was going to get this cold out tonight." He was giving her a skeptical look now. "Okay. You have a point," she said. "But I just decided to come see you and I left the house in the same thing I was wearing all day."

Clancy had to laugh. "I can't believe you just showed up like that, all hell-bent on proving I'm your daddy."

Mia looked up at him incredulously. "Are you trying to tell me you're not? That's you in the picture. And Mom wasn't much older than that when she had me."

"Yeah, that's me in the picture. But that picture doesn't tell the whole story. It's just one moment in time. A frozen second before life or fate or whatever it is puts its own plans in motion and does what it wants to do."

"You mean like how life lets a guy walk out on his pregnant girlfriend?"

"You got it all wrong, kiddo. I mean . . . I wasn't a prince. I'll admit that." Mia was reminded of all the lousy things Constance said her father had done, whoever he was. "But it's really not my place. . . . I know your mother wouldn't want you to hear about things from me. And you're her daughter."

Mia sighed and turned to look out the window.

Clancy reached out and tapped her on the shoulder. "Listen, you can ask what you want, and I'll answer what I can. Okay?"

Mia searched his face, to see if he was just toying with her. But he was waiting for her to begin. "Okay. Is this the same car as in the picture?"

"Yup. She's my baby. Sixty-five Mustang."

"So you knew my mom. Obviously, right?"

"Yes, I did."

"How well?"

Clancy stuttered a bit. "You want to know if we . . . if we . . . were . . . together?"

"Yeah, like were you her boyfriend or not?"

"No. No I wasn't."

"But you slept together."

Clancy braked a little too hard at a red light. "Again, that's something for you to ask your mother about."

Mia sighed. "Did Mom drink a lot back then? Can you tell me that?"

"Oh, yeah. We all did."

"Who's all? You guys were part of the same crowd, then?"

"No, I had the bar and she came in a lot."

"She used to drink at the Common Ground? When she was my age?"

"I wasn't very careful about things back then."

"How old were you?'

"Around twenty-six or so."

Mia let that sink in. "Around Robbie's age?"

"Something like that," Clancy said. "Listen. You think twenty-six is old. But believe me, it's not. I was stupid about a lot of things."

"Was she losing her shit back then, too? Because she's completely out of control now. It seems like all she wants to do is drink. She got fired from her job, you know?"

"Mia, alcoholism is a disease, not a question of will-power."

That was the first time this word had been used about her mother. *Disease.* Constance was ill.

"But she's like a completely different person."

"I know," Clancy said sadly.

They arrived at the Marriott just then, and Clancy pulled the car into a space near the front doors. For some reason, Mia felt Constance was in there. She just knew it. She sighed. "I don't know what to do. Part of me wants to march in there and make her . . ." Mia didn't finish.

"Honestly, there's not much you can do. You can try to bring her home, but it's up to her to stop drinking altogether. She has to want that. Believe me. I know what I'm talking about. Took me years to deal with my drinking, and it wasn't easy. But I'm okay now."

Mia looked hard at Clancy. "Are you really okay? Because I look at you and you just seem sad. And you work in a bar. Isn't that a bit odd? You spend all your time around the very thing you can't have."

"That's life, kiddo."

"There. That's what I'm talking about. You've got a very gloomy view of things. Like the world has let you down."

Clancy laughed gruffly. "Do I? Maybe you're right."

They sat there quietly until Mia said, "I hate her sometimes."

"No. You don't."

Now the sad smile came again, but this time it was Mia flashing it at Clancy. "Yeah, you're right," she said. Mia glanced toward the hotel entrance. "Will you come in with me, Clancy?"

"Don't you think Constance might have a bad reaction at seeing us together? With no explanation of how we know each other?"

Mia fixed Clancy with a meaningful look. "Or what we are to each other."

Clancy's turned away to stare out the windshield, looking ahead into the blackness.

"We need you," Mia said resolutely. "Because otherwise all we're going to do is fight. It's what we always do. Can't you come in? Be our referee. Just this once?"

Clancy didn't move.

"Please? For a friend? For new ones and old." Mia was talking about herself as well as Constance.

She could have sworn she saw Clancy swallow down something, something he didn't know how to deal with. Like some of the sorrow he carried was exactly the same as what her mother suffered from. Then he said, "Let's go," and got out of the car before Mia did.

Seeing that, she felt the beating thing inside her chest might burst wide open, and she knew she was ready to face whatever trouble lay ahead of them.

## 21

*Inside the lobby* of the hotel, there was a sign for a bar called the YeeMeeLoo. It looked like an old-style Chinese restaurant. The only light came from red paper lanterns, some hanging low and some scattered on the tables. Small drawings of dragons and snarling tigers in fake bamboo frames were placed all around. There were a couple of men in business suits sitting at the bar.

At the end of the lineup, four seats away from everyone else, Mia spotted a blond woman. She couldn't even be sure it was her mother. The blonde sat slumped over, with one hand on a glass of white wine. With the other hand, she scribbled something onto a pad of paper. The pen looked loose in her hand, like a floppy toy. She drank down the contents of the glass and turned to the bartender to order another. "Pee-no Gri-jo," she said in an unmistakable voice, and Mia knew that slurring woman was her mother.

The shock of it sent a feeling like ice through Mia's veins. "Oh, God     's worse than I thought."

Clancy reached out and touched her arm. "You don't have to do this. It's not your job, kid."

*My job.* Mia flashed on flies giving birth to maggots. How she had to brave that moment, too. And how she knew she could.

Mia turned to Clancy. "I want to try to talk to her. Will you wait for me back there for a minute?" she said, indicating a semicircular red booth away from the bar.

"Sure thing. Try not to argue with her, Mia. It won't go well. Just try to get her home. And try to understand."

"Okay, Clancy."

Mia approached the bar. Constance scribbled away, her head hovering over the page by just a few inches. Mia pulled out the heavy stool next to her, slowly and carefully as if she were approaching a dangerous stranger. She put her elbows on the bar and kept her voice low. "Hi, Mom."

Constance turned and acted like everything was normal and they were meeting up again after a long trip. "Hey!" she said enthusiastically.

"How did you get here, Mom?" Mia asked.

"Well, it's twenty-seven steps from the front row of the parking lot."

Mia was silenced for a moment. Her mother was talking nonsense.

"Seventy-eight from the bus stop," Constance continued. "So, quicker by cab. But the bus is cheaper."

And Mia finally understood. She remembered counting her own steps in the department store. It had helped her figure out exactly how long it would take to get the thing she wanted—in her mother's case, counting until that next drink was in her hand.

"I didn't mean this bar. I meant . . ." Mia looked down at what her mother had been writing. It was a small lined notepad, and on the page was a numbered list of things that made no sense. Pick up stock. Clean out first, dump it. It was Constance trying to keep her life in order, control things, but her mind was so fogged she couldn't even think about what it was she wanted to remember to do. She didn't want Mia to see the book and took it away. "Not your business," she said, and tried to stuff it in the pocket of her jacket. She wasn't coordinated enough to pull it off. The book fell on the floor. Constance didn't notice. Mia got off the stool and retrieved it for her.

"Got stuff in there," Constance said as Mia handed it back. "Gotta keep it all straight."

"I think we should head home, what do you say?"

"No. No! Not going there. Daddy will be mad." Then Constance cracked up, pounding her hand on the bar. "Ouch. That hurts."

Mia thought for a second about telling her the truth about Grandpa Andy. But now wasn't the time. "He's not there, Mom."

"Good." Constance took another gulp at her glass. It was nearly empty. She drained it and pushed it forward, calling to the bartender at the same time. "'Nother one down here!"

The bartender looked their way and Mia caught his eye, giving him a silent shake of the head to indicate he should not refill her mother's glass. The bartender turned away.

"They can be kind of slow around here," Constance said.

"Why do you like drinking so much, Mom? Is it really so great?"

"I like everything about it. It just feels good. I like holding on to the cold glass. I like the warm feeling going down my throat, and how it settles on me, reaches down to the bottom of me somehow. Bartender!"

He didn't even turn around this time.

"Best of all, it changes everything." Constance leaned in, confessing. "Sends me in a different direction. I'm much more *re-lax-ed.*" She drew out the word, relaxing as she said it. "You know?"

"I do know. But do you think you could stop if you wanted to?"

"Why would I do that?"

"I just think you'd feel better. You'd be better off."

"Never good enough." Constance shook her head back and forth.

"That's not what I'm saying. I'm not criticizing. It's just that drinking the way you do . . . it's all you want to do." Constance looked directly at her for the first time that night, and Mia felt a surge of hope that she was getting through. "Come on, Mom, why don't we talk about it at home?"

"You think I should restrain myself, do you?" Constance was talking very loudly now. "Walk a straight line. Your grandfather insisted on that. That *bastard*!" She practically spit as she said it.

"Don't say that, Mom!" Mia took a deep breath to calm herself. "Listen to me. I know that Grandpa Andy gave you a hard time. I saw it. Many times. But that doesn't mean he didn't want the best for you. He just didn't know what that was."

Constance calmed down a little. "Damn right he didn't."

"But he's your father. Doesn't that mean anything to you?"

"I don't care about him anymore. . . . He can't stop me *now*!"

From the corner of her eye, Mia saw that Clancy had gotten up from the table where she'd sent him.

"And when he's gone? How will you feel then?" Mia felt her throat constrict. She tried to stop herself, to swallow the tears jamming up against her eyes. But she couldn't.

"You don't know how lucky you were to have a father! Even one who didn't get it." Out of her control, her whole face let go with a quiver. Tears spilled fast down her face.

Clancy stood only a few feet away from them now. Mia watched through watery eyes as he tried to decide whether to interrupt, as if an invisible barrier held him back.

"Doesn't matter. He's dead to me now," Constance said, and slumped in her chair.

It was a horrible thing to say, and Mia no longer cared how drunk she was. A stone-cold hardness crept into her voice. "Yeah, you're right. He is dead."

Her mother sat up then, and the next thing said came from Clancy.

"Hey there, Constance. It's really late. And it's time to go home."

Constance turned and took in the man who was speaking to her. Her eyes went wide and her mouth opened, as if to scream, but no sound came out. And then the shock seemed to take her over in an even bigger way. She slid off the barstool, and fell forward, crumpling into Clancy, who caught her and held her.

"Did she faint?" Mia asked.

"I don't know," Clancy said. Everyone in the bar was looking at the three of them. Constance was flopped over his arm like deadweight. "Bartender," he said, "I think we need an ambulance."

The next few hours that night felt like they happened in the bowels of hell. Constance, who'd revived in the ambulance on the way to the hospital, wanted to be let out and fought with the emergency worker. She'd had to be re-strained. At the hospital, they found out that the alcohol level in her blood was so high, she'd poisoned herself. So now she was in the hospital for who knew how long, to detox.

Clancy didn't want to be listed as the responsible adult on the hospital's intake sheets, so the task fell to Mia to sign the papers, giving them the go-ahead to treat her mother for alcoholism. That had been on Clancy's advice, who'd said, "It's the best thing for her."

Before Mia left the hospital, she'd viewed her grand-father's body. She wanted to see him one more time, but when she found him lying on that cold metal slab of a table, looking like nothing more than an imitation of himself, stark light beating down on his empty body, she said a hur-ried good-bye and ran out of the room. She directed the hospital to arrange a cremation at a funeral parlor down the road, which seemed like the easiest thing to do. She wondered why he hadn't made any arrangements himself.

After all that, Clancy dropped Mia off at home. And it was as if things between them were no different from the first night they'd met. She said good night. He gave her the sad smile. She got out of his car and swung the door shut, and he disappeared into the last little bit of night without a word about when she might see him again. Quite frankly, she felt like it was his turn to reach out. She'd done all she could.

Mia felt so old.

———

The apartment was a total mess. Old bedding was strewn across the couch from nights Mia had spent waiting there for Constance to come home, plates were stacked in the sink and on the table, rotted garbage was stinking up the pail in the kitchen.

Mia threw her bag on a chair and started to clean up, going after it real fast, just wanting to make things disappear. Dishes went into the dishwasher, and she set the machine humming. She cleared the fridge of everything rotting, dried up, or empty. Then she took out the trash.

On the back porch, she found the cans were full. There wasn't room for even one more bag. She'd have to take them down to the street. As she pulled out the one on top, it made an ungodly racket, the sound of glass banging against glass. She tore it open and looked at all the bottles, only bottles, that were crammed inside. Huge fifths of bourbon, gallon jugs of red wine, and hundreds of those tiny shot-size liquor bottles, the kind you pick up at the cash register on your way out of the store. All of them drained dry. She pulled out the other bags stacked in the can and found more of the same.

Mia stood several of the bottles on the warped wooden floorboards of the back porch. They glimmered, even in the dull porch light. Still calling out for attention, even though they were used up. Studying them, she noticed how each one had a personality. Some looked tubby and jolly, others were narrow with a long neck that made them look mean and miserly. All kinds of interesting shapes.

She gathered up a bunch and took them inside. In her room she placed the bottles neatly on her desk, then just sat there staring at the glass shapes, trying to decide what to do with them. Her first impulse was to get a hammer and smash them to bits. Destroying them could be a creative act. But then what would be left, and what would be said once they were gone? She wanted to make something that would last. Like a photograph. For all time.

Mia got up from her desk and opened the old photo album. She looked at the bottles. And then at the photos. And soon she knew what she wanted to do. She pulled all her art supplies off the shelves in a hurry. The glitter, the glue, the tracing paper and scissors and acrylic paints, too. Beneath the goddess on the wall, she spread out her magazine stash and got to work.

The first thing she made was for her mother. What had once been a fifth of Gordon's gin became a narrow-necked vase, perfect for maybe three flower stems, and decorated to look like some kind of crazy road trip. Mia covered it over completely. A decoupage of mountains and green gardens and lakes, all the beauty of nature she could cull from those magazines were pasted to the surface of the bottle. On the very front, she added a hand-colored tracing she'd made of that telling photograph. Young Clancy in the driver's seat holding on to the steering wheel and Constance hanging on, ready for a wild ride. Mia decided they were trying to escape together into that perfect world. But in their way, on the road ahead, was a baby courtesy of Ivory soap, a rosy-cheeked child utterly unaware of the two crazy adults barreling down the road.

She might never know the true story between Clancy and her mother, the real story of how they were linked. But for some reason it made sense to her that this was their story as far as it could be told. Some promise held them fast.

She made several more of these artworks like the one for Constance. Bud vases and jugs with traced photos and the pictures of bugs that Mia drew from the Audubon book. Each one told a different story.

About a birthday cake made of fire. About a glowing golden girl about to fall down from her horse.

And a little innocent baby on a red blanket, who was both mother and child. She painted thick letters on this one. *M + C.* For mother and child. And it stood for Mia and Constance, too, she realized. Funny how she'd never before noticed that coincidence of their initials, how it was all backward now.

And it was all that was left.

Experience is not what happens
to a man; it's what a man does
with what happens to him.

—ALDOUS HUXLEY

## 22

*On the Friday* afternoon following the YeeMeeLoo disaster, Mia arrived to an empty lab. There was a note waiting for her. She flopped down at her desk, disappointed that Finkelstein wasn't around, and sat there for a moment trying to pull herself together, still reeling from what had to be the worst night of her life.

She knew she should stand up and take the day's count, but she didn't have an ounce of energy left for the flies. She reached for the note Finkelstein had left.

> *Dear Mia,*
>
> *Professor Deacon has summoned me for a conference.*
> *I'll be with him until late this afternoon.*
> *I may not get back before you go.*
> *Be sure to check on your young ones.*
>
> > *Signed,*
> > *J.F.*

It took her a moment to realize what he meant by telling her to "check on your young ones." But then she got it. The flies were born! They were waiting for her in the sawdust boxes of the breeding room. She was sure of it. Mia went down the hall to see for herself.

She found them in their April 16 boxes, milling around as if awaiting instructions. All six boxes had tiny little flies, breathing heavily, their brand-new lungs practically pumping right through their still-soft exoskeletons. They glanced up at her innocently as she pushed the sawdust off them, exposing them to the light. Mia checked the boxes dated two days later. These had maggots and appeared to be right on schedule.

But the helpless fly babies seemed to be unsure of what they should do or even what they were. Mia scooped them up with a spoon, as Finkelstein had instructed, transferring them to clear plastic boxes to start them breeding. She set all six boxes on a tray and took them back to the lab.

As she began placing the new flies on an empty shelf next to their parents, she noticed that in one box a few had gotten their wings working already. It was that fast. They zoomed around like kamikaze pilots, squealing through figure-eight turns and flying low over their buddies on the bottom of the box, who looked up in awe and then began to shake and pivot in place until finally one and then another lifted off, buzzing madly in pursuit.

A few minutes later, every one of the new boxes had flying flies. They went bouncing off the walls of the box, crashing into one another. Mia watched them for some time, until she finally grew tired of seeing them fly in circles. She walked over to the shelves where the mature flies were busy eating and laying their eggs.

When she turned her attention back to the babies, she found most had already spent that first burst of energy and now were moving around in their confinement like all the other adults. A step, a turn, a stop, a hop. And she hadn't even put the food in yet. When she did that, it would be all they cared about.

They'd never really fly. Not free. Unless . . .

Mia stood considering two very distinct courses of action she could take at that moment.

Let them exist for their short lives in a box.

Or give them back their lives, the ones they were meant to have.

Which was the right thing to do? There was a choice waiting for her. And how did she know? She felt that familiar rush, the one that came on with a buzzing *zap*. She had to admit, she still really liked the feeling. But this time she had to think things through.

If she let the baby flies go, they might get eaten by birds or swatted flat as a pancake. All sorts of terrible things might happen. But what if they got up in the sky? Away from this world with its plastic boxes and dead grandfathers and sick mothers and friends who no longer cared? Including one who never really would, no matter how much she might want him to?

They'd fly above it all.

Mia put the boxes full of baby flies back on the tray, walked briskly down the hall and up the stairs. She slipped outdoors and placed the tray beneath a bunch of privet bushes. Smoothly and carefully, she removed the lids and shooed the flies from the boxes.

They were reluctant at first, but one by one they got the idea, alert to the open sky above. She wondered if they experienced that special rush of energy, too. It happened fast after that. They flew out in a swarm, a black cloud of bugs. She reared back, and then she laughed at herself because after all this time she still wasn't completely used to them. She watched as some of her flies circled the bushes; others landed on the tiny leaves and clung there to get their bearings. The sun was still strong, and the warm light brought out the phosphorescent color in their wings. For the first time ever, these specimens looked like real flies to her. And she liked what she saw.

It wasn't long before her flies disappeared into the big wild world and she was alone again. Mia eventually returned to the basement. And once she was down there, the rush was over and she realized what she'd done didn't make any sense. Not at all. Mia took a deep breath and felt some of that flyaway freedom again. She wanted to believe in that. She wanted to feel her actions hadn't been pointless.

She stowed the empty boxes under the sink and left Finkelstein a note about a family emergency. Exiting the lab, she bumped straight into Graham. "Hey, Mia. I'm done for the day. How about it . . . are you free?"

For all she knew, she had just ended everything forever at the lab. But looking at Graham, Mia felt good. Kind of instantly. Another small miracle in the basement of Sutton Hall, the most unexpected place in the world.


Mia and Graham sat outside at a round table. The sun was squeezing down between two old buildings and the warm patio was caught up in a rosy glow. As they sat silently for a minute sipping at their drinks, Mia wondered whether to tell Graham what she'd done back in the lab.

"Well, I'm glad we finally got together," he said.

"I am, too."

"Remember that day in my office . . . the way you grabbed my hand when you were drawing?" Graham asked.

"Oh. I shouldn't have done that, I guess. I was worried you didn't like it. That I'd made you uncomfortable."

"Are you kidding? It was great."

"It was?"

"Most people would think twice about doing something bold like that. And then they'd probably stop themselves. But not you."

"Right, not me."

"It might have taken me weeks to work up the courage to ask you out if you hadn't done that."

Mia laughed. "That's good, I guess." Given what she'd done with the baby flies, these bold moves seemed more like a case of temporary insanity.

"So tell me something about yourself." Graham fixed her with an eager look. "Whatever you want. I want us to get to know each other. You know, like friends."

Mia stirred her ginger tea to play for time. She didn't want to keep secrets. But the whole truth was too much. "You go first," she said.

"Okay . . . I like long-distance biking. I've been around Lake Champlain twice."

She laughed. "I've got a bike," Mia told him.

"Where do you go?"

"Oh, mostly out to the reservoir."

"Where's that?"

"Out on Route 29. It's great for swimming. You haven't been there?"

"No. I'll have to check that out."

They were quiet again, and Mia thought hard about what to ask, since it seemed to be her turn. Why was she so nervous? "Maybe this is boring," she said, "but how did you wind up at the college?"

"This school was my first choice. My father went here as an undergrad. He studied to be an ornithologist. Great program."

"What's that?"

"A bird man."

Mia laughed. "It makes sense that you're into science, in that case."

"Like father, like son, you mean?"

"Yes, exactly. But it's not a put-down. I think it's a good thing."

"Yeah, it is. I'm just joking around. I couldn't believe how happy it made my father when I told him what I wanted to do. I hadn't expected that."

Mia thought of Grandpa Andy and how he never really got to experience how it would feel to have someone in the family carry on the scientific tradition. That's why he liked to hear her talking about the lab so much.

"And what about your mother?" she asked Graham.

"She's not in the picture. Lives in California. Likes warm weather. Not us so much. But she's happy. And we're fine. Me and my brothers see her a couple times a year and try not to get into fights in front of her. She really can't take that." He stopped talking then.

"You don't get along with them?" Mia asked.

"Not really. There's three of us. I'm the oldest by four years, and they were always in my stuff growing up, and in my way mostly. They say I boss them around."

"Are they right?"

"Yeah, of course. They were little punks. It was self-preservation. But there was one time, when I did something . . . let's just say not good."

"So . . . did you light them on fire, or what?"

"Almost that bad. When I was thirteen I chained them to a tree and left them there all afternoon while my dad was at work." He shook his head. "A neighbor had to come over with bolt cutters."

"You chained them?"

"I see I've shocked you. Okay, so what else can I tell you? Many of my shirts are this color," he said, obviously trying to change the subject while pulling at the dark green collar of the button-down he was wearing. "And once, when was a little kid, maybe seven years old, I ran away from home and hid under a tree in the backyard."

"You did? How come?"

"I don't know . . . I was mad at my mom for leaving and hated my brothers, and Dad was always working, and I thought things would be better if I was on my own."

And there it was. The thing she didn't know she was looking for. That they'd have something in common. Mia felt herself melt just a bit. "So, you really weren't happy growing up?"

"No. But have I said too much? Maybe I've said too much."

"I don't think so."

"I've been going on about myself since we sat down," Graham said. "Your turn. Tell me about you. Where did you grow up?"

"Right here," she told him.

"At this Gimme! Coffee shop we're sitting in?"

"No, goofball. In town. I've lived here all my life. Never been anywhere else."

"You know, this place reminds me of where I grew up in Ontario," Graham said. "Lots of houses that look exhausted from surviving winter year after year. Lots of people who look the same."

"Here's the thing about this town," Mia told him. "It basically stinks, but only someone from here is allowed to say that."

He laughed. "Okay. Rule number one. No ranking on the town. So tell me, why does it stink?"

"There's just nothing going on. So, out of boredom and emptiness, I think, people do stuff that's bad. Things they shouldn't." She stopped herself. She really didn't want to get into all that she'd done. "Anyway . . . the only good thing here is the college," Mia said. "But hardly anyone from town goes there."

"But you do."

"No. I don't. I'm a sophomore in high school."

Graham pretended to choke on his coffee. "No way!"

"I'm not fooling."

"Fooled me."

"How old are you?"

"I'm fifteen."

"Huh."

"Do you have a problem with my age?"

Graham thought about it for a moment. "No. It's fine."

Mia smiled, relieved that the truth was out. "So how old are you?"

"Twenty-one," he told her. "And very mature for my age."

Mia laughed. "Twenty-one is not really that old." Isn't that what Clancy would say? But she had a moment of worry, wondering if he'd disapprove of Graham, as he had Robbie.

"When do you turn sixteen?"

"In June."

"Good. That's soon."

"So you *do* have a problem with my age!"

"No, I'm just making a mental note. What day did you say?"

"I didn't. June twelfth."

"Will you save the day for me?"

"You're making some very bold assumptions."

"No, hopeful assumptions. So let's get back to the bad stuff you were talking about . . . want to be more specific?"

"You don't really want to hear about all my problems, do you?"

"Try me! C'mon . . . I just told you the whole tale of my messed-up family."

Like friends, he'd said. Right? "Okay, you asked for it." The whole tale came out of her in a rush. "I'm a shoplifter trying really hard to reform. Luckily it's not as hard as I thought. But my mother's an alcoholic, something I found out only recently because she's been very good at hiding it. She went on a binge and is in the hospital right now so she can detox. My grandfather, who is my favorite person in the world, just died, but right before he did, he kind of let my mother know that he didn't love her. My father has been a missing person my whole life, and I thought I'd found him, but he won't step up and admit it. I don't have any true friends anymore, if I ever did. Except for Finkelstein, and he's going to fire me from the only job I've ever had. Pretty messed up, right?"

"Wow. That's a lot. For sure. But Finkelstein fire you? I don't think so."

"I did something . . . let's say not so good."

"Did you chain him to a tree?"

"Almost as bad." Mia took a deep breath. "I let a batch of new flies go. They were my first batch and I set them free. Outside the building."

He laughed. "No way! Why'd you do that?"

She shrugged. "I wanted to see them fly free."

"Really?"

"Yes. I didn't want . . . it didn't feel right to make them live in a box."

Graham was wide-eyed with amusement. Not the reaction she'd expected. "What did Finkelstein say?"

"He doesn't know yet."

"Huh. Well, honestly it's not such a big deal. You could just tell him the flies all croaked and you tossed them out."

"Oh. I hadn't thought of that." Mia took another sip of her tea. "But I don't want to lie to him."

Graham nodded. "Right. So now I know you're honest. But go back to all that other stuff for a minute. Your mother being sick and your grandfather dying. Are you all right?"

"I'm not. And I am. Even though it's hard, I think that all this bad stuff is just a phase. It's like the flies. They go from egg to maggoty worm and then they become a baby fly. I've seen how things can change really fast. They have to change for me. I just have to live through it. Do you know what I mean?"

"But Mia, it sounds really hard. And what about your father?"

"Yeah. I don't even know him, but I miss him so much."

Mia felt a great weight drop off her. Maybe it was because Graham had so easily confessed some of the drama in his own life. Or maybe it was that everything she'd felt for the last few terrible weeks had finally jelled into something she could finally say to someone, without feeling like it was the heavy awful truth, just the facts of life. Her life.

"You're right. The things that happen to change us are all part of cycles," Graham said. "We pass through them. It's the strange and wonderful metamorphosis of the human bug."

Mia looked down at the table. There were a couple of flies buzzing around after spilled sugar. She said, "Of course, I have no idea whether my mother is really going to get through. She went so far over the edge with her drinking, I don't know if she can turn herself completely around and recover."

"Maybe you just need to believe she can." Graham grabbed for his backpack. "Can I show you something? It's kind of a little bit of magic."

Mia wasn't sure what he had in mind, but she was curious. "Yeah, sure. Is it a trick?"

"No. It's more like a transformation." Graham pulled out a used ziplock bag.

"So now I know you like to carry dirty plastic bags around with you."

"Listen, Miss Wiseass Pants, do you have any idea how long discarded plastic takes to disintegrate in the environment?

That's why I bring my lunch to school in this one every day. After I wash it, of course. Saves money, too."

He took his glass of water and poured it into the plastic bag, then sat it upright on the table so it didn't spill. "Now we need to catch a fly." He cupped his palm over a fly feasting on the spilled sugar, which he then dropped into the bag and zipped shut.

"Oh my God . . . you're going to kill it!"

"Just watch." Graham picked up the bag and shook it, so that the water flowed all around the fuzzy body. It drifted from top to bottom and back again. The insect was completely lifeless, just floating. It looked more like a speck of dust than a bug.

"It drowned," she said, sadly.

"So it would appear." He placed the bag on the table, as if his simple trick were now done, but then he picked up a saltshaker, unscrewed the top, and poured out the white granules, until a tiny hill formed on the tabletop.

"What a strange boy you are," Mia said.

"That's why you like me, right?"

"It's too soon to tell. Besides, you're a fly-killer."

Graham looked up at her with mock disappointment. "Poor me. Well, maybe this will convince you otherwise." He smiled as he unzipped the bag and took out the drowned fly, delicately pinching it between two fingers, and placing it gently on the salt hill. Then he pushed some of the granules onto the feathery black body with the tip of his finger, taking care, as if he didn't want to wake the thing, covering it up under a blanket of white. "We'll give it just a minute," he said.

"Before what, the funeral?" she said sadly.

They sat there silently observing the pile of salt. Mia stared at it so long that she couldn't be sure what she was looking at anymore, because it seemed like something was moving in that white pile. A point emerged, the tip of something, perhaps a wing or a leg. And then there was a quick movement, fast like only an insect could make. "No way," she said.

"Here we go," Graham told her, pushing away some of the salt as carefully as he buried the bug a few minutes before. The fly lay there exposed. It seemed to be disoriented and lazy as if emerging from a deep sleep. But then it shook itself and got onto its legs. The wings shuddered, the proboscis tested the salt. It took a step.

"Oh . . . my . . ." Mia said. And the fly flew away. "How did you do that?" she asked.

"It's simple really. The salt absorbed all the water in its body. It just needed to dry out."

"But it was dead."

"Yet it lives again."

"That's so great!" Mia cried out loud, causing the people at the nearby table to turn in surprise.

"See? It's like you were saying," Graham told her. "Things change. Even the worst situation can completely turn around." Graham reached out for her hand this time and just held it across the table. And they didn't talk anymore, because the thing both of them wanted, to become friends, was happening for real and not just in their heads.

———————

At home that night Mia made a vase for Graham, from a liquor bottle of the clearest glass. A man and a woman sitting on grass among the bugs. She'd drawn magnifying glasses in their hands. But they were observing each other through them, not the insects.

She couldn't wait to give it to him.

## 23

*Mia woke up* on Saturday morning to find the mailbox stuffed with a huge manila envelope from the Law Offices of Jacobsen & Brant, two names she'd never heard before. But she did recognize her own. The package was addressed to her.

She opened it right away, while she was still standing in the downstairs hallway outside Grandpa Andy's door. Inside was a blue legal-size folder containing pages and pages of type tagged with little sticky notes, that read "sign here" in at least five different places. She closed the folder and opened a letter-size envelope paper-clipped to the front.

Inside were two letters. One was a formal correspondence on the lawyer's stationery stating she was the sole beneficiary of the estate of Mr. Andrew Morrow, which was being held in trust by Jacobsen & Brant. It included the house and the land it stood on, which had been paid in full before she was born. In addition there was a lump sum of two hundred and seventy-five thousand dollars that could be used prior to her twenty-fifth birthday only if Mia planned to go to college. In lawyer-speak, the letter stated it was the final wish of Mr. Morrow that she pursue a higher education, at a college of her choice.

The letter was short, but she had to read it twice to make sure she understood what it said.

But there was no mistake.

That was it. G.A.'s will left her everything. He expected

her to go to college. And her mother got nothing. Mia didn't know how to feel. She was stunned.

The other letter was more of a note, actually, handwritten on piece of onion paper.

>*My dear girl . . . remember the birds?*
>*I know that you can take care of things.*
>*I know this is for the best, for you and your mother.*

And in that instant Mia felt again that it was all too much. It was more than she could bear. He must have been out of his mind . . . what kind of lawyer would allow G.A. to leave everything to her? She found it very hard to breathe at that moment.

Slipping into his apartment, Mia closed the door behind her and stood in her grandfather's living room. It was unchanged from his last day there, with everything in its place. "Damn it, G.A.," she said out loud. "How could you leave such a mess?"

What would they live on? And what about Constance? She was sick and would have to be taken care of. Exactly what kind of care would she need? Could Mia provide it? And Mia worried most of all that even if her mother got better, this inheritance thing would mess her up again. That she'd try, in that old familiar way, to bury the way it made her feel.

Mia stared at his worn-out chair, and in a flash she pictured him sitting there, smiling at her like he did because he believed in her. It had always given her courage. Mia pulled open the drapes and let the morning light in. She wandered through his apartment, noticing how all his things seemed to be waiting to be taken out. Lovingly, and maybe with Constance's help, she would empty the place. Just the thought of it seemed to open up possibilities.

Her first thought was that she could move into Grandpa Andy's apartment by herself. That way she and Constance would each have more space to themselves. And they wouldn't be in each other's way, arguing all the time anymore. They could live apart but still near each other.

Or, better yet, they could rent this apartment, and use the money to live on, or for things they needed. Combine that with the rent George was paying, and maybe her mother wouldn't have to work at some awful job where she wasn't appreciated. Maybe she could do something much more meaningful to her, whatever that might be. As long as it didn't include drinking. Good, good. This would be good.

Mia went out the kitchen door and took the two steps down into the backyard. There was the hole. And she knew, without even having to think about it, that the reason Grandpa Andy hadn't planned for his funeral was that he wanted his ashes to be buried there. This was where they belonged.

But Grandpa Andy, bless him, had wanted her to see that for herself. Maybe he wasn't so crazy after all, giving her control of their future. Maybe he did it out of love.


Mia picked three daisies on the grounds outside the hospital. One for herself, one for her mother, and one for Clancy, because he might be gone, but he'd helped them out that night for sure. She placed them in the road-trip vase she'd made for Constance and took the elevator up to the ninth floor, where she stopped at the nurses' station to ask if her mother was feeling well enough for a visit.

"Oh, yes, she's doing fine," a nurse told her. "Has a visitor now, but I'm sure she'd like to see you. Go right in."

Her mother must have called Brenda when she'd sobered up. "Thanks." Mia went down the hall, and just outside her mother's closed door she heard Constance's voice speaking calmly. She was definitely feeling better. Mia knocked and entered slowly.

Constance's face brightened when she saw her. "Mia. They told me you were coming. I'm so glad. I wasn't sure you'd want to." Her mother's visitor was sitting in a chair with both feet up on the bed's metal guardrail. He pushed back to get out of the way now.

It was Clancy.

Mia went over to her mother's outstretched arms and gave her a hug. Constance's sweaty body felt as hot as something just out of the oven. She clung for a second more and then let Mia go.

Mia turned to Clancy. "What are you doing here?" she asked, adding quickly, "I mean, I'm glad to see you, but this is a surprise."

Clancy gave her a wink. "I know, kiddo."

"Didn't you say you didn't want any part of this? I thought you were bailing." She wasn't sure why she was giving him a hard time, but she couldn't help it.

"Well, it's more a question of what your mother wants."

They both looked at Constance.

"Here. I made this for you." Mia held out the object in her hands, her mother's present.

Constance immediately locked onto the image on the front. "So, from that old photo you figured out we knew each other?"

Mia nodded.

"Look, Clancy." Constance turned the vase so he could see. "Do you remember the day this was taken?" she asked.

"I do," he said to Constance, who stared at the vase in her hands. Mia saw tears well up under her mother's swollen lids. Clancy stood up from the chair. "I'm going to let you two talk," he said to both of them. Constance nodded and swallowed back a sniffle. Mia waved good-bye.

"You need a ride home, Mia?" Clancy asked. "I can wait outside. If that's okay with you?"

Mia's heart felt like it beat about ten times as fast as normal. "Yeah. That'd be good," she squeaked.

"Great to see you feeling better, Constance," Clancy said. "And thanks." He slipped quickly out the door, and it clicked shut, leaving the two of them alone.

"*Are* you better, Mom?"

"Well, I'm not drunk. But I'm not completely better. Apparently it's going to take some time."

"Oh."

"But now I know what's wrong. That I've got a big, big problem. So that's something." Constance shook her head. "Did I tell you anything about the day this picture was taken?"

"I used to ask you about all your pictures, all the time. Remember how I used to practically study your album? All you'd say about that one was that the guy was just a friend of yours. Nothing more."

Constance looked shyly up at Mia. "This was taken the day I told Clancy I was pregnant."

Mia took the vase out of her hands and looked more closely at the image she'd made. This time Mia wasn't looking at the guy. Something different captured her attention now. The young woman had a killer attitude. Determined. Unafraid. Mia saw it clearly, and for the first time. "You were glad you were pregnant."

"Of course, Mia . . . of course."

"Did Clancy feel that way?"

"He did."

"But he's not my father."

"No. But he wanted to be."

"What does that mean?"

"He offered to be . . . was willing to . . ." She trailed off, looking out the window.

"Just tell me what happened, Mom."

Constance let out a big sigh. "We were together. It was only a few months, and it was way before this picture. I was so crazy about him. But I was very young at the time. Too young. I was seventeen and Clancy was twelve years older, and it was a lot of difference back then. So he ended it."

"But Clancy loved you. Didn't he?"

"I guess he really did. Because when he found out I was pregnant"—she pointed to the vase in Mia's hands—"and that the guy had taken off on me, he said he'd take care of me and the baby. He wanted us to be a family." Constance paused then.

"Really?"

"It didn't work out."

"Gosh, Mom. Why not? Didn't you want to be with him?"

"More than anything." Constance hesitated then, and Mia saw the feelings building up inside of her. And at that moment, she knew why Clancy wasn't part of the family. She could feel the truth of it blowing full-steam toward her.

"Grandpa Andy. Right?"

Constance said, "Your grandfather didn't approve. Didn't think Clancy was good enough for me. He wasn't . . . you know . . . the straight-and-narrow sort of fellow your grandfather would like. He owned a bar, for one thing." Constance shrugged. "Little did your grandfather know just how much drinking I'd do on my own."

"So Clancy might have been my father?"

"Your stepfather. Yes. If I had stood up for what I wanted." Constance looked at her and smiled that sad Clancy smile. "Biggest mistake of my life. I sent him away. To please your grandfather. Something I never managed to do. Not ever."

Mia slumped back in her chair. "That must have been so hard."

"It was. But then again, I wasn't alone. I had you. Did you ever wonder why I named you Mia?"

"No, not really. Figured you just liked the name."

"Because it means *mine*. And that's what I decided you would be. All mine." She reached for the vase again, studied it. "It's so funny how you put things together. I wish I could do something like this. Make something beautiful. It looks like it's alive."

Mia was taken aback. She'd never heard her mother talk like that. Not about her. Not about anything. "I really hope you're going to keep getting better, Mom."

Constance nodded slowly. "There's a difference. I can feel it for the first time." Her mother looked up, her eyes bright and clear. "I know how much you loved Grandpa Andy. I do. And I know the relationship you had with him was very different from mine . . . but you have no idea how much I hated him. And now that he's gone . . ."

Mia imagined her mother was going to let loose with some horrible feelings of regret, for all that could never be fixed with Grandpa Andy. She reached for Constance's hand, to help her get through it.

Constance squeezed back, her face bright as a moonbeam. "I can't describe it. But whatever was holding me just let go. Do you know what I mean? And all those angry feelings, now I only want to get past them. They aren't doing any of us any good. That's what Clancy said to me today. It's all in the past. And he's right."

Mia smiled. "You know, I understand how hard it is to grow up without a father who loves you."

"I know you do," Constance said.

"But I'm not just talking about me. I really know how it must have felt, because now I know what it did to you."

Constance burst out crying. "Thanks, sweetie." She sniffled through her tears.

Mia sat there for a while, and then as the light started to leave the sky, Constance said it was probably best if she got some rest and Mia stood up. At the door, Constance called out to her. "Hey, Mia?"

"Yeah, Mom?"

"I'm so glad you came to see me today."

"Me too." Mia quietly slipped out of the room. As amazing as her mother's sobriety seemed, it was equally amazing for Mia to find Clancy waiting on the other side of the door. Just as he'd promised he would.

Clancy stood, and without a word they started walking down the long hall together. It felt awkward between them for the first time. Mia realized it was because she knew all about him, he knew she knew, and now that the past had been finished, the future seemed like one big blank. It really could go either way. A happy ending. Or not.

Once they got to the car, Clancy turned the engine over, but he didn't drive. He put his arm across the back of Mia's seat. "Sorry about all this, kid. It's an awful lot to deal with all at once. It is for me."

"What made you decide to go see her?"

Clancy turned toward her. His voice got real low, serious and sadder than she'd ever heard it. "I lost you both a long time ago. I didn't want that to happen again. But I couldn't just force myself into the picture. Not if she didn't want me there. On the other hand, it didn't make sense anymore that you and I shouldn't know each other. Especially since we already did. I couldn't go backward and pretend you didn't exist. So I had to talk to her."

"But you're not my dad. So what should we be?"

"I thought maybe . . . like you said that night . . . we can be friends."

"But there's so much history now."

"Look, we don't have to name it. Let's just say I got your back, kid. I'll be looking out for you. Isn't that good enough?"

Mia had to laugh. "Yeah. It'd be nice to be looked out for. I don't want to be on my own anymore."

Clancy let out a huge sigh. "Me neither. So, good. Good."

And then she saw a different version of his smile. It started out small and unsure, and then it grew until it lit up his whole face. It was a sweet smile, quite promising, really.

"Okay. Where to? Home now?" he asked.

He drove her back, and as he pulled in front of the house, Mia asked if he wanted to come in.

Clancy said, "Sorry, Mia, but I've got to get down to the Ground and get it ready for tonight." But before he left, he gave Mia a few numbers where he could be reached. At the club, at his apartment, and his cell phone, too. And then she got caught up in the first and only fatherly bear hug she'd ever had in her whole life. It took her in completely. The leather of his old jacket was much softer than she would have thought.

A kiss on the forehead sealed the deal. As she delivered it, it had a strange effect on Clancy, who began to stutter. "So, then. Should I . . . I guess I'll wait for you to call?"

"You won't have to wait long," she told him.

## 24

*On her way* to gym, Mia stared up at huge clouds streaking the sky, threatening rain, all in various shades of gray. She knew who would be in class with her, so she took her time just to avoid them in the locker room, and then changed her clothes extra quick. Taking a seat a couple of rows back on the bleachers, she had a chance to steel herself before setting eyes on her old friends.

Michele and Gael were sitting near each other but not talking. Gael was busy checking out her nails, and Michele already had a book out, as if they were purposely ignoring each other.

Maybe she was reading too much into it. Maybe nothing had changed.

But wasn't Gael looking so, so . . . plainly miserable?

Soon Coach Barnes came in and told everyone soccer was canceled due to the weather. A vote was taken for an alternate activity, and volleyball won out over basketball and calisthenics.

Mia felt a surge of energy. She raised her hand almost immediately. "I call captain." Barnes did a double take, but he gave it to her. She surveyed potential teammates from the group of girls hanging about like a bunch of used towels on the metal benches. Not one of them seemed particularly eager that day.

"Gael. Blue team," Mia called out.

Michele looked up then, her brow in a snag, while Gael

went over to Mia's side. The opposition captain chose next, and when the teams were picked, Michele was left benched. Coach Barnes said, "The rest of you . . . ten times around the gym." There were groans from the bleachers, Michele's brassy complaint heard above the rest while the players got in position.

Gael had taken the spot next to Mia's on the court and was standing there looking at her. "Hi . . . so how come you picked me for your team?" she asked.

"Because you know how to play?"

"Is that the only reason?"

"Maybe not. Is that okay with you?"

Gael smiled. "I'm glad. That's all."

"Great. Just don't wuss out on me. Let's play to win today."

"All right. I'll do my best."

Coach Barnes yelled, "Coin toss!" and Mia went to center court, where she won it for the team. Everyone cheered, even Gael.

"Blue team serves," Barnes said. With a firm swat, Mia got the game started, and she played it fair but hard. She and Gael even shared a key play, a low flyer that forced Gael to drop fast to one knee in order to set it up for Mia to spike at the net. They pulled the move off like a couple of pros. Gael didn't cry out when her kneecap hit the gymnasium floor, making an audible cracking sound, and Mia helped her to her feet once the point was secure.

"Not bad," Mia said.

"I'm trying," Gael said.

"I can tell. How's your knee?"

"Hurts a little." Gael bent her leg a couple of times.

"Maybe you should sit this round out," Mia said, not wanting to get blamed for another injury.

Gael looked up, smirking. "Don't worry. I'm fine. I'm not as lame as Michele."

They went back to playing and fifteen minutes later the blue team was up by ten points. Barnes called a time-out, releasing the girls who wanted out and pulling a few off the bench. Michele didn't get picked, but she shot a dirty look at Gael, who'd chosen not to walk.

As the teams switched courts, Gael went around to the other side with Mia. "You play really well. I had no idea how good you were. I mean . . . you always used to mess the game up."

Mia shrugged. "I guess it bugged me that there were rules and we had to follow them. I just wanted to have fun with it, you know?"

"Well, I like seeing you wearing your game face instead."

"Like this?" Mia bulged her eyes out at Gael, who laughed out loud.

Coach Barnes called out, "Enough with the gab session, girls. Get into position."

It was a great game. Everyone was sweaty and winded, and when it was over, Mia's teammates surrounded her and tried to pick her up to celebrate their win, but they were all laughing too hard to do it.

"Way to play," Barnes said, giving Mia a hard pat on the back.

The bell signaling the end of the period rang. Michele stormed off to catch her next class without waiting for Gael. Mia and Gael shared a look.

"Guess she's in a rush," Mia said.

"No. That's not it. She hates it when I don't do what she wants."

"You're supposed to stay away from me or something, is that it?"

Gael looked embarrassed. "Something like that." They headed for the locker room together. As they changed back into day clothes, Gael said, "She's just really stubborn. I'm so tired of it." Gael sighed. "Forget about her. You know I can't help remembering the last time we played volleyball, and how different you were. But it was only a few weeks ago."

Mia nodded. "I know."

"I always knew you were into the game," Gael continued. "Very into it, but you used to pretend the opposite. Like you didn't care, or it was too silly for you."

"I know, but now it doesn't make sense to me anymore, to pretend to not be good at something I am good at."

"Funny, that sounds like Michele, the way she'd described her superabilities in math."

"Yeah, well. Much as I hate to admit it, she was right about some things. But not all."

Mia walked out of the locker room and Gael went with her. They passed through a set of glass doors to the outside. Gael took a deep breath. "Mia, I want to tell you something."

Mia braced herself, unsure of what new and devastating thing Gael might say. "Okay."

"I want you to know I'm really sorry about what happened with us."

"You are?"

"Yeah, things were really messed up back then. You were

acting out all the time and I . . ." Gael hesitated, not wanting to go on.

"Say what you were going to say. Don't stop now."

"I didn't want to be around you because of it." Gael sighed heavily again.

"And now?"

"That's not how I feel now," she said. "Listen, I never thought you were a lost cause. Michele did. And now that you *have* gotten better, I hope we can be friends again. Or at least try." Gael scrunched up her face, like she really meant what she was saying.

Mia felt her whole chest filling up with hope. She'd wanted this so much, hadn't she? But something wasn't right. "You want to be friends now that you think I'm different?"

"Now that you're doing so much better."

This was so unexpected. And it should have made her happy. But it didn't. "I think what happened with us was that you decided all the bad things Michele thought about me were true, that I was a total loser, and that it was best to end our friendship."

"That's not it!" Gael objected. "I care about you. I always have. I still do."

Mia's eyes welled up, the way they always did in the past when Gael spoke to her this way. But she still didn't feel okay. Mia realized she didn't believe her old friend. "So you ended things to prove how much you cared?"

Gael had no answer. It started to rain, hard. "I've got to go," Mia said. "I've got class."

"Call me later, okay?" Gael said, but Mia was already running into the building.

Mia's last class was American history, covering the pre–Civil War period. She took a seat and opened her books, but couldn't keep her mind on the lesson about the differences between North and South and why it seemed they couldn't be joined together.

The problem, as Mia sat there analyzing it, was that the balance was still off between them—her and Gael, that is. Gael assumed that saying she cared should be enough to erase what she'd done, but it didn't match how much Gael had hurt her, how much Mia had suffered being dropped like that. And what was her explanation? That Mia was messing up?

What was friendship worth if it ended when one person was losing it or behaving badly?

Mia thought Gael was right. She had changed. But the difference was, she knew what it really meant to care for somebody. You shouldn't give up on that person. Mia knew for certain she herself wouldn't have done that.


The sky had cleared by the time she got to the college campus. Mia sat down on the damp grass of the arts quad to think. She wasn't mulling over what had happened with Gael. Instead, she was trying to figure out what she could possibly say to Finkelstein about letting the flies go. He would never understand that she'd had to do it. She hardly understood it herself.

Maybe the best thing would be if she didn't do anything. Didn't defend herself. Didn't argue. After all, she'd done the deed. Now she just had to face the consequences.

Mia checked her watch. She still had five minutes before she was due in the basement of Sutton Hall. Looking around, she noticed there were more people out on the lawn than a couple of weeks ago, but most had their books in their hands now. College students always got more serious about work as the end of semester approached, she thought. Hoping to change the outcome of it all. Of course, it was worth trying.

Then she saw a white-blond head in the crowd. Peter York was there, not playing Frisbee but sitting under a tree surrounded by textbooks like everybody else. He was taking notes on a laptop.

Her first panicked thought was to get out of there, fast. She remembered his angry face from that night in the park and how it seemed directed at her. But a very different impulse took hold of her in the next instant. Mia wasn't sure what she'd say as she crossed the quad to talk to him. All she knew was that she'd lied to this person, over and over. No wonder things hadn't worked out right.

Peter didn't look up, even when she was only a few feet away. That's how focused he was on his work. She didn't know he wore glasses. She tapped the sole of his shoe with the tip of her sandal to get his attention.

"Wow. Mia. Never expected I'd see you up here." He was genuinely surprised. And not mad.

"So you know that I don't go to school here, right?"

"Yeah. Figured that out when I couldn't look you up in the roster."

"That's because I'm still a sophomore in high school in town. I live with my mother and . . ." She almost said "grandfather," then remembered he wasn't there anymore. "And I always have."

"What about the flies? Was that part true?"

She didn't tell him it was only for one more day. "Yes. I've got a job in the fly lab in the basement of Sutton. I'm on my way there now."

Peter nodded and didn't seem to have anything else to say to her.

"I'm sorry I lied to you. Just wanted to tell you that." Mia turned to go.

"Why'd you do it?" Peter asked.

"Guess I wanted to change into someone else," Mia told him. "Thought you'd like me better. Or I thought I'd like me better. It didn't work out that way."

Peter had a very serious look on his face. "I know what you mean. I didn't like myself after that night in the park. I felt bad about what happened. I tried to call and tell you that, but I couldn't find you."

"It's okay."

"No, not really. It was my fault we were down there in the first place. The fight was my fault, too. If I hadn't been drinking, I would have used my head and backed away from those guys rather than try to take them on all by myself. I got mad because I was buzzed from the beer. Henry and Dan really got on me to straighten up after that and get serious about school." He held up the textbook in his hands. "I'm trying."

Mia nodded. There wasn't much else she wanted to say to him, except she hoped drinking wouldn't be a problem for him. But she didn't know him well enough to say it. She took a step away. "Good luck with all that."

"Same to you, Mia. See you around, I guess."

She waved good-bye and he waved back, and then he went back to studying. She heard the tap-tapping of his fingers on the keyboard of the laptop as she walked away. It sounded like he'd changed, too, and she was surprised how glad she was that all the lies she'd told him couldn't bug her anymore or make her feel like she'd messed things up. All that was cleared away.

Mia realized she felt ready for anything. Good or bad. And she headed for the basement of Sutton Hall, hoping she could hold on to that feeling.

## 25

*Mia found Finkelstein* kneeling down beside the fly shelves. He looked scared, or maybe angry. As soon as he spoke, his voice halting and sharp, she knew it was both. "I can't find your new batch of flies," he said. "I've looked everywhere. Where did you put them?"

Mia set her bag down on her desk, taking care not to break the glass vase she'd made for him that was inside.

"I looked in the breeding room and on everyone else's shelves, in case you misplaced them," Finkelstein continued. "They all think I'm nuts now, looking for my lost flies. Are you going to tell me where they are?"

"I don't know where they are exactly," she said, "but they're not in the building."

He was pacing now. "What happened? Did none of them mature? They were doing fine, I thought—" He stopped dead in his tracks, his eyes narrowing to small dots behind his glasses. "What do you mean they're not in the building?"

Mia looked him in the eye. "I released them."

"You . . ." He stared back at her with total disbelief, as if she'd just told him she'd learned how to fly herself. "What?"

"When they hatched and I saw them for the first time, something happened. They weren't just experiments anymore. They were living creatures and I couldn't stand to keep them in a box. It seemed wrong." Her voice dropped low. "So I took them outside to live the way they were meant to. To be free."

"You dumped them outside?"

"I didn't dump them. I released them. There's a difference."

"Mia, when you let those flies go, you threw away three months of work. They were fifth generation. A control group exposed to a point-thirteen-ounce dosage of PZ841. There's a huge hole in the data without them."

"I'm so sorry. It was wrong of me to ruin your work," she said. "I know that."

Finkelstein smacked himself in the forehead, harder than he meant to, and cried out. "Damn it!" He stomped away to the other side of the room, where he began to mutter angrily. It took several long seconds, but he finally turned back to her. "I can't keep you on after this. Professor Deacon called me in on Friday to tell me two of his other students have written up their results already. He says the work is of publishable quality." Finkelstein hung his head. "I'm starting to look bad compared with everyone else. Like I can't even keep up."

"It's not a race. That's just how you see it."

He shot her a pained look. "You are very naive if you don't think all of us in this program aren't competing with one another . . . for funding, for jobs, for acclaim. For everything."

"I'm sure that's not totally true. Graham Stoddard told me that he finds it unusual the way you keep to yourself. You never share any of your work with anyone else here."

"He did? Well, he's new here. That's why. The point is, it doesn't help me to have an assistant who lets the test subjects go free. Why don't you ask Graham if he would ever do something like that? For goodness' sake, Mia."

Mia shrugged sadly. "I could say a lot of things. My family was totally messed up. I felt lost and I wasn't thinking clearly. But the real reason I did it is because it's what *they* wanted."

"That's ridiculous."

"It's not. My grandfather taught me that science is all about observation, plain and simple. And I think he was right. If you took an honest look," she explained, taking a step closer to the fly shelves, "you'd see how crazy it makes them to be stuck here." She gestured to him to come over. "Think about it, they can fly and they have to live in a box. It's not natural. I couldn't do it to them. So I screwed up."

He came up and looked at the specimens with her. "But they're just flies, insects. They're perfectly happy in a box."

"No way. All living things want to have a good life. Even the flies. They're just like you or me."

A smile came slowly to Finkelstein's face, and Mia watched it grow into a big goofy grin, the same one that always used to bug her. What a relief it was to see it now. "I just realized something," he said. "Never thought I'd see the day."

"Okay . . . what are you talking about?"

"Mia Morrow! Who'd have ever thought you'd go all soft on me. You were one tough customer when you first walked in here. Not that I didn't admire it. Not at all. I just never expected I would ever accuse you of being overly sentimental. But that's exactly what's happened. You've changed. You're just a big softie!"

Mia shrugged. "Think so?"

"Can't ignore the proof."

"Well, I guess you're right, then. I am."

"I hope this whole episode doesn't set you back. I mean, I never knew how much you cared about the flies until you let them go. Who would have thought? Then to get in trouble for it seems sad and so unfair and . . . and I liked having you in my lab. I really did."

"And we became friends. Didn't we?"

"I thought so. But now . . ." Finkelstein kicked at the floor. "You probably hate me for firing you."

"I understand that you have to fire me, so don't worry. I knew it the second I let the flies go. I don't hate you at all. And I can prove it." Mia went for her bag and carefully pulled out the fly vessel she'd made the night before. On it, lines of flies marched one by one like a column of numbers written in black ink, over the lip of the bottle and down the sides. The bottle was ringed with two black handprints, dripping and sorrowful.

Finkelstein reached for it like he was taking hold of a charmed chalice. "Did you make this? You painted these flies?"

Mia nodded.

"How amazing." He turned the bottle around and took in all the details. "Look at how they're marching out as if they're escaping," Finkelstein said. "And the black hands look like some kind of evil force trying to keep them in. This is fantastic. I mean . . . I can really see how you feel about everything from this." He looked up at her, and of all the looks he'd ever cast her way, she'd never seen him in awe of her before.

Mia realized how good the piece was. In the frenzy of having created it, she had no idea. But now, standing apart from it and seeing it in the hands of the person she'd made

269

it for, Mia realized she'd made something that was greater than her, perfect in so many ways.

"It's so sad-looking. Isn't it?" Finkelstein said.

"I was trying to tell you I was sorry."

Finkelstein nodded, and she knew he believed her. But he stayed slumped against his shelves of flies, as if he were too sad to move.

"Hey, want to hear a joke?" she asked.

"Sure," he said.

"What goes *zzub, zzub, zzub?*"

"I don't know."

*You didn't even try*, Mia thought. "A bee flying backward," she told him.

Finkelstein laughed. "Good one."

"Use it anytime you want."

"I will," Finkelstein said dejectedly, and turned to regard his escaping-flies vessel again.

There was only one thing left to say. "You know I'm really sad to leave here. Because everything changed for me when I started working for you," Mia told him. "This job was exactly what I needed. I had a real routine here. It was something I kind of got lost in. And because you made me do things right . . . it made me do everything right."

Finkelstein put down the vase and said, "I'm so very glad I could help, Mia. I truly am. And I suppose if you really don't want to leave . . ."

"When the next box of flies is born, I'm going to want to do the same thing. Let them fly away."

Finkelstein understood that, too. He swallowed hard. "I'll walk you out," he said, and stood up.

The two of them went out into the sunshine, to the very place where Mia had let the flies go. "This is where I released them," she said. Finkelstein looked at the privet bushes and right then a fly came in for a landing, hovering for a bit and then settling down. But it was only a moment or two before it was off again.

"Wonder if that's one of your flies?" Mia asked.

"Not anymore," Finkelstein said.

"Are you going to be all right? Your experiment, I mean."

"I'll figure something out." Finkelstein looked down and smiled at her. "Off you go now, Mia."

When she was at the end of the path that led away from Sutton Hall, Mia turned around to look at the building one more time and saw that Finkelstein was still standing there. But he wasn't watching her walk away. His face was turned up to enjoy the rays of the sun, and he didn't seem like he was planning to go back inside anytime soon, now that he, too, was out and feeling free.

On the way home, Mia walked by the window of Jewel Moon. She saw something there she'd never seen before. There was a handwritten HELP WANTED sign posted behind the glass. SALESPERSON NEEDED. Mia's heart skipped a beat. There wasn't any place on earth she'd rather work, no place she'd rather be, than Jewel Moon.

A week ago, she wouldn't have known what to do about that sign. But now she could go for it. She was free as a fly. She stepped inside the cozy shop.

Margo greeted her. "Hi, Mia. How's your life?"

"Constantly changing," she said.

"That's so true."

"So how come you're hiring another salesperson? Has it been getting busier in here?"

"We're thinking we'd bring on another person this summer so we can take some time off. But then Janet decided to go back to school in the fall for her business degree, and now we want to get an additional person to take up the slack. Are you interested?"

"You bet!"

"Do you have any retail experience?"

*Only as a shoplifter,* Mia thought. "I love to shop . . ." she said lamely.

Margo laughed lightly. "That doesn't surprise me. But we're looking for someone who's done sales before," Margo said. "You already have a job, though. Don't you?"

"I worked in the entomology department at the college. But that just ended."

"Breeding flies, right?"

"Yes, but I learned a lot of different things." Mia explained the way she assisted during the stages of fly development and was in charge of recording the primary sets of data about the bugs. Realizing that sounded dull, she talked about the breeding room and the miracles she'd seen there.

Margo said, "It sounds like you have two qualities we're looking for: someone who can help maintain our business records *and* has a good eye for the well-made object. And I imagine that if you could do such a technical job up at the college, you could certainly handle this one."

"I'm sure I could. But . . . Margo? I have to tell you something first." And then Mia confessed what had happened up the street at the department store. "But I swear I never once thought about stealing from Jewel Moon. Not once."

Margo stopped her. "I never worried about you in here. Even when Roger Brady put out a rap sheet on you at the Commons Business Association meeting last month."

"He did? And you trusted me after that?"

"Why don't you fill out an application, and I'll talk things over with Janet." She retrieved one from a drawer beneath the cash register.

"Thanks so much! It's really nice of you to give me a chance to—"

"I have faith in you, Mia. Because I know what this place means to you. After all, you come in here practically every other day."

Then Margo went back to her office while Mia looked the application over. Most of the sections were easy to fill out, but two of them stopped her. An adult had to give consent for her to work. And she had to get a recommendation from a previous employer. Both caused problems that she couldn't solve standing there in Jewel Moon.

"Margo, I need to take this home and bring it back. Is that okay?"

She stuck her head out the door of the office in back. "We're not going to rush a decision, so don't worry."

Mia stopped at the small creek near her home. Compared to all she'd been through, getting the application done wasn't going to be difficult. Her mother would be home soon. And though Constance would be disappointed Mia had been fired, at least there was another job. One that Mia really wanted to do. Constance would sign. And Finkelstein? Maybe he'd recommend her even though she'd messed up in the lab. Hopefully he'd understand the shop was where she belonged.

What other reason could there be for that sign appearing on the very day she was done at the lab? It was meant to be. She just knew it.

## 26

*At ten minutes* to eight, Mia put a pot of coffee on. Her timing was perfect. Just as the coffee machine beeped to let her know the brew was ready, she heard the key turn in the lock downstairs. She burst out of the apartment and flung herself down the stairs to welcome her mother home.

Glowing in the morning light, Constance looked like a brand-new version of herself, and backing her up was Clancy, who seemed to be in good spirits even though it was early in the day for him. "Here she is," he said. He could have been talking about Constance, who looked happy to be back, or Mia, who was eagerly waiting for her. A first for both of them.

Mia caught their entrance with a disposable camera she'd bought for this very purpose, to capture them coming through the door before they could object. There should be pictures of this. And, of course, she knew she'd find some interesting way to use them in her art.

The three of them bumped up the stairs, Clancy carrying her mother's bag. Constance looked around the apartment, as if it wasn't the place she'd been living in for most of her adult life. But a lot had changed. The biggest difference was that all the walls had been painted clean white.

"Do you like it?" Mia asked. "Or do you miss all the old colors?"

Constance shook her head. "No. It was so dark before. I had no idea."

"I wanted it to feel like a blank canvas in here, so we can start all over."

Constance spun around to take it all in. "I think you read my mind. Because I wanted everything to feel different. To be different. So this is great." She stopped to address Mia. "Did you do all this by yourself?"

"He helped," Mia said, pointing to Clancy, who took a comical little bow.

"You guys . . . I don't know what to say." Constance was grinning ear to ear, and Mia was glad to see her so pleased. "It's amazing."

They went into the kitchen, and Mia poured two coffees, and a juice for herself, and they all took a seat at the table, which wasn't rickety anymore because Clancy had braced it with a couple of simple pieces of wood. Clancy lightly tapped his fingers on the table and just sat there nodding, clearly not wanting to be the one to speak up first. Constance put down her cup, looking agitated all of a sudden.

"What's the matter, Mom?"

"Well, Mia, as part of my recovery, I have to make amends. It's just a fancy way of saying I've got to talk to the people I've hurt because of my drinking, and the way I behaved." Constance took another sip of hot coffee. "Is that okay with you?"

Mia nodded.

"Okay. Here goes. What I want to say to you, Mia, is that I'm very sorry for leaving you like I did. I made you think I didn't care about you, when the opposite is true. I have always loved you and wanted the best for you, even though I've mostly shown it the wrong way. I'm truly sorry for that."

"I'm sorry, too, Mom. For all the fights we had. I thought you were trying to control me, and I hated it."

"Well . . . I was mostly trying to make sure you didn't turn out like me."

They were silent for a moment. So Constance had been hard on her only because she was afraid for her. Mia wished she'd figured this out herself, and earlier. But it was the past, right? "You know what? All that time you were gone, all I could think about was how much better it would be if you were back. I missed how much you cared."

"Thank you, baby. That's good to hear."

After that, Constance explained it was going to take her some time before it wouldn't feel like she was trying to stay sober, but right now she had no urge for a drink. And all she had to do was feel that way for the rest of the day. And then the days would add up, and then the weeks, the months. And on and on.

"It gets easier," Clancy said, "not harder."

"Yay," said Constance, somewhat meekly.

"Well," Clancy said, pushing back from the table like somebody done with a big meal, "you guys seem in good shape. I'm going to let you get settled." And then he was at the door so fast it left them speechless. Mia got up to follow him out.

"Clancy, thanks a lot," Constance said, poking her head out from the kitchen. "Thanks for everything."

"Anytime, Constance," he said. "You'll let me know if you want to go to a meeting together. Okay?"

Constance smiled at him, "I will . . ." she said as she waved good-bye. Then she left Mia and Clancy alone in the hall.

"And how about you and I have breakfast one morning next weekend?" he said to her.

"Okay!" Mia answered. "Let's do it on Sunday."

She followed him down to lock the door behind him, and gave him a quick peck on the cheek on the way out. A few steps down the path, he spun back around. "She did good, don't you think?"

"I do," Mia said. "Thanks for helping us out, Clancy."

"Just doing my job, ma'am." He tipped his baseball hat to her, and she watched him as he jauntily walked to his car. Back when she'd spotted him glowering at her in the dark club, she never could have imagined this version of Clancy.

Mia climbed back up to the apartment and found Constance sitting on the edge of her bed, her lips tightly pursed. "I don't know what to do with myself," she said as she looked up. "Unpack or lie down? I've never been at a loss for some *thing* I should be doing."

Mia sat down next to her. "Hey, Mom, so what's up with you and Clancy? Something? Nothing?"

Constance shrugged. "He's been so supportive. I think mostly because he really cares about you. And it's just good for me to have someone to talk to, someone who knows what I've been through. Now and before. He's been through it, too. Turns out talking is the cure for alcoholics. Who knew? So spending time with him is good therapy, but that's all."

"For now?"

"For now."

"He's great, though, isn't he?" Mia raised an eyebrow.

"He is. And I hope we'll be friends. But I need to get my life on track. Figure out what I'm going to do, and I can't get involved with anyone yet. I'm not ready."

"You've said that for years. You know that, right?"

"Fair enough, but now is not the time. You know that, right?"

"Yup. I get it. I do."

They both smiled. Constance stood up and went to her closet. "I feel like I want to clean out this room, too, just like the rest of the place." She started pulling out her clothing. "This isn't me. This ugly stuff is all about me trying to be somebody else. Somebody in control." She tossed the clothes on the floor.

Mia picked them up. "Some of these are kind of decent clothes. I mean, they're not in bad shape. Hey! You know what? We should have a yard sale."

Constance poked her head out of the closet. "Absolutely. Let's do it."

"And then we can use the money to buy things you like better. Things that are right for you."

"What a good idea."

"I know."

Constance started chucking pieces of her wardrobe out the closet door. "Oh, hell. I almost forgot about this again." She came out holding up the fringed black leather vest. "Keep it or toss it?"

Mia took it from her. "This thing. I never told you I wore it one night."

Constance pretended to reach for it. "No! Not my rock-and-roll-ain't-I-hot vest?"

"Yup. And it was one of the worst nights of my life." She handed it back.

"It was one of the worst years of mine. This we should burn."

"Do you really mean it?" Mia asked. "Because I can think of something even better."

"What?"

"Let's cut it up," Mia whispered, as if she was saying something especially wicked. "Just slice it to bits! Doesn't that sound like a cool idea?"

"Should I get the scissors?" Constance was jumping up and down.

"Do it!" Mia urged.

Constance ran out and came back holding the scissors aloft.

"Are you ready to be the destroyer of your past?" Mia asked her, picking up the slinky vest and holding it up under the bedroom's ceiling light. It looked like a carcass, wilted and lifeless now, ready to meet its fate.

Constance nodded enthusiastically. "Ready!"

Mia told her, "I think we should both say something about one time that we wore it. Something we want to forget or rid ourselves of as we cut it up. Okay?"

"One thing only?"

"Say as much as you want."

"Who goes first?"

"I will," Mia said. "Since I wore it last." She took a deep breath. "I wore this the night I went to the Common Ground and met Clancy and took drugs and got attacked by a stranger while I was nearly passed out." Then she made the first cut, a diagonal across the left chest piece all the way to the armpit.

"Oh my God!" Constance exclaimed.

Mia looked at her, concerned. "Are you okay with this?"

"Yes. I'm just so sorry that happened to you."

"So am I. Now it's your turn."

Constance shook the thing hard and then picked up the scissors. "I, too, wore this the night I met Clancy and got so drunk he had to drive me home and met Grandpa Andy, who said I was never to bring him home again."

Mia gasped. "That was the first time?"

Constance nodded. "They never met again. He refused to give Clancy another chance."

She cut into the leather across the other breast, just as Mia had. Then they took turns cutting, at first seriously and then with more zest, saying things like, "I didn't know who I was," and "I gave up on myself way too soon," as the vest went from being a garment to a bunch of scraps at their feet. When they were done, Mia gathered the pieces and placed them neatly in a pile.

"Can I have these?" Mia asked Constance.

"What are you going to do with them?"

"You'll see."

"Be my guest."

"Thanks, Mom."

Then Mia got ready to go. Before she left, she didn't think to question her mother about whether she'd be home when she got back that afternoon. Instead, she said, "Have a nice day!" and went out into the new morning, feeling calm and ready for anything.


Mia walked to the Commons for her first day of work at Jewel Moon. Clancy had signed the application for her, back when Constance was still in the hospital, listing himself as her temporary guardian. He knew Margo, through the town business owners' association, so she had no problem accepting his signature. And Finkelstein had been so eager to write her a recommendation that Mia had to convince him to wait until Jewel Moon asked for one.

As she walked along, taking her usual route over the gorge bridge and into the neighborhood that belonged to her old friends, she thought about how she'd avoided going there since the breakup, feeling like she was no longer welcome on those few blocks with the nicer houses and older trees on bigger lots.

Today it didn't matter. This was just another street in the town where she lived. Now she was curious to see if it had changed, too, the way everything else in her life had.

But it was the same. Picture-perfect as always. She kept going, down to the end of the block where she usually turned left for Gael's house. Only a few weeks ago, it would have been easier to walk on, avoiding it altogether. Now that wasn't necessary. She made the left.

Mia hadn't said anything more than a brief hello to Gael since that day in gym class when Gael had said she wanted to be friends again. But Mia noticed Michele and Gael no longer sat together in the cafeteria, or in math class, either. It appeared as if the thing that had wrecked her and Gael's friendship, mistake or whatever it was, had run itself out.

After giving it lots of thought, Mia decided that she wasn't mad at Gael anymore. Ultimately what her old friend had done by giving her the boot turned out to be for the best, even though Gael probably hadn't meant it to be for her own good. The truth was, that kick in the butt had forced Mia to shape up.

Arriving at her old friend's house, Mia saw the detached garage at the end of the driveway was open, and Gael and her mother were sorting through boxes. She could hear their voices, strained as only mothers' and daughters' can sound.

"We're not saving these old toys anymore. They're rotting in this box," said Gael's mom.

"These are my things. You can't just throw them away," complained Gael.

So it seemed everyone was cleaning house today.

"Hey there," Mia shouted down the drive. Gael's mother stood up straight and smiled as if nothing were wrong, and Gael exited the garage in a hurry.

"Mia. Hi," she called, then walked down the driveway. "My mother's ready to give away my childhood. She calls it pushing me out of the nest."

"Better get ready to fly," Mia said.

Gael laughed. "Yeah, you're probably right. I was hoping my stuff would always have a home here, but I guess not."

"Mom and I are having a yard sale one day this summer. If you want, you can join in with us."

"Really? You mean it? That would be great. That early edition of Candy Land is worth something. So . . . how is your mom?"

They hadn't talked about Mia's family for a very long time, so Mia didn't know how much Gael knew. "She's good." And that wasn't a lie, because she was.

"I heard what happened, you know."

"How?"

"Oh, the usual grapevine. My mom was talking to some mom whose kids are on the swim team with some kids whose mom is a nurse, I think. Something like that."

"Really. Well, for all the talk, no one offered to help. Ever. Even after my grandfather died and I was by myself. But I guess it was interesting as a topic of conversation."

"But she's doing good, you said. So that's great."

"Yeah, she knows she has a problem. That seems to me to be a big step. For her or anyone."

"Right," said Gael, shuffling her feet. "So, what are you up to today?" she asked.

"Going to the Commons."

"Shopping, huh? Better stay out of trouble."

"No, Gael. There's a job at Jewel Moon and I'm not at the fly lab anymore, so—"

"Mia, what makes you think they're going to hire you? You're a shoplifter."

A shocked silence hung between them for only a moment. "You don't get it," Mia told her. "I already got the job at Jewel Moon. I'm on my way there now for my first day of work."

"Oh. Oh, that's great!" Gael said, covering her mistake with a big smile.

"And I paid my debt to the department store. It's over and done with, so I'd appreciate if you didn't bring it up again."

"I didn't . . . I didn't know. . . ."

"Now you do." Mia didn't wait for her to answer again. Mia knew one thing for certain. Her old friend hadn't changed. Not really. She only saw the worst. "Well, I've got to go or I'll be late for work," Mia told her.

"Okay, well, good luck. At work and everything, I mean."

Mia turned around even though she was already at the sidewalk. "Good luck getting rid of your old stuff, Gael." And she quickly waved as if she were actually saying good luck instead of good-bye. It seemed better to end things that way, now that they were obviously over.

She had five minutes to get to her new job, and she ran the rest of the way. She didn't want to be one second late. And if she ran faster, she might get there early. That would be even better.

If you cannot get rid of the family skeleton, you may as well make it dance.

—George Bernard Shaw

*It's the middle* of June. School is out, but Mia is busy. Spread in front of her on the floor are newspaper fragments, colored pencils, paint chips, and an astounding collection of buttons. Her putty knives, manicure scissors, tape, glue, and pots of dye are nearby, too. Every little thing she likes to use. She likes to work on her hands and knees, kneeling over her projects.

The living room is her studio now. She grabs a black thumbtack, on which she paints two enormous compound eyes, not in great detail, but just to suggest the fly. And then she searches through a prime selection of G.A. memorabilia. She knows what she wants, hunts for it now. Suddenly the image appears. Hands. There is a smidgen of the caption.

"Andrew Morrow . . . receives . . . Lambert Prize . . ."

The voice in her head says, *This is the one.*

She pins it inside a box that used to hold shoes. She has lined this container inside and out with scraps of black leather glued in place to make a tiny room Grandpa Andy might like. There's a wooden chair made from sticks dyed a deep red. It's a squat and bulky seat fit for an old man. And there's a rug made from onionskin typing paper. On it Mia has pecked out a promise to her grandfather, to take good care of things, as he once noticed she was quite able to do. And now, with the tap of a tiny hammer, the thumbtack will keep watch like a fly on a wall.

It is done. She'll name the piece *The Handshake.*

Mia put the leather box on an empty shelf. Picking up her camera, an early birthday present from Constance, she checked the flash settings and took her shot. The photos, when she was done, would be for the portfolio she was putting together to apply to a summer art program offered at the college. Choosing which ones to send would be the hard part. There were so many favorites.

Constance appeared in the doorway, ready to go. "Sure you don't want to come with us?" she asked.

"I have a date, Mom."

"Well, bring him along. I'd like to get to know this young man."

"You will. I promise."

"Mia . . ."

"Soon."

"Anyone you like, I'll like. You know that, don't you?"

"Give me a chance to make sure I like him . . . like that, anyway. We've been friends till now, so this is different for us."

"All right. I'll try to be patient."

A horn honked out on the street. It sounded like a happy toot. Constance practically jumped for the door. "That's my ride," she said.

Thursday mornings Clancy came to pick her up. They went to an AA meeting together and afterward blasted out on the highway to a few country markets so Constance could pick the freshest produce she could find. From there she'd start planning what to make and serve over the weekend, at the bar. She had certain things that were now standards on her menu. A crispy eggplant dish was Mia's favorite.

But for Constance, the fun was improvising. Clancy was open to it, too, once he realized that people were coming in for something other than drinks.

So now they opened the Common Ground an hour earlier every night, took back a piece of the parking lot, and made an outdoor patio that would serve food throughout the night. Constance ran it. Her idea. When she'd first suggested it to Clancy, he'd said, "If it means you'll be hanging around me more, you can do anything you want at the club. Except drink."

They named the café Take Two.

A giggle escaped Constance as the horn tooted once more. "Gotta go!"

The door slammed downstairs and Mia heard another toot, which she knew was for her. And then she heard the roar of the black car as it drove away.

A quiet fell on the room. It was just what she needed to finish up before her date arrived at noon.

When the doorbell rang exactly on time, Mia was pleased. She let Graham in and showed him around the studio. He zeroed right in on *The Handshake*. "I didn't know your grandfather won the Lambert. That's impressive. And so's this piece. I really like it."

"Thanks. I think he would, too."

"Hey, did I tell you Finkelstein came up to me in the hall the other day? Said he wanted to talk. And boy, did he! Took me back to his office and I didn't think I'd ever get out of there."

Mia laughed. "Yeah, he can go on when he's got a captive audience. So what did he say?"

"Well, he asked if we'd ever lost any flies in our lab, and what we did about it. I told him we handed in the results without the data. You can calculate the rate of aberration in the populations and chalk it up to that. It's really no big deal. I went and looked at some of his numbers and he is so incredibly precise—"

"Wait a second. He let you look in his books?"

"Yeah, and I mean he's got everything timed down to the hour, even. It's a bit obsessive. It's so perfect that he really shouldn't worry about one box of flies. I told him that. But when I teased him a little about how neat his books were, he got kind of quiet, so I knew I'd hurt his feelings. Then he said maybe he drove you out of the lab by being too strict."

"He did? Oh, no. I'll go talk to him," she said, worried for old Fink now.

"Yeah, I'm sure he misses you."

After they'd finished looking at all of Mia's work, Graham said, "There's someplace special I want to show you today. Are you ready for an adventure?"

"Always," Mia told him.

Graham rode a beat-up Peugeot bicycle he'd salvaged from a junk shop and restored himself. They pedaled side by side when there were no cars, but as soon as they heard one coming up behind, Graham dropped to the rear to be safe.

When he wasn't watching the road, Graham was turned

to her, delivering a pep talk. "Go, Mia. Keep going." They were climbing the longest and steepest hill she'd ever attempted. It was steady up and up, and the tops of her thighs were burning. She wasn't sure she'd make it all the way.

"You're almost there!" Graham's breathing sounded perfectly normal. Were his legs made of steel?

She peeked up the road to see for herself and felt a drop of sweat run down her face. "Argh! Not close enough."

He reached out and grabbed ahold of her saddle to give her a tow. It was like being hitched to a truck. Mia looked down at his arm with its long muscles firm and tensed. His strong hand held her in its clench, helping her along. She still had to pedal, but she felt weightless, and the top was getting ever closer.

"It's worth it," Graham said. "You'll see."

It was hard for her to speak. "I'm. Not. Giving. Up!"

"Good for you. You're doing great!"

The road finally leveled out, and Mia felt the strain drain from her entire body. Graham let go. He said, "We'll pull off just up on the right," then he leaped ahead on his bike to show her the way.

Soon they were heading down a paved path. At the end was a park bench, and there the vista opened up. She could see the whole town. It looked like a pretty postcard with its white church steeples and quaint clapboard houses. She could even see the little stone bridge that crossed the gorge near her home. Beyond that were the dairy farms and the finger of a lake reaching the edge of town. In the distance was the college. The glittering castle on the opposite hill. She was higher than it now.

She stood there with a bug's-eye view of all of it, thinking how strange it was that this place she'd lived all her life could keep on giving her new and wonderful experiences. Graham put his arm around her shoulder. "Happy Birthday, Mia." He kissed her hot cheek.

They stood there like that together, when suddenly the sound of insect song surrounded them. It had a rhythm, starting off so low as to be practically inaudible, then rising with vibrato as if every leaf in every treetop were occupied. When it suddenly stopped, Mia wondered whether the insects quit because they got tired, or did they just need a moment to catch their breath? And all of sudden those harmonious insects started up again, but from farther away this time.

"Let's keep going," she said to Graham, and they flew down the road, following their cue.

The only transformation
that interests me is a total
transformation—however minute.

—SUSAN SONTAG

# Acknowledgments

I must pay tribute to Caroline Knapp, author of the memoir *Drinking: A Love Story*, for providing the clearest and deepest of insights into the heart of what it means to be a "functional alcoholic." I've never read a book as unblinkingly honest.

For his artwork that inspires by constantly pushing boundaries, kudos go to Mike Kelley. Many of the quotes used here were garnered from his powerful installation *Pay for Your Pleasure*, which is in the permanent collection at the Museum of Contemporary Art, Los Angeles.